"WILLOWS' TRAIL"

The sequel to~

"ENDLESS POSSIBILITIES"

In the series~

TAILS OF THE CROW!

Frank J. Sconzo, Sr.
Samantha Hayes

WILLOWS' TRAIL... is a work of fiction, Names, characters, places and incidents are products of the author's imaginations or are used fictitiously and not to be construed as real. Any resemblance to actual events, local organizations or persons, living or dead is entirely coincidental.

Printed USA by Sconzo Printers

This book is dedicated to all those who aided in the making of this story.

To Jackie, for all his help in the research of this work and giving us a birds' eye view of Camelot.

And to a dear friend Debbie! Heal quickly dear!

THE BEGINNING

"Who are you? Where are you? I can hear you, but the fog makes it impossible to see!" He sits up in bed, anxiously searches through the semi-darkness of his room for the disembodied voice. It concerns him, her calling for 'help'.

"I am here," the sound wafts to his ear. "I am in the field. Are you through the 'looking glass'?" the young woman nervously asks, more desperate with each passing moment.

"Looking Glass? What is a 'looking glass'?" He sees an oval shape; something akin to a mirror sticking partway up through the floor. The edges glow and shimmer; sparks flying.

"The brigands are coming back and we need help!

They kidnapped my young sisters." He hears a sigh. "Who are you?"

"I am called Dean."

"Dean, I am 'Beth'. Help us, please?"

"DEAN! *DEAN*, wake up!" The lit candle his Dad holds brightens the room, somewhat.

"Dad, I-I am awake; I think," he answers, still sitting upright, asleep, or is it a trance?

"What was that all about, son?" His dad, the Wizard Jere inquires. "You were having some kind of strange dream?"

"Yes, very strange, a girl needed help from somewhere. A young girl, something to do with brigands and a 'looking glass'; whatever that is?"

He was explaining; trying to remember the dream as it partially fades, but still remains; not sure if he was sleeping and dreaming, or in a type of trance. Or is this all real?

"It was in a field, a tilled field. I could smell the earth." He takes a breath as if to help him remember. A smile comes to his memory. "You remember that scent right after the rain; the clean smell of fresh loam?"

"All right, Son, go back to sleep," Jere says. "We will figure it out in the morning."

"Thanks, Dad," he replies stretching back out.

"She said her name is '*Beth*'. What a pretty name," he closes his eyes, smiles to himself as he drifts to sleep.

CHAPTER 1 Beginning Again

It is a wonderful spring day, but it is always spring here. The temperature is warm; the slight breezes sway the tree tops.

It is a typical, quiet morning; the ones' we enjoy here in Camelot. The birds sing; frogs from the nearby pond croak their sonnets along with the crickets; a quiet that most modern people could never experience. Here, there is no extraneous noises of cars, trains or busses. The ringing of a phone is unheard of. Turbine engines running power plants do not exist... a quiet that lulls and super-sensitizes your hearing.

It brings a peace; making you uniquely aware of any sound out of place.

Merlyns' head lifted in an instant, tracking towards the pathway as if on a swivel, bringing her immediately to her paws. Dagwood, who had been hunting in the forest, bounds to the table to stand next to his mate. Both watch expectantly, tails move in rhythm to some unheard noise, almost unheard any ways.

A sound drifts on the air, not any sound but an unusual sound. Pleasant, musical; a lute strums; the voice we can nearly discern; light and melodically different in its' own unique way.

"This is the Magical story of Miss Abigail, The wizard from that faraway place. She came to defend, with her older friend Frank, Bringing power of iron and lace!"

"*Oh no*, he'd better not be singing that again," she exclaims, threateningly, rising from her seat, both hands as fists. Abby's demeanor is frightful, but her eyes couldn't disguise the smile.

Allain Alan, the wandering minstrel and agent for Sir Jackie will grace our abode. Now we know why the cats are so quick to attend.

When we first met him at the fair, he lavished much attention on both felines. No matter how sentient and intelligent, they love being scratched.

Abby rises shaking her head; the cats stand still, only tails moving in eager anticipation of the visit.

A hand goes up and we hear the familiar, *"Hail the Manor!"* We wave; well, I wave. A signal, all is good, welcoming him.

"*Hello the Minstrel*," I hail back.

Abby isn't angry about the ballad. She is impressed and proud, understanding the need for wandering minstrels relaying news and stories. It is the exaggeration of making her bigger than life she objects to.

It is how he makes his living. No one ever pays to listen to a mundane tale more than once. Stories need to excite, entertain; to make people hold their breaths in eager anticipation. The good songs get patrons stomping their feet; funny stories bring tears of laughter and joy. That is what brings people into the pubs and taverns and sells food and ales. A good minstrel works for room and board, an occasional coin and favor. Manor houses will ask you back time after time the more entertaining you are.

He has visited several times since we have met. Our Manors are not huge, but comfortable. Not massive like most others, but we are ever expanding.

At Jackie's, he would have to entertain daily for his supper and room. Here, he can just be himself, practice songs, jokes and rest. We treat him as one of the family.

It's amazing; he strolls up, packs on his back and hasn't even broken a sweat. I was jealous.

Someone had alerted Ana in the kitchen and the pages race out to place the food trays down on the table. A good staff makes life easy.

With his charming smile, he hugs Abby, engulfing her in broad arms as if she was the only woman in Camelot.

Her pretend sour mood façade drops quickly. He shakes my hand as the cats, with tails swiping, pounce, wrangling to get their backs scratched while Abby serves up refreshments.

'A long quaff of ale, cool and refreshing washes the dust off the pipes', he told us at one of our first meetings. He still looks like a kid, even though he is our age.

"So," Abby quips, "what brings you out this way? Hiding from an irate Father wanting you to marry his daughter?"

We all have a quick laugh. The cats are not happy since he has stopped scratching.

"Actually, this is part of my regular run before the fairs begin," he relates. "I do the circuit to give and receive what news there is; pass on greetings between friends, tell people when and where the fairs are. But this has been a fairly quiet trip," he admits. "Except for one thing. Have you noticed an overabundance of fish dying?" he asks with an inquisitive look.

"Where there are streams and lakes, there are dead fish," I mention.

"No, not like this," he responds in all seriousness.

"We are talking several farmilies[1] in different areas all mentioning fish dying." He helps himself to the meats we get from the other place. He enjoys it as much as Jackie does. "I don't pretend to recognize what it means or portends; I am passing along the news," he muses, adding cheese to his plate. His appetite is like several of our kids and grand kids.

"So! Do you have time to visit, or are you off again to places unknown?' Abby asks in anticipation.

"I have to be at the Sir Jackie's in a few days, so I can stay and visit," he answers. The cats stare up, expectantly. If felines smile, I am sure this is what they would look like. "I have been on the road for several days, sleeping in odd

1A family of farmers not necessary related by blood or marriage.

places," he relates with a smile. "I could use a nice bath, a warm bed and a home cooked meal."

"Then get married," Abby retorts smiling.

"It is not the first time I have heard that from a pretty woman," he grins, encompassing her hand with his. "Several of the young ladies at Jackie's tell me that all evening. Several can be quite compelling in their statement, and quite exhausting in their endeavors," he brags with a hint of a smirk. "They keep me on my toes, so to speak. But I would not run near as fast around here, dear lady, as I do there," he quips with a sly wink at her.

And then…

Quiet!

"The birds are gone," she mentions, looking around, "Again".

And I feel more than hear the hush that settles over the lands. The quiet that envelopes us is as before the first snowflake falls gently to the ground.

Then the tickle starts at the back of my brain.

"You should get more choice pieces of beef and coffee," I say. "Our friend is back!"

"Jackie's back," she queries? "Whatever could he want this time," as she slowly rises from her seat? "Whatever it is, though, the answer is, I can't wait to go," she smiles expectantly.

We hear a '*CAW*' from the meadow to our left, where the sun appears every morning, giving us spectacular displays.

The large crow so black as to appear almost dark purple glides towards us and lands gracefully upon the picnic table.

It took some getting used to. I hear the words in my head, moments before my ears pick up the uttered sounds. Back when I first met 'Jackie', it was quite disconcerting. I would hear him in almost stereo with a few Nano-second time delay. The same echo heard at Yankee Stadium when Bob Shepard[2] would announce a batter.

He looks towards us, his head shaking slowly. As he speaks, steaming coffee and meat appear beside him on the table. He chuckles to Abby and bows, almost.

We all chuckle.

"Allain, it is so good to see you again. I trust you will be gracing my Manor House soon with your great songs and jokes?" he wonders with a wistful air, a wing raised in greeting.

"Most definitely, Sir Jackie, your hospitality is known far and wide, as is your generosity towards wandering minstrels!" He begins the spiel we have heard time and again. "And the food from your kitchens is unsurpassed by any other," he praises with a sly smile.

"I am sure Cook will love to hear all that from your very own lips," Jackie suggests, "and she will; three days hence! That is all you can goof off hiding out here," he finishes with a caw.

We stare at him bewildered.

2Bob Sheppard- New York Yankee announcer from 1951-2007 died in Oct 2010 age 99

"I am having a special celebration for Kaye's birthday and you are all invited. Allain will grace us with his presence and singing voice." He hops from claw to claw, eager in his announcement.

"I would be most honored Sir Jackie," he replies with a small bow. "I may hap am able to create a little ditty in her honor."

With a nod towards me, Abby answers, "Thank you, from both of us."

"Thank you all, I was hoping for a great turn out," Jackie says as he sips coffee, his wings out as if eager to depart. "You are the first invitations in a long list I must deliver. I sent Kaye on an errand to keep her occupied so she knows nothing of this," he informs us with a sly look.

"You mean this is a surprise party?" I hastily query.

He nods. Even though we share a link in our brains; and are telepathic, we seldom use it to avoid intruding upon each other's privacy.

"And you *will* bring that special gift with you?" He asks directing his gaze towards Abby.

"Is that for her?"

"Yes! I did not want anyone giving hints of what was going on. I did not mean to deceive; you would never divulge privileged information. But there *are* ways that she has of finding things out," he sighs, shaking his head, his feathers fluffing. "I did not want to take any chances."

"Uh, Sir Jackie, before you leave," Allain starts his question, "has there been any talk of an unusual amount of fish dying?"

"Fish dying," he restates, his head bobbing with thoughtfulness. "I do recall hearing something of this."

"It was a complaint I heard from several farms farther to our south." Allain explains. "I am trying to find how wide spread it may be, if it is a problem at all."

"I will check with Rebekah when I get home and see if she has heard anything further. We will discuss this when I see you nice folks for the party." With a quick nod and a wink, he poofs out.

Abby glances around; "I think I will go make a necklace for our birthday girl," rising from the seat, "I have a great idea to put the new beads...!" And that faraway look possesses her as she is off to her workshop.

I smile, "There she goes! The world could end, a tidal wave could wash away the manor and she would be oblivious until the piece is done."

I also rise.

"Frank," he stops me, "can we talk for a minute? I need to discuss something."

"Sure! Walk with me while I get my fishing pole." I ask, "What's the difficulty," as he has a serious look; unusual for him.

"It seems that I have begun walking faster than usual." Allain mentions.

"And that seems to be a problem, how?" I ask, with a puzzled look.

"Not that it is a problem, so much as I cannot figure out why it is happening. I did not plan to be here for two more nights. The places I normally would stay for the night, I arrive in mid-morning. It throws off my schedule and I have not a clue why it is happening."

"When did this begin, and has anything changed since this started? Did you bang your head; get hit by lightning, anything like that," I ask, half serious.

"No," he states with certainty. "Although, when I left Sir Jeres' Manor House I did notice some strange marks on the forest floor. It seemed as if someone had tried to plow the ground. There were furrows under the trees."

I stop walking and look at him questioningly.

"I also found these lying along the digs," he mentions, reaching into his pack to produce several, pretty stones. They are gems, though I could not tell what type. Abby will be better to examine them, being more knowledgeable.

He hands me four and pockets the rest. A strange feeling runs up my arm and LH quivers.

"So, what exactly happens while you are traveling," I query, picking up my rod and bait.

"I would be walking along, working out a lyric or tune, I would start whistling or singing it aloud to get the feel for it and I would suddenly find I am further along the path than I normally would be, as if by magic. I want you to know, I do not have a magical bone in my body!"

"I can see where that could throw off your schedule," I admit. "Let me look further into these stones, show them to Abby and we will see what we can find out."

"Okay, thanks Frank. Just do not tell anyone. If the young ladies find out that I may have magickal abilities along with my good looks, quick wit, charm and fabulous singing voice, they will redouble their efforts to marry me," he says playfully.

"No problem, Allain. I can identify with that," I quip back. "Oh, before I forget, be sure not to miss dinner; Ana has found some interesting herbs and is creating a new barbecue sauce. She will try it out on the ribs tonight."

"She is one of the best chefs around, I will surely be there." I notice him salivating as he walks on to his room and I continue on towards the lake.

It still is a beautiful day and I look forward to the half hour walk. This spring weather reminds me of that great entertainer, Al Jolson and his famous song, 'April Showers'. I have been singing that song for over 50 years.

"Though April showers may come your way," I warble.

"They bring the flowers that bloom in May; and if it's raining, have no regrets; because, it isn't raining rain, you know, it's raining violets."

My voice won't win America's Got Talent, but it is not completely without its pleasantness.

"And when you see clouds upon the hill, you soon will see crowds of daffodils; so, keep on looking for the bluebird, and listening for his song, whenever April showers come along."

I begin another verse as I trod the trail to the pond.

"Though April showers may come your way, they bring the flowers that bloom in May; and if it's raining, have no regrets.

A squirrel in the branches above chitters along as I sing my refrain, or maybe chittering that I would refrain from singing. Everybody's a critic.

"Because, it isn't raining rain, you know, it's raining violets. And when you see clouds upon the hill, you soon will see crowds of daffodils; so, keep on looking for the bluebird, and listening for his song, whenever April showers come along!"

I enjoy singing while I walk; it helps pass the time and Jolie inspires me! It is something in his voice that makes you feel things. He is one of the greatest entertainers! Er- well... he will be in a few hundred years.

LH quivers, bringing me out of my reverie. I am at the lake – but, how? Normally – I will sing several verses to get here. I barely finish one.

My pocket is warm; very warm and I hurriedly yank those stones out. They have increased to an unpleasant temperature, and the luster has amplified! Can these stones somehow facilitate travel when combined with the musical notes? All thoughts of fishing depart. Abby will want to examine these gemstones right away. Maybe the power of the crystals will speed my trip back.

CHAPTER 2 Abby's Chain of Thought

'It's amazing how many gems and stones I use here. Frank says,' 'Abby, you sit there and string beads; how can that be so tiring?'

'He doesn't realize the beads need holes to string them. Mechanical means are available, but some of these stones are toxic when heated. I would feel bad if someone became ill drilling them. So, I hold each bead and feel where the hole should be and place it there, magickally.'

'A silver smith is crafting chains for some of my finer pieces, and a tanner is slitting strips of hide, to be cured and rubbed with beeswax for most of the others.'

'I do bring beads from Earth. No one will be able to tell the difference and it gives me a wider range of colors and textures to choose from.'

"Miss Abby, should I bring lunch here, or will you dine in the hall?"

"Thank you, Janet, but I will dine later. Please see that no one disturbs me, unless it is urgent."

"Yes, Miss, but you will remember to eat?" *Janet always watches out for me.*

'I remember when Alex used to watch out for me at the bead shows; I would spend hours wandering through the displays, judging color, textures, shapes. Examining piece by piece to find the right vibration of stone. He would get upset with me not eating or drinking. Then again, the cost for certain stones would upset him.

'Couldn't you choose a less expensive piece,' he would complain.

Eventually, he'd give in and I would buy the gemstone I felt was proper. My spectacular jewelry showed that I made the right decision.'

"Alex! I do miss you! There I go talking to myself again. The good years we had together. Damn! I promised myself I wouldn't cry anymore. It's not like it happened yesterday. It has been a while since he disappeared. It's just that, I feel so frustrated with what happened, a stupid accident we might have been able to avoid."

"And poor Frankie, he should feel it worse. It wasn't Eves' fault for the accident. She walked into the room when Alex experiment went haywire. If it weren't for her cat, Baby, she would never have even gone into the room. I have to stop feeling this way and get myself under control! I will have to tough it out and make the best of it."

"Let see what other color beads we can use for this piece for Kaye. The amber coloring should be nice, going with her red hair.

What's that? Footsteps?"

"Oh, Come in Frank!" *He rarely comes to my workshop. He doesn't want to disturb my 'creativity'.*

"Abby, don't blame Janet. She tried to stop me, and I don't normally bother you when you are creating. But I have something that may be of interest."

He holds out his hand and there lay four very strange, but interesting stones. They almost *glisten*!

"I think they have magick," he announces.

I gape up at him with my one eyebrow arched. "Allain found them near Jeres' property.

They seem to help some people travel faster, which is why he showed up today." He explains Allains' and his own experience, hiking to the lake.

I listen in rapt attention. There is something in those stones that bears investigation.

"All right," I tell him. "Let me see what I can determine. Maybe we have found a new crystal?"

"I don't know," he states, "But since my fishing trip has been canceled, I think I will go to Jackie's and talk to Cook about an idea I have for Kaye's party."

His eyes seem to glaze over, so I know he is thinking of some recipe or idea for cooking or baking. It happens to him when he gets near a kitchen.

We say our goodbyes and he wanders off to Jackie's.

Though it does show me how to finish Kaye's necklace.

CHAPTER 3 Back to Me

Back when our Manor Homes were first being constructed, I started a quest for talented people to run my affairs. The first was a head chef. Food was important as Jackie has reminded me. We would need many workers and they all needed to eat. If it was just a few staff, there would be no need, since I spent enough hours preparing meals for many people. I've loved being in the kitchen concocting new and exciting foods.

Luckily, I found Ana at Sir Guy's. His head chef has served for many years and will serve for many more. Ana was the second, but a first-rate chef in her own right; and the baby sister to Cook, Jackie's chef. So, I bartered her away from Sir Guy at Cook's bidding.

I do help out in the kitchen occasionally. I will ask for a certain meal prepared in a certain way or show a special dish I learned that was not in her repertoire.

And she is always on the lookout for new and exciting things to feed us. Tonight, she promised would be memorable.

We have been experimenting with a barbecue sauce, and she fell in love with it; almost.

"There is something not quite right with the flavor, Sir Frank." My eyebrow went up at the "sir"; she knows I hate titles.

She thought something was missing, some little taste throwing the sauce out of balance. She continued experimenting with different herbs and spices.

Yesterday she came running "I found it; I found it, Sir Frank."

"Found what?" I query. She sees my frown and bobs her head in recognition. Someday she will remember my name is Frank, not 'Sir Frank'. I will patiently await for that habit to change.

"The special herb for the sauce," she raises an eyebrow. "I am letting the ribs marinate as we speak. Tomorrow we will barbecue them over a fire until the meat just falls off the bone."

I eye her with certain apprehensions. Barbecue sauce is a new concept here.

"So, what did you finally end up using?"

"It is called 'Lovage leaf'. A friend sent it from the other side of the world," she answers showing me a sprig.

It appears celery-like, but the taste is remarkably different. "I think that will definitely impact the flavor. I cannot wait to try it." The anticipation causes me to salivate.

And finally, we sit, in anticipation of this gastronomical miraculous experience. Abby is not overly excited as she does not partake of many spicy offerings but will simply enjoy her meal with the standard fare of beef or lamb.

But for the adventurous of us, *we have ribs*!

The trays arrive, the sound of the diners will continue to increase to a crescendo until the food enters the mouth, and then it will die off to a dull din. Tonight, it hushes quickly to a total silence. I glance around thinking I've gone deaf.

Allain, seeing my expression laughs out loud.

"What?" I inquire.

"They are awaiting your reaction to the new dish. You have the honor of the first taste," he informs me.

"Oh! What an honor," I reply.

"Yes," he continues, "and if you survive, then the rest of us can eat," he jokes.

The entire room erupts in laughter.

"And if I do not survive," I question, with eyebrow raised.

"Let them eat lamb," Abby quips to the sounds of louder laughter, mine own included, as she takes another bite of her steak.

Ana makes a big deal of pushing several ribs upon my plate. I smile and nod as she steps back to await the verdict.

I sniff, the fragrance wafts, my nostrils expand to breathe the deliciousness and I sigh.

I pause a moment longer, checking the texture, admiring the look of it. I break a piece from the bigger slab, check the perfume again; milking the theatrics for all it is worth. I raise the piece up to my lips and take the first bite. It is tender and the burst of flavor awes me. My face lights up like a neon sign. I chew, savoring the taste as it rolls around in my mouth, the layers of seasonings and herbs meld together. Swallowing, I nod to her, stand and applaud; acknowledging the splendor of the dish. I point to the chair near me for her to sit and eat.

We enjoy a spectacular meal and great conversations with friends. At the completion, we even persuade Allain to entertain us with songs.

We have singing and entertainment each night. Many of the staff and their families have musical skills, along with other means to amuse. It was a most fulfilling night all around, and after a proper wait, I leave to go to bed. There is much to do for Kaye's Party.

CHAPTER 4 Dream On

"Where are you? Keep calling, I'll find you!"

"Dean, *Dean!*" She calls again, frightened, lonely. He has to find her.

"DEAN!" Another voice, deeper, more commanding, "*DEAN*," someone grabs his shoulder. "Wake up boy, you are dreaming again." his father tells him.

"Huh? What? I'm up! I'm up," he assures his dad groggily.

"Was it the same dream?"

"Yeah, Dad, it was," he sighs mightily. "I could almost see her, nearly touch her. Then nothing, she was gone," he closes his eyes to savor the moment.

"I would have let you sleep, boy, but you were levitating and I was unsure what was going to happen," he admits to the lad.

"Thanks! I saw what appeared to be a plowed field surrounded by trees. The scene is as if I am looking through an oblong window. The previous dream was dense fog. But this did not look like anywhere around here," he reported with perplexity in his voice. "But I do not think that they are dreams

"Do try to get some rest", Jere advises his son.

"Yes Dad! I will try," he answers.

"And try and keep your feet on the ground," his father jokes as he walks back to his own room, wife and bed. He hears his son chuckling.

CHAPTER 5 Flowery Thoughts

"I haven't had bad dreams since I was a child," said almost as an apology to Dagwood for disturbing his rest. "I wonder what brought that one on."

The night had troubled me. I awoke with strange thoughts racing through my mind. As a consequence, I am more tired upon waking than when I had gone to bed the night before.

I vaguely remember giant plants stalking the grounds, looking for victims, reminding me of the movie, "Day of the Triffids[3]." But these creatures looked like the lavage plants we used for the sauce.

I shrug, dress and poof directly to Jackie's where we spend an arduous day in the kitchens with Cook and her staff. After much trial and error, we tiredly called the day a success.

Using techniques not yet invented, we did it right and proper. Helped by Jackie's pastry chef Olivia, we attain a most spectacular effect.

I return home just in time for dinner, as Ana thought to try the sauce on steaks the butcher carved special. The grilling of the meats is perfect. The added sauce makes a wonderful accompaniment. At this rate, I will need to diet

---

3DAY OF THE TRIFFIDS, starring Howard Keel, Nicole Murray, Janette Scott and Kieron Moore. An Allied Artist Picture Corp. 1962

extensively or run a hundred miles a day to work off the extra calories.

I peer around the hall and sigh.

I miss Abby. She is away teaching healing techniques and on the never-ending quest for plants, for making salves and tonics. There was a brief mention of a troublesome incident she had handled. That could wait until tomorrow.

Allain is at Sir George's Manor for dinner and to entertain. He picks up extra coins and information by doing that. I imagine those stones he found helped make his trip there and back a mite easier.

Dagwood and I have a quiet dinner. Well, as quiet as it can be with several dozen people dining together.

This huge hall is looking like one right out of an old English castle. The fire places we designed to heat the entire room, with enough heat left over to warm the upper regions. Abby has artisans creating stained glass to cover the openings. Weavers are making tapestries depicting the history of Camelot to cover the rock walls to keep out drafts. I helped the carpenters build the tables, chairs and benches used to seat the people. And there are many people, with more coming in each ten-day.

But as I see Abby's empty seat, it did remind me she can go where she wants and return when she cares to. I have no hold upon her, except my feelings.

And it is not unusual for her to spend a night or two away, though I do miss her company. We have spent many days together since we reunited that night long ago with Jackie during the blizzard. And many spent since that day when our spouses were tragically taken from us.

I slowly rise, heading for the stairs and bed; Dagwood has beaten me to our room and is already staking out his territory on the bed. I get a lonely 'meow'. It stands to reason; with Abby away, Merlyn is also gone.

"Yeah, it is a bit quiet around here without the ladies," I mentioned. He is a more than normal feline; intelligent in his own right. I often make statements to him which garner odd looks from those unfamiliar with us.

Abby and I do not share a bed; we are still in mourning. Though, hopefully our sorrow becomes bearable and we are able to move on.

With my feelings for her left unsaid, I didn't want to push the relationship. It was still too soon and I was unsure of her feelings towards me. Things will sort themselves out, eventually. These are the last thoughts I have as I doze.

I awake with much to do. First, I send a page to remind Ana to prepare barbecue sauce. Then, I have hours of kitchen work at Jackie's to finish the birthday surprise. And with all the other details, I promised The Crow I will supervise for the party. It will be a busy day.

Abby still has not returned and I do need to talk to her. Especially after last night's dream.

I am hoping it is not a harbinger of things to come. Giant grasshoppers had invaded the countryside, as in the old movie, "The

Beginning of the End[4]." May hap I am missing my library of sci-fi books and movies. I poof directly to Jackie's, breakfasting there. Overseeing his kitchen staff, it turns out to be an easier day than I had anticipated. The surprise is complete, Olivia's bakery staff is amazing and talented, and the task done with little interference from me.

By early afternoon, I am able to poof home to dress for the gala.

4***Beginning of the End*** 1957 Peter Graves, Peggie Castle, Morris Ankrum |

CHAPTER 6   The Pirate's World

"You be gentle with those young'uns, Hans," the woman warns. "You hurt them and their Father will tear worlds apart to get at you."

"Have not a fear, Betta; I will handle them like the milk cows they are." He laughs as he pushes the girls into the windowless back room. It is a small cabin needing much repair.

The girls scream as the door slams leaving them alone and in darkness.

Betta also screams as he trips over her turning to leave.

"Out of my way fool woman," he snarls pushing her roughly aside.

She regains her balance and turns to face him.

"You cannot leave them in that cold, dark room. They are frightened, perhaps hungry and apt to hurt themselves. There be no where they could run, you said so yourself." She places a hand on his chest to soothe his demeanor.

"Their family cannot reach them, nor can anyone cross to save them," she reminds him. "Once we have the things we need they can be put back home with no worries for us," his wife smiles.

"She is right, Da," Leif says, at sixteen he is nearly of a height with his father. "Once we have the gems we need for land and tools..."

"Is that what you think this is?" Hans yells. "Gems for land and tools? I am planning on a castle, with servants!" He slams his hand on the table. "I need not grub or grovel for a bit of grain and some stringy meats ever again. We have milk cows, let us milk them!"

"But there is still no reason to leave them locked in there," she argues back. "With no place to run and all of us to watch, where could they go?"

"Fine," he relents, "but it is on your head. I want nothing to do with it," he yells slamming the outer door behind him.

Beta brings the girls, who hang on to each other dearly into the main room. The younger girl, Anne is twelve; while Grace is nearer sixteen and outspoken.

"What do you think to gain from abducting us? My Fathers' guards will cut you down like vermin," she warns.

"You heard my Da," Leif reminds, "We are nowhere near your lands or your family. They cannot cut down what they cannot find," he says smugly. "And once we get what we need, he will send you back."

"Why did you not ask for help if you needed it," she questions, standing a little taller, looking closer at the young man. "Is there not a king or such that can offer aid when needed?"

"My Da asks no king or man for help. He is no beggar. He is strong and takes what he wants," Leif defends loudly.

"Strong," Grace throws back at him with a slight laugh. "He abducts two small girls. That is strong?"

Leif surges forward as if to grapple with her. Betta steps between them to halt the quarrel, grabbing her son in an iron grip inches from Grace.

He stands transfixed, stares hard into those young, pretty eyes.

Betta cannot stop the thought she sees running behind his eyes. He shakes his head, confused, then walks away, unsure of what has transpired, slamming the door, much like his Da minutes before. But the young girl is right; what Hans has done is not proper and it is up to Betta to correct it by taking good care of the girls. Why did they not ask for help? But it cannot be stopped now.

The other thing that cannot be stopped is what she saw pass between the girl and her son. She has seen that look before in a man's eyes. She saw it in Hans' eyes the night he and she fell in love.

"So, what is it you want from us ma'am," Grace demands of Betta. "We are but two small girls..."

Betta sighs and says, "You are not such small girls where I will sugar-coat the truth. My husband is of a mind to ransom you both for gems. He really is not such a mean-spirited man, but short-tempered. Be mindful of him. I will protect you both as if you were my own daughters." She lets out a small whimper that startles young Grace.

Anne looks up from where she kneels on the floor. "Why not let us go home? Our father will not rest until we are found," she pleads, trying to choke back a sob of her own.

"I wish it were that simple," Betta answers. "Your home is a very long way off. So," she says turning, "we will have to make the best of this. If you want to eat, you have to work and help with the chores."

They give her dubious looks.

"You heard what my husband said. He does not care what happens to you, but I do. Mind me as you would your Ma and I will protect you best I can," she warns.

The young girls, after a brief, whispered conference nod to each other.

"Annie, you look old enough to use a knife," Betta motions to the chopping block and greens bin. She opens the door and shouts, "Leif, if you want supper, bring water."

He soon returns with two bucketfuls, pouring one in the stove hopper and the other he leaves by the chopping block. Somewhat embarrassed, he avoids the eyes of either girl.

"Take Grace out to the stables. Those horses need looking after. I sure your Da left them unattended before heading to the fields."

He bristles at that comment and his sneer, as he tears the door open is not cordial.

Betta shoos her after him as the young girl hesitates, shaking her head.

Once in the yard she sees it filled with farm equipment, most in disrepair. She spies fields in the distance being worked. Rough cabins range in an unorderly row skirting the fields.

Several smaller children, poorly dressed stop their play to watch the new girl. Most know of her and Anne and why they are there. They wave to Leif.

The barn also had seen better days. The roof needs patching, the doors sag and the wall planks could use repair.

"Is it safe," as she enters hesitantly.

"It has held together this long, though it could use work," he answers sharply. "We will have a new building soon enough with many new workers."

"But is it right, where the building comes from," she accuses. "How can you even think of such a thing? Were you not taught right from wrong?"

"Is it right the children go hungry most nights, or that our roofs leak?" He bites back some anger. "Is it right that some die for want of a healer?" He leads two horses over and they work as they speak. Several others, engaged in chores stop to watch the interchange.

"Do you not have leaders to aid you? Do not neighbors help neighbors here," she spat back to him. "You have to resort to abducting young girls?"

He rounds on her with that. "My Da is doing what he must. There is no help here. Our Barons take and take and when we are used up, they throw us out."

The others all nod and murmur in agreement.

"You never asked us for help," she says to them all, but with a look at Leif directly. A sad smile plays across her lips.

"And I am sure your people, in the magnificent homes would jump to help us," he states with grand gestures. "My Da told us of the houses you all live in." For all his harsh words and hard demeanor, she watches him work the horse. It surprises her at his gentleness with the mare. He talks and pets while carefully working over every spot. What surprises her more is she is liking him.

Another young man, Eric leads the last horse over and works. A silence shrouds them, both with secretive glances when they think the other is not looking.

Soon the chores done, the horses curried. With the call to supper, Leif leads the horses to the paddock.

Eric stops her and shyly begins, "He would not have me tell this." He glances over his shoulder to make sure Leif is not returning. "They buried his baby sister several months back." Grace stares at him with horror. "She had the sickness and no healer would be sent. There was no coin. Do not say I told," Eric pleads. "He would not want pity."

Leif waves from the well and draws a bucket to wash. She notices he will take a quick glance when he thinks she will not see. He smiles as they go to eat.

CHAPTER 7 Happy Birthday

"Allain," Abby calls, "are you ready to go?"

"I will be there anon, just dusting my jacket," he answers from his room at the top of the stairs.

She looks at me, her eyebrow up in a question. I shrug. "Like it's my fault he's so vain? It is the part he plays as a minstrel, to look presentable."

He finally comes down, smiling and brushing his sleeve with his hand.

She smiles despite herself, takes his arm and...

...We are at Jackie's, in the main room and it was crowded.

He said he had invited everyone; and I think they all came and brought friends.

We gawk in amazement.

"It seems as if the entire planet is here," Allain says echoing my own thoughts.

"Well Kaye is beloved by all," Abby notes and watches as Allain waves to several young ladies whose faces light upon seeing him. With-in moments, he is spirited away by the young, eligible attendees.

"That boy is going to have a heap of trouble," she remarks, smiling.

"You forget that 'boy' is our age," I remind her, laughingly.

Taking her hand, we make our way to

Jackie's table, greeting people as we go. Everyone also knows of us. That is the power of Allain writing songs of Abby's 'heroic deed'.

"So, what is your plan for getting Kaye to her own party," she asks Jackie after we exchange greetings.

"As I mentioned, I had sent her to help with the inventory at one of the larger holdings. The wife gave birth, but there were complications. Kaye helped with the birthing, and then stayed to help the new mother and daughter recuperate. She has just returned and Rebekah advised her of this special meeting," he finishes with a smirk in his voice and a small caw.

He dips his beak into the coffee. It still steams, smelling delightful. His wing points to the carafe, *"Help yourself, while it is still hot,"* I hear in my head.

Turning to Abby, he comments, "I hear you made a beautiful necklace with some of the local beads and stones."

"Yes, I spent several days getting it right. I am sure she will love it."

Both of their heads then track towards me.

"What? Don't worry," I defend, with both palms towards them to ward off that look. "Our contribution came out fabulous. 'Carlos Bakery[5]' and 'Ace of Cakes[6]' combined couldn't compete with what we pulled off," I reassure. "Cook, Olivia

---

5Specialty bakery in Hoboken, NJ.

6Specialty bakery in Baltimore MD.

and their staff *really* came through. We tried *new* techniques and it came out great."

Kaye, carrying her basket of paperwork walks into the hall with every eye upon her. She nervously clears her throat, not thinking there is this many people in all Camelot.

Slowly, the room grows quiet as people shush others with slight giggles of happy anticipation.

"Miss Kaye," Jackie greets heartily. "We are so very happy that you have returned to us and at the proper hour.

"For what, Sir Jackie," she queries formally?

"For our new tradition in Camelot! The celebration of the anniversary of a birth," he informs her.

Still confused, she looks around the room, "What… who… *anniversary of what*?"

Her parents stand up, "your 110th anniversary of the day of your birth," her mother exclaims.

Kaye's jaw drops. With all that went on with the farmer's wife and the baby, she had forgotten her own birthday. There is always some small recognition of the date but never anything like this. She stares back at him quizzically.

"Miss Kaye, since Miss Abigail and Frank brought this tradition from their home, let them explain it. But first…,"

He hops from the tabletop to the large stand I had built for him, making it easier to be seen by the crowd. Cawing loud to gather everyone's attention, he turns towards the center of the immense hall. With grand gestures he weaves a spell unlike no other; banners magically unfurl from the rafters, candles and torches sparkle with a bountiful of colors. Bunting races literally around the room, attaching to walls while streamers stream, connecting everything together.

The entire hall magically transforms with lights and decorations befitting a grand gala! Not since the days of that young, upstart Wizard Harry has there been such a decorous transformation for a celebration.

Abby explains the traditions and the meanings. Guests approach bearing gifts or tokens of friendship. She hugs everyone, Oohing and ahhing' at the spectacle around her.

The band plays mood music as pages and servers dish up delectable food and drink.

Cook used my barbecue sauce to marinate the roasts. Everyone commented on the fabulous new taste.

At the end of the meal, when all has had their fill, they settle back. The band, which has played sweetly throughout the meal, takes a break.

Allain comes center-stage and motions for Kaye to join him. As prearranged, I poof a chair for her to sit.

He takes her hand and gallantly touches his lips to the back.

Retreating a step, a flamboyant bow, a strum of his lute:

"The anniversary of your birth

Gives us reason to attend
This festive celebration
Hosted by Jackie,"

He flourishes his hand, gesturing to the crow sitting atop his perch.

"Your greatest friend!"

Several guests clap and whistle.

We have come from far and wide
To proclaim our tidings to thee.
To share a meal,
Hear a song,"

He grasps his mug and holds it up to the crowd.

"And have a drink, or three."

Mugs clink together throughout the hall.

"Friends attend to show they love you,
They join us to show they care, and
Of course, they come to listen"
"To me,"

This time, a flourish of his hand above his own head in grand gesture.

"The greatest Minstrel in the land!"

There are laughs and titters among the crowd.

Allain grows a bit more serious, and with head bowed slightly-

"We thank you for all you have done
And hold you in high admiration.
We gather here to show you our love"

A row of horns blow a "ta-Ta TAA!"

"WITH THIS GALA BIRTHDAY CELEBRATION!"

He takes a deep bow, first to Kaye, then Jackie before escorting her back to the table. Tears stream down her cheeks. It is emotional.

Even Jackie's eyes shine as he flutters down with a package in his beak, tied with expensive ribbons and kerchiefs of silk. Back home that would have been its own expensive gift. Apparently, she thought so too, until Abby instructs her to untie the ribbons to expose the beautiful ring nestling in and amongst the silk. Tears spring from Kaye's bottomless well of emotions. A soulful look passes between her and Jackie.

I know what he will tell her. We have had our share of man to man conversations, so to speak. I explain that women want and need to hear of how they are thought. Maybe marriage is not in the near future, but she should understand his true feelings. I know that later tonight they will have a long conversation. But for now, the gift is important!

Abby is the last to bestow her gift, the necklace with that new stone. Kaye's eyes sparkle as much as the crystals.

I wait for the unexpected to happen, and... A spark jumps from the strange stone to Kaye's hand. Their expressions freeze and they glance to see who else notices. Abby's eyes meet mine and I shrug.

Then it is my turn, since Cook and her staff are bringing out the main attraction.

We had, in only days created an exact replica of the Manor House, including figures of Jackie, Kaye, Me and Abby as herself along with the Purple Dragon and the White Unicorn. Merlyn and Dagwood lounge outside by the moat, all done in cake and sugar. Kaye stares at it in wonderment.

With a blink, I light 111 candles. Abby explains to make a wish and blow them all out. Still not suspecting, she closes her eyes, takes a breath and with help extinguishes them all. Everyone claps, laughs and whistles.

"What do we do with it?" she asks with hesitation in her voice.

"Why, we eat it!" I proffer my sword for her to make the ceremonial first cut.

She gapes at me with eyes wide.

Cook whispers to her, "Miss Kaye, we made you a cake."

"That is a cake?" Kaye exclaims, eyes growing bigger. The story spreads, for it is of mammoth proportions with all the turrets and spires, the drawbridge and moat.

Olivia and her pastry staff have many of the skills needed to create the masterpiece and I added my little bits. I will put them up against the specialty bakeries, any day.

She slices the first piece and then turns over the rest of cutting and serving to Cooks' staff.

~<>~<>~<>~<>~<>~<>~<>~

Allain huddles with Sir Jere and Jackie behind his stand. Several other people attending shake their heads. I have a quick thought from Jackie, *'some nonsense of fish dying'.*

Abby is still involved with Kaye; and now Rebekah and her friend Judith has joined them.

As my eyes track around the room, they alight upon Sir Dean, Jeres' oldest son sitting alone, looking dejected with his head held in his hands. I take my coffee and head his way.

"Dean, are you all right?" I inquire.

He glances up at me, recognition coming to his glazed eyes, "Oh! Yes, Sir Frank. I think I am all right, but strange dreams have been keeping me up nights. At least I think they are dreams," he admits with some hesitancy.

"What kind of dreams would keep a young man like you awake?" I ask innocently, thinking of my own strange dreams.

"I hear a young woman's plea for help," he begins. "I have not yet seen her and not sure what trouble she is in. But as soon as I close my eyes, I hear her," he further explains.

"Can you tell me of the surrounding area? Do you see what or where it is?" I question him as Sherlock Holmes might have done? "Does she explain anything more?"

"She says something concerning a looking glass buried in the soil. I have never heard of a 'looking glass'. I see a large rounded shape growing partway out of the dirt. The frame shines and sparkles. I see fog, and once when the wind blew, I saw tilled soil of a field or garden," he gasps. "It does not look like anywhere around here. It seems alien, somehow."

"What do you mean, alien?"

"The trees and brush look the same, but somehow different. They feel odd, the energy seems..., it is hard to explain." He stops, shakes his head and with a little lost boy look, "Then she mentions brigands," he finishes with a small shrug.

"Brigands?" I shake my head, trying to take it all in? "Are you heading home tonight?"

"No! We have business first thing on the morrow, so we plan to stay here. I have the rooms next to your suite."

Abby may have an interest in Dean's dreams, if they are dreams. She is talking to Jonathon, who walks away with a big smile on his face.

I signal for her to join us.

With greetings exchanged, I explain what problems Dean faces. She half-listens snacking on cheeses and vegetables, but her eyes keep darting to the main table, until; "Abby! What is going on?

Abby!" I grab her arm, *finally* getting her attention. She glances towards me and smiles.

"Watch," she points back to where Jackie converses with Jonathon. He listens intently to the lad for a moment and then hops back to his high roost.

Kaye calls for quiet as Jackie pronounces "Is Rebekah's family in attendance? Please come up to the table."

They make their way with their son, Brendon and his family. Jackie recognizes them and shudders. It was at their farm where he met his untimely demise as a human, transferring into the Crow.

Her family is looking puzzled and worried.

"Jonathon, you are acquainted with Rebekah's Father, Master Farmer Donald," Jackie queries? "Ye-ye-yes Sir," the lad stammers.

"Then do what must be done."

He nods his head, obviously nervous. "Master Donald, Sir," the lad begins at almost a whisper in his voice.

"Louder, Young Man, everyone wants to hear," The Crow commands. Several people laugh until he turns a baleful eye upon them.

"Sir," Jonathon starts again, louder, "I would like your permission and blessings to marry your daughter, Rebekah," he blurts out in a quick rush of air.

Rebekah's mother Helen gasps; a hand to her bosom as the tears well.

The two men shake hands. Then Brendon shakes Jonathon's hand and the whole room cheers.

Rebekah sits with mouth open in complete surprise and shock.

"*Quiet Everyone*!" Jackie's magicked voice shakes the very rafters. "Let the young ones' finish," he commands in a somewhat quieter tone.

Jonathon, all shades of red turns to Rebekah, bends down on one knee, he takes her hand. "Rebekah my Love, my life, since we have met, I have adored you and I cannot live without you. You are in my thoughts all the day and night. I would be proud if you will consent to be my wife, please?" He stutters and stammers but he gets it out. She nods, crying, as he places the ring on her finger.

"He got the proper finger, finally," Abby exclaims.

Everyone shakes hands, bangs each other on backs, hugging and crying.

I turn to Abby and ask, "What do you mean, 'he got the proper finger?' You knew all along what was going on tonight, didn't you?" I glance back to the happy couple and the demonstration of happiness. "And you didn't tell me?"

She smiles, "Some things need to be kept secret."

"How many other rings are you making for guys to give to girls?" I ask, smiling myself.

She is misty-eyed as I put my arm around her shoulder.

Women can be so mushy that way.

"FRANK!" I hear Jackie in my mind.

"Yes Jackie?"

"Are you all right," he inquires.

Abby, seeing the far-away look in my eyes, mouths "Jackie?" I nod.

"Yes, why," I answer.

"I called to you several times without a response!"

"Sorry, caught up in the moment," I acknowledge.

"We need to have a meeting in the Council Chambers. Have Miss Abigail attend. If you see young Dean, bring him along, also," he states.

"Abby is with me. Dean headed for bed moments ago. He has had several bad nights," I relate.

"Let him rest then. He would be no use sleeping during the meeting," he surmises.

"What," Abby asks.

"Jackie needs us at a meeting." I relate to her.

I notice people moving towards the small meeting room. It is less noticeable to walk out than to poof out. He wants to minimize the importance of this meeting.

Fifteen people meet to talk of dead fish.

"So how many fish are dying," Sir Henry inquires.

William the Younger answers first. "We have dozens in lakes all over the properties." Williams land is adjacent to Jeres lands.

"And Jere," Jackie queries, "you are finding birds and small animals have also died?"

"Yes, even a raccoon was found lying next to a dead fish," he continues.

"I did not think coons would eat something that would be harmful," Sir Albert interrupts.

"Maybe we should begin a formal investigation," Sir James interjects.

Jackie glances. My senses tell me this is something that he wants us to handle. A quick thought in my head tells me I am correct.

"Actually, James," I interrupt, "Abby and I have some free time and will be very happy to look into this to see what we find."

Her head swivels towards me; she glares.

"If you think you can," he relents with no real argument. Jackie bobs his head in acquiescence.

"I am sure we will find a simple reason for what is happening," I assure all concerned.

CHAPTER 8 The Brigands Are Coming

"Elizabeth," The Queen queries, "To whom do you speak?"

"Hopefully," Beth answers, "someone who can help save us, Mother!"

"Well, hide them dear. The brigands come again," she warns softly.

"He is not here; his voice came through the looking glass."

"What looking glass, I see nothing," she says in quiet exasperation.

"No Mother, it disappeared. But it sat as if growing out of that very soil."

"Your Majesty!" The brigand, Hans nods to the Queen. "Your Highness," he tips his head again observing proper protocol. "Where is the King?" he sneers.

"My Father went to rest," Beth throws back at him in an insolent tone. "It is unseemly for someone of Royal Blood to be made to do menial labor. And at his age, it could be fatal," she finishes loudly.

"As long as I hold your two younger sisters hostage, you will do as I say," he throws back at her. "But I will relent. I would want nothing untoward to happen to his Royalness." He laughs at the strange word he created. "But in exchange, I want extra jewels," he snaps at them.

"You do remember that we told you it is dangerous to your health to handle those stones," The Queen reminds the man. "Over exposure is deadly."

One of his two companions make move to ask a question. A slight arm movement from Hans cuts off the query before it is even asked.

"That is our problem, Madam! You deliver them or you will never see your daughters again." He smacks his palm across his thigh for emphasis. "We will be back to collect our jewels soon," and he storms off with the others trailing behind.

The two women are shaken but compose themselves, they are royalty, after-all.

"Now dear," The Queen asks after several deep breaths, "What is this about the looking glass?"

"Mother, I saw a looking glass! The same type the brigands stepped through that first day. This was a bit smaller."

"Were you able to see anything," her mother asks. "Did you see who was speaking?"

"It seemed to be a young man upon his pallet in his room, asleep," she explains. "But strangely, he was several inches above it, as if levitating. There was a deeper voice, and older voice calling to him, as if to waken him. Then the brigands came and the glass disappeared," Beth finishes.

"Be careful," Her mother warns, "we don't want them to learn we may have garnered help. If anything happens to my babies...," The Queen says tiredly.

"Mother, you go rest," Beth suggests with concern in her voice.

They walk slowly back towards the castle. "You have been doing much and need peace," Beth insists. "They have no understanding of how the Stones are created. That once I hold my jewel, I have the power to control the movement of the 'Creative Ones'." She wraps her hand around the jewel and smiles as the power tickles her hand. "Look around! The brigands have gone and several loyal subjects have promised to help with the harvest." She stops to sob as the strain of the invasion is getting to her, also.

"You are a good daughter," her Mother proclaims, hugging her. "I am very tired. Things will change once we get out from under these thieves. I will reopen the Royal Gardens for all to enjoy. I had care of them many years ago when your father and I were first married, before he became King."

"Yes, Mother! You told us that wonderful story," Beth remembers, lovingly. "Go, rest! Tell Father we will be all right, soon."

Turning from her Mother, she makes her way back to the fields, pulling a stone from beneath her bodice. It shines and sparkles upon her touch.

"Now is my chance," she states aloud to no one. Holding the gem in both hands up near her face, she begins a chant; slow and melodic; the prayer that brings the Creative Ones to the field to intermingle with the soil, consecrating the earth and turning it so the new growth can flourish and an occasional gemstone is produced.

"LUMBRICUS TERRESTRIS, I CALL; please

attend this field and magic weave. For in your spirit, we do most believe. Please honor this humble request and bless us with a bountiful harvest!"

It was a simple intoning, repeated while holding the magical gem.

After several minutes, the soil trembles, shakes and then roils. It churns violently all around her. Up through the soil the Creative Ones writhe. They are a foot in diameter and range from seven to ten feet in length. They glisten in the sun, which can be deadly to them. With no discernible faces, they come in answer to the Princess' call. They understand what is being asked.

They churn the loam in the field, passing through it, consuming what they consume, leaving their droppings, which occasionally are small colorful stones, different from the adjacent rock.

Some people find those stones precious; others deem them harmful. Keeping them close can cause sores, bleeding and flesh to burn and slough off.

The rocks are generally collected wearing special safety clothing, and then piled away from the fields in earthen containers. If left in the soil, it kills the immediate surrounding plants for the season. If they are left in containers, it heats up, facilitating their breakdown. It can then be feed back to the soil in small quantities to promote plant growth. But if left wet, to cool slowly, the resulting stone can become beautiful and/or more powerful than any gem.

CHAPTER 9 In My Room

I sit in my room enjoying a cup of coffee. Dagwood lies across the bed, napping. Suddenly, his head comes up and he pops to his paws. The door opens and Abby enters with Merlyn by her side. Without a word, she removes a bottle of 'Mountain Dew' from a small wooden box. A moment later, it is chilled and the cap popped.

"Ah! That's what I needed," she smiles, giving a quick scratch to Dagwood right behind the ear. Putting the bottle down as she sits on the bed, "Now, why are dead fish and animals important for us to look into it? Isn't this a normal phenomenon, something like the algae that forms on top of lakes and oceans?"

"I am not sure. We have been here a few years, and we have never encountered this," I mention. "We will have to investigate since Jackie is concerned; which is why he insisted we look into it."

"But I need to discuss another matter with you," I admit getting comfortable on the seat. "I have been having strange dreams the last couple of nights."

At the mention of dreams, she sits up to pay rapt attention.

"Several nights ago, I had a dream that plants walked, like in 'Day of the Triffids'. I haven't had dreams of that type since the Wizard Orson was around. Could it be a harbinger of things to come?" I ask.

Her face blanches when I mention the plants and turns pale at the mention of Triffids. "Are you all right?"

"The other morning as I readied to leave, I was in the kitchen gathering my herb pouches when Ana ran in looking for help. Two of the girls were trapped in the garden by plants that walk. They literally grew up overnight, as I didn't see them the night before." She stops to take a sip of her soda. "Every movement of the girls, the plants blocked them. I set a fire spell and burned them. Maybe I should have used salt water, as in the movie?" she laughs.

"That is not funny," I comment, "At least not to the girls. Somebody could have been hurt. I wonder why no one mentioned it?"

"I don't know. I left directly after. I presumed Ana would have said something," She remarks.

"That was the morning I left early to work on the cake at Jackie's. No one said anything when I returned, figuring you had told me," I reasons.

"It is strange you would begin to have premonitions," Abby cites.

"LH gave me no sign that anything was untoward. So, I am not sure what is happening."

"There was no direct danger to you, so LH would have no reason to alert you," she assumes. "There was another dream?"

"Yes, last night I dreamt of giant grasshoppers."

"Oh, my goodness! Really?" She asks with eyes wide. "That's eerie. When I got home this afternoon, John said the fields had been inundated with crickets the size of his fist. He had never seen anything that large. Sir Thom had stopped by for herbs and magicked the critters away. There was no real harm done, but we need to find out what is happening," she cautions.

"Yes," I muse, "Am I picking up on future events that are natural or am I picking up the thoughts of someone playing with magick?" I wonder.

"Or are your dreams simply coming to fruition?" she ponders innocently. "Is there some reason why you might conjure up ideas from your mind and they become real?"

"I don't have a reason and why would it start now? I have had dreams before and things don't show up the next day crawling, walking or flying around," I say, getting up to pace the room. "Why would this start suddenly?"

"Did you bang your head, get hit by lightning? Have you changed your eating habits or drinking something different?" she interrogates.

"Not really, just the new herb Ana mixed with the barbecue sauce.

Six eyes followed me as I pace back and forth. "I am not sure..."

Both of the feline's ears twitched up.

"What is that noise," she asks. "Someone calling 'Beth?"

We venture into the hall. Voices float to us from Dean's rooms.

I knock. Getting no response, I open the door and see he is alone on his pallet. Strangely, we hear another voice, a female voice from the far corner of the room.

"Dean, help us, please," it implores.

I will attempt the impossible. If it works, I will make the invisible, visible. To hold what we hear and make it seen. I want to converse with the girl of his dreams.

A quick word, a slight hand movement of the spell and a portal materializes.

I see trees and a field, two women stare back at me. Then Dean sits up calling for Beth; the portal pops closed, leaving us all in the dark.

Jackie poofs in having heard my consternation.

Everyone talks at once. Jere comes in to investigate the commotion with Dean still puzzling of what went on, wondering why all these people were in his room.

He re-tells the story he related downstairs, of Beth calling for help. Brigands had invaded. He never heard anymore because he woke to soon. We settle everyone down. Jere will stay with his son. The rest of us venture back to my room.

"So!" Jackie begins, "What did *you* see?"

"I for one," Abby starts, "didn't see much. I glimpsed what may have been a portal."

"Jackie, it was a portal! The same as we use," I answer. "Two women stood in a field surrounded by trees. They appeared human like us, but not us. There was an alien feel to it. They were from another world, another alternative," I finish.

"All right," she says. "How can someone not familiar with the portals create one?"

"Well," Begins Jackie, "that is how I first came to your world!"

"True," she agrees.

"What if these Brigands knew of portals? Learning from Sir Orson while he transported through the alternatives," I inquire.

"That could be a possibility," my two friends agree.

"I guess tomorrow we start investigating dying fish to see if somehow the two are related," Abby mentions.

"I don't see how a portal could be causing fish to die, unless it opened right in the water," I object.

"Yes Merlyn," Abby states looking down to the feline, "taking Allain with us might be a good idea. He is familiar with the problem. I do think you want someone along that pays you extra attention," she comments laughingly.

Merlyns' fur bristles slightly and her back arches during a quick hiss.

Abby smiles at me. "She thinks I hang out with you and your sense of humor too much."

"So? What is so terrible?" I joke. "Let's get back to the other problem," I request.

Jackie turns a baleful eye on me, "What other problem? Is there something you are not telling me?"

I let him read it directly from the mind link we share.

"So, you have no idea who, or what or even why any of this is happening. It very well may be of your own creation. If something is affecting your dream state sufficiently, you may be creating these phenomena," Jackie caws, lecturing.

"Yes," Abby takes over. "In REM sleep you dream; certain enzymes are released by your body to immobilize you. If that process is disrupted, you can move, throw things, slap, hit, punch or even walk in your sleep. Possibly this process is slightly disrupted allowing your mind to create what you dream, or at least a bit of it. So, if it is the new barbecue marinade causing your condition, stay off the sauce," she quips.

"Sure! Now you tell me," I gulp.

They each do a double take.

"I had the sauce basted on the roast beef tonight," I mention with a sheepish grin looking down at my feet. "It *was* delicious, though," I admit, looking back up.

"Uh oh," Abby comments. "We will have to be on our guard tonight."

"Not much we can do about it," Jackie mentions shifting from claw to claw. "Just try to dream something harmless."

A gleam comes to Abby's eyes, "The 'Sta-Puft Marshmallow Man."

I instantly get the connection to 'Ghost Busters[7]" and we both break out in laughter. Jackie perching on the chair back just shakes his head.

We chuckle as we say our good nights.

7**Ghostbusters 1984** produced, directed by Ivan Reitman written by Dan Aykroyd and Harold Ramis. With Bill Murray, dan Aykroyd Harold Ramis, eccentric parapsychologists with a ghost-catching business in New York City.

CHAPTER 10 Here, There Be Dragons

The next morning dawns bright and clear with a warm breeze wafting through the window. I arise, stretch, thinking how wonderful a good night's sleep is. There is something dim, almost in my conscious. A piece of a dream, just out of reach of...

...A piercing scream and a commotion in Jackie's herb garden.

I poof there to find Cook and Thomas face to um-face with a small dragon. I guess it is small, comparing it to the only other dragon I have ever encountered. This one is not so large.

The dragon stands, poised, head swinging, very lost and confused. Then it focuses on me and bellows. With wings waving, eyes whirring different colors, it bounds at me.

LH remains dead in my hand, so I trust that I am under no threat. The dragons tongue comes out and tastes the air around me. Then the thought strikes me – FIDO! The dragons name is 'Fido'.

Who names a dragon 'Fido'?

Abby and Jackie both poof in with Allain following by the normal mode of transportation along with other members of the staff. The guards have swords drawn.

The dragon places his head on my shoulder and I am hit with another shock. I can communicate with him. I can hear him clearly. Not the same communication I have with Jackie, but communicate, none the less.

Fido is a young dragon from an unfamiliar alternative, very confused and lonely.

Jackie breaks in on our conversation. *"Frank, where did that Dragon come from and what are you going to do with him?"*

Abby sidles up next to me with another question, "What did you dream last night?"

My memory returns, the dream comes back. I smile to her. "Anne McCaffrey and the 'Pern Series," I tell her.

"So, this dragon is from her world," she gasps out.

"I would guess so," I answer.

Fido is bending down to have a sniff at Merlyn and Dagwood, to see if they are his new playmates.

I let Jackie have a quick look into my memory to explain of what we talk.

"This dragon comes from a series of sci-fi books that you have read over the years?" he asks. I nod.

"Friends," I hear the voice ask in my head.

"Yes Fido. These are our friends," I tell him, both mind to mind and verbally.

"And as for what I am going to do with him..."

I smirk to Abby, then to Jackie and once again back to Abby with the grin growing on my face.

She immediately shakes her head, "No!"

She repeats emphatically, "*NO*!"

"Can I keep him? Can I, can I, huh, huh? *PLEASE!* He followed me home. Can I keep him?" I am laughing so hard I can barely stand.

Abby breaks down laughing, holding onto the fence that Jackie perches upon.

He stares askance at our antics.

We finally calm, almost.

Abby, with a deep breath to help calm her asks, "Well, if you were to keep him, where would he stay," and at that moment she knows it was the wrong question.

I laugh again and almost can not breathe. I finally gasp out, "Anywhere he wants to!"

We both break into paroxysms of laughter again.

After several moments I stand without doubling over in laughter.

"Seriously though, I have to keep him, for a little while, at least."

Several heads turn glaring as if I have three heads myself.

"What else can I do with him? He is a tame, intelligent creature, so he does understand.

"You had better give this much thought," she suggests.

I take his head in my hands and gaze into his eyes. Well one eye, anyway. I see the love and intelligence there along with a questioning look. "What the hell! I always wanted a dragon for a friend!"

Fido's eyes whirl; his tongue comes out and licks my face.

"Down Fido, down, good boy," I say and he stops licking and steps back a pace.

"So, now seriously," Jackie asks. "What are you going to do with him?"

"I am going to keep him," I explain. "There is no place to send him. I can't destroy him as was done to the Triffids and the crickets. So, he stays with me."

"Make sure that he stays out of my gardens," Jackie mentions.

I talk with Fido, show him where to go, what areas to avoid. I glean from his mind what he eats. Small animals and fish are his main diet, with an occasional fruit or vegetable thrown in. I put hunting areas in his mind. And assure him we are friends.

I caution him about scaring people. With a simple thought I show him I will return later.

Once he is familiar in the area, I can bring him on trips with us. We watch him wing home. If he ventures further afield, he will be at Abby's and that will be all right too. We don't have many people working our lands, yet.

We go on to breakfast. I am hungry enough to eat a... never mind!

The discussion of the day concerns Fido. Some worry a fire-breathing dragon in the neighborhood is dangerous, remembering the previous instances a Dragon flew the skies

Allain whispers for me to stand and say something to alleviate the peoples fear. I'm sure he is already working on a song of dragons.

I stand and garner every ones' attention.

"Most of you have heard about my friend, Fido the Dragon. He is intelligent, probably as intelligent as some of us. He will be staying with me. I want no one teasing or bothering him!" I state with authority.

"He is young, large and friendly. In his exuberance, he can easily hurt you just rushing to meet you. Otherwise he is harmless. So, I want no one to worry. If you see him doing something that he should not, tell me. Thank you! Go on with your meal." I wave to all as I sit.

I fill Allain in to what is planned for the day. He is relieved. Several eligible girls want to spend quality time with him.

Jackie also wants to go, but with meetings and other duties he needs to perform, he stays behind. But he does make me promise to tell him of anything unusual that we might stumble across.

He cautions with fish dying, it might cause harm to humans.

It is Sir Jere farms we would search, so I asked his permission. It is just a formality, though he agrees most readily, as it is to his advantage for this investigation to conclude with due haste.

Cook brings supplies out knowing we need a snack or two to work properly. With all the investigations we have done for Jackie, she knows what we enjoy.

As the supplies are being assembled, we finish our meal.

"So, Jackie," Abby questions? "How did you conclude with Kaye last night? She seemed quite happy with the party and the gifts."

"Yeah, Jackie, did you manage to give all that cake away? I think people around here will be eating it for the next three weeks." I joke.

"Ah! Yes, the cake." he takes my cue having to not talk about Kaye if he doesn't feel comfortable with the subject. "Magnificent piece of engineering you and Olivia came up with, nearly lifelike. Even the details on the pattern of the walls," he goes on to say. Abby glances at me, I shake my head and mouth, 'later'.

"You have a meeting with Jere this morning?"

"Yes! Yes, I do," he agrees. "I do not want to keep him waiting." He bids us good-bye and poofs out.

"What was that?" she rounds on me. "I ask a simple little question and get it side tracked into everything else. Does she like her ring and necklace, or not?"

"That wasn't what you had asked. I heard the discomfort in my head from him. I think she loved it all, but cannot love him the way things are," I suggest. "I cannot guess the exact outcome of the conversation, but I am sure it was not entirely happy," I conclude.

"We need to resolve his being a bird. How long can he live in that crows' body," she wonder, now in a sour mood.

Dagwood enters. His many relatives throughout the forest will aide us in our quest.

Allain reminds us all of Jackie's warning for caution. I mention 'careful is my middle name'. He thinks my parents fools for naming me that.

CHAPTER 11 Getting to The Root of It

We transport to where the first dead fish had been spied. The numbers are now startling and we use wet cloths over our noses for masks to not choke on the stench. We count a squirrel and two foxes among the dead.

Not seeing any obvious contamination, we hike upstream. Back on Earth we would look for businesses dumping poisons and or toxins into the water supply.

With limited industrialization, there are few polluters. Smelters and smithies are two trades that might poison the water. A tannery can also have that effect. I don't think there is sufficient volumes of business to cause this amount of contamination.

We do find furrows in the earth looking remarkably similar to what a plow might do. The differences do become apparent. First there are no prints from oxen or people and two, a plow can't cut roots with the ease which this cut root.

"Abby! Allain!" I kneel near one furrow. "Look! This root doesn't look like it was whacked with a plow or cut with an ax. The ends are smooth," I suggest.

Abby takes root in hand. "This has the feel of being chewed," she states, opening her eyes wide in amazement.

Chewed?" Allain questions looking around. "What could be large enough to chew a root the thickness of my arm?"

"Whatever it is had no trouble at all with the roots or hard soils," Abby mentions. "The farmers here would love to harness a creature which could till for them, as long as it isn't big enough to eat them first," she jokes.

"Now, now," I chided, "We don't know *what* made these furrows! May hap it is something natural," I caution.

We scout further afield, poking here and there. Merlyn was digging in the dirt, I thought covering something.

I get a strange look, as if to say, 'excuse me', along with a quick growl.

Abby gets there first.

"This looks like one of the stones you showed me," she comments, brushing away the dirt.

We concur.

Merlyn gives a quiet meow as she places a paw on it.

"She thinks there is a power to it. Different than what we found in the 'crystal cavern', but still a power. And she suggests we visit the 'crystal cavern' as soon as possible."

I see looks pass between them. "She won't say why, just that we should. You can explain soon!"

She stands with a blank look on her face. "This is another instance she shut me out. I do not like it one bit."

"Okay," I begin. "Here is what I can say. When we get to the caverns, you will understand what is going on. Until then, I have been sworn to secrecy." I admit.

She picks up the stone and remarks that it is still warm.

We spend several hours more hunting around lakes and streams and find additional dead and dying fish, along with furrows scarring the land. It is frightening to think we could have an epidemic of staggering proportions.

CHAPTER 12 What's for Dinner?

We find just enough information to know we are well out of our league.

Jackie is at his usual spot in the main hall. Those who live and work for him use this room for meals and meetings; it is filling fast.

Abby explains, "we need to bring samples back to Earth for analysis. We have no idea what is causing the fish and small animals to die," she continues. "A good Biologist should be able to point us in the right direction."

"So, what is the trouble," he asks, picking up a piece of fruit in his claw.

I pick up the explanation, "As soon as a qualified scientist begins examining a fish sample, they will wonder where it came from," I pause to let him understand. "With no toxins, poisons or pollutants in the cells, they will have many more questions for us than we can answer." I take another sip of coffee from my ceramic mug.

Jackie's head bobs up and down. A habit he picked up since becoming a crow. When he thinks deeply on a subject, some of the original crow habits come to the surface.

"Unless," Abby remarks, "we can talk to my neighbor, Diana? She is a biologist and would not ask too many questions."

"Yes," I say, remembering. "The neighbor with the big roses I always admire?"

"They are chrysanthemums and that was not what you were admiring," Abby jokes.

"Well, whatever they are, they are big and I admire them. It's not my fault she is a widow and dresses like that," I tease.

"We could approach her and see what she says," Abby suggests.

"Nothing ventured, nothing gained; I always say," Jackie adds.

"We will head back in the morning and see what we can find out. We will poof from the lake with fresh samples, and transport a live one for comparison," I propose.

CHAPTER 13 Home Again?

Early the next morning, there is a light knock and Abby opens my door as I was pushing my foot into my boot.

"All ready?" She queries.

I nod, and in a blink, we are back at the lake.

I wish she would warn a guy, first.

We spend several minutes gathering the samples. Then she opens a portal into her garage. It is the easiest place to walk into without attracting attention. The windows are masked to keep nosy neighbors from seeing in.

I don't know why we consider this going home. Yeah, we have relatives on Earth and houses we own. But I am not sure, anymore. With so many friends in Camelot, better weather, better quality of life, it is home. And as Abby is quick to point out, 'In Camelot, 'there is the magick!'

I give a sheepish shrug as she watches me place those contaminated samples into her clean refrigerator. The live fish splash around in the bucket. We wish there were ways to save them all, but it is beyond our meager capabilities.

I go for groceries and she visits Diana. We both know what it might mean, having to tell what and where. But considering the losses; the deaths, maybe higher up the food chain; it will be worth the risk.

Merlyn pace the kitchen, hungry, awaiting my return. It was a quick shopping trip. With

Merlyn satisfied, I bring refreshments to the patio where the women chat.

"So, any idea on what may be killing these fish," Diana queries.

"No," I answer. "Jackie said fish are going belly-up in his lake."

"It upsets him," Abby remarks. "And he worries it will spread. If the small animals eat the fish or if it is something that can infect the small game."

I am getting hungry and suggest we continue our discussion at the local diner. We take a booth near the back and peruse the menu.

"So, who's for the fish?" Diana quips. We find she does have a sense of humor.

"Jackie sent samples over for you to look at."

"I do have a lab. It will be a simple matter to do some preliminary investigations. I might find an enzyme missing or some poison leeching into the surroundings." She has the same far-away look Abby gets when designing a piece of jewelry.

Then she mentions cell structure, DNA, water evaporation ratios. I glance to Abby to comment. But she is staring passed Diana at a woman wearing a very lovely necklace with colorful stones. And so, the meal went. The only one listening to me is Merlyn.

"Merlyn, what do you think of the Yankees chances this year?" She purrs at me, then with a quiet meow, slowly shakes her head.

"That bad, Huh?"

The two women give me a double-take as I rise to pay the bill.

We transfer the samples to Diana's lab and she is already muttering, absorbed in the investigation, promising a preliminary report the next afternoon. I am not sure she even hears us say 'thank you', as we leave.

Walking back to Abby's it is hard to catch my breath. The pollutants on earth are taking their toll on my breathing. Camelot has no trucks, trains or jets. The pollution and cacophony that is Earth makes me realize the perils we face while away from Camelot.

I prepare dinner. It is not rocket science, or even biology. Two steaks on the grill, potatoes in the microwave and a tossed salad will be a change of pace for us. I pop open a cold bottle of beer. While there are many intoxicating beverages back home, including ales, but nothing beats an ice-cold Michelob Lager! *

We sit comfortably on the patio, shielded from the elements. The garage and house act as wind breaks. I light the fire pit for effective lighting and residual heat. It as a bit chilly after sundown.

A quick flash from the garage and the side door swings open with Jackie winging onto the patio.

"Hello," Abby greets with a smile. "It's surprising to see you here."

He neatly lands on the picnic table. "We had a little incident and since our link does not work between worlds, I thought I would visit, instead." His look is such, as if expecting something.

A smaller flash and coffee and London broil appear from nowhere.

"Thank you, kind lady for your hospitality," Jackie mentions, hopping to the mug and sipping.

I hear a sigh of satisfaction.

"You need to bring the communicating stones with you. It would simplify things," he advises, taking another bit of meat. "It seems that Dean was able to find further information concerning his dream girl. Beth is real as we suspected. A band of outlaws invaded their world, abducted her two younger sisters and is holding them hostage."

"What is it they want," I inquire, taking another sip of beer.

"They want jewels mined from the fields," Jackie answers. "Then Dean awoke and we found out little else."

Abby shares that it is a troubling incident and we will help investigate that after we solve the dying fish problem. We bring him up to speed on Diana doing a preliminary analysis.

A strange noise echoes from the back yard. A bang and then a quiet curse as someone apparently trips over something.

"Hello!" A call comes a moment later, and Diana appears from the side of the garage.

"I saw a flash of light from the garage and took a chance you were still awake." She has questions to ask.

I stand, more to shield her view of Jackie, than for any archaic manners.

I need not have bothered. "Oh, a tame crow," she exclaims as she sits.

I offer her refreshments, and nearly magick the coffee before realizing where I am. Abby gives me a funny smile. Maybe she was thinking the same. Using powers becomes second nature living in the land of Camelot. I return in minutes with a carafe and cups for coffee.

Diana is eyeing the extra coffee mug and dish of meat on the table. "I thought you had a radio on from the sounds of conversation; unless the Crow talks," she laughs. The look that comes across Jackie's face is priceless. His thought is one of playing a regular crow.

"Yeah," I laugh, "The crow talks."

She gets serious for a moment. "There is something strange happening."

Jackie stiffens, sitting on the perch he has hopped to a moment ago.

"I heard another voice as I walked through your yard. Now, unless the cat can talk, there is another explanation?" She finishes with a look to both of us. Merlyn picks her head up and meows daggers at the woman.

"And then there are the fish and water samples," she continues. "All through this land we find pollutants; except for in the samples you gave me. I can't name a place where there is not some type of poisons in our waters. Pesticides, mercury, fertilizers, medicines or salts leech from the sewers, roadways and fields, yet you manage to bring me samples with none of these. It may as well be from the year 1600," She is looking at us with an accusing stare.

I am perspiring slightly.

"I found nothing in those samples to suggest 21th century earth. Would either of you care to fill me in?"

I lean over to pour coffee in the cups. She nods her thanks and takes a sip.

"And those two fish came from completely different places," she advises, looking straight at me. I nearly drop the pot.

"Dear Lady," Jackie states, "That is entirely impossible."

She nearly drops her coffee and sits back quickly, choking on the sip she had taken. "We aren't on 'Candid camera?" she asks, her face ashen.

"No," Abby assures her, "no television cameras anywhere."

She takes another sip and clears her throat as Jackie hops to the table to his coffee.

"Now dear Lady," he begins, "both those fish came from the same place," looking to Abby and me for confirmation.

"Yes, that's true," I answer. "I got the live one further upstream, but in the same stream."

Diana takes a breath, looks at the three of us, one at a time and realizes that we were not playing a joke on her. Being a scientist, she takes the facts in rather quickly, makes her determination and runs with it.

"No," she insists. "One fish came from a completely different place. The atomic numbers are off. The DNA readings are different. The molecular structure of the water sample is different enough to show me they were from different environments," she finishes up with a sip of coffee.

"Okay," I ask, "can we put this into terms I might be able to understand?"

"I can," she admits, "but first you need to explain to me what is going on, and why I am sitting here having a conversation with a crow."

"All right," Abby jumps in. "Here is the short form of the story." She then fills Diana in on what went on and how things progressed. How the Wizard Merlin became a crow in our alternative; finding Frank and his wife Eve who helped him through his bout with amnesia. "Frank called to me through a mind link that materialized being around the Magicks of Merlin, now called Jackie.

"So, you can travel between worlds using portals," she asks with skepticism.

"That is correct," I admit

"Could it possibly be you are calling up 'wormholes' and traveling 'black holes'," she asks.

"We are not entirely sure," I answer. "We never thought scientifically. But we have fish and wildlife dying unnaturally and we are afraid it might travel up the food chain into human losses."

"Let me see if I can put this into simpler terms," she says, taking a deep breath. "An analogy might be helpful. You are both gardeners, so I will use that. It is as if a base loving plant was trying to live in an acidic world." She stops for a minute to let that sink in. Then she continues. "That is not precise, but it is almost as if one fish is out of phase, a little off of the normal readings. It is so very hard to explain. I have additional tests to run. I hesitate to send any of the samples to other labs. Any good technician would immediately see something amiss," she finishes.

"Any idea how much longer these tests will take," Jackie inquires.

"A few days, but then I still may have to come out and inspect the site," she states, holding her breath and looking from one to another of us.

"Miss Diana," Jackie begins, "You realize we live in an alternative world?"

"I wouldn't miss seeing this site for anything in this world," she says breathlessly.

"I am sure you wouldn't," Abby acknowledges with a smile.

"So, how many intelligent, talking crows are there where you're from," she asks, looking to Jackie, humorously.

"I am the only one," Jackie remarks with a sigh. "The rest are merely humanoid," he says with such a straight face; I almost think he is serious.

"Maybe we should plan for your visit. This way if you need additional equipment, you can procure it," he suggests.

"That would be great," Diana agrees. "I have a minimum of 24 hours of testing. The remainder can sit and await my return."

"Would Wednesday be too soon for you," Abby inquires.

Jackie hops from his perch on the back of the chair to the table top. Looking up at Diana, he caws to attract her attention. "Dear lady, this must be completely secret. You can tell no one!" He wants her to understand the seriousness. If word leaks out, every Government agency will want to get to Camelot.

"Jackie, I am well aware of what secrecy means. Just because I am a scientist doesn't mean I have a loose tongue," she soothes his skepticism somewhat. "Besides, who would believe me if I said I had an intelligent conversation with a crow," she remarks with a sly smile. "Most scientists are aware a bird's brain pan is too small for intelligence!"

After a moment's silence, we all laugh. A sense of humor is definitely something needed here. We spend the evening planning her visit and talking of what we might have to do to save the fish. She leaves to check tests she has running and Jackie returns to Camelot.

Abby and I enjoy some quiet minutes in the back patio planning our visit to the Crystal Cave. Finally, with all the details set, I lock up the house and head to bed.

She has a comfortable spare room.

CHAPTER 14 The Guardian

We again use the garage, but this time to transport to the Crystal Cavern.

Abby still is not happy. "So, you've kept secrets from me." A hurt look crosses her face.

I counter, "Let me explain this in simple terms. When I am asked to keep a secret, I keep it. It is called integrity."

I have not yet told her of the 'Guardian'. All she knows is the little Merlyn has told her. Soon the secret will be shared, but she is more mad at me than she is at Merlyn. Even Dagwood knows enough to keep out of the way. The felines skulk into the cave ahead of us, leaving me with a very irate friend.

"I don't care who told you or what you promised to whom... This is me, Abby, Your Friend," she rants. "I am entitled to be informed. We have been through so much together; you can't keep me in the dark on things."

I let her continue to prattle on while we wend our way to the back of the cave and enter the cavern. I hope I can let her in on the secret soon.

We light glow balls.

As often as we have come in here, it still overwhelms our senses. The Cavern illuminates with thousands of crystals twinkling as if stars in the night sky.

It subdues her temper, a little.

It is a crime to argue in all this beauty.

I lead her to the rear and to the opening of the small cavern. She hesitates, giving me a questioning glance. I shrug as we follow the two felines through the slim opening.

It is still the same quiet grotto I spent an interesting afternoon in. And is as I remember; peaceful, calm; the small pool gurgles. A sense of serenity overtakes us. I hear her sigh.

Then a voice in the front of my mind, quiet and deep; commanding, yet friendly, intelligent and exceedingly old, says, *"Welcome to you all!"*

Abby stiffens. *"Yes, Miss Abigail, you are hearing me! I am known as the Guardian."* The voice hesitates for a moment to let her acclimate to the sensation. *"I am the secret that was kept from you."*

He relates to her the very story he told me that day in this cavern. He told of the life forms that destroyed themselves out of greed for power, after trying to destroy him. How he insinuated his essence in the rocks and followed the new humans from the quagmire, guiding and educating them from a distance. How his friends, another sentient species were brought in to aid in these duties.

She was much involved in his story.

"I used hidden crystals to extend my realm of influence outside the cavern." He let her see one of them. It was the large one in The Crow's laboratory.

"You have been using that stone to gather information all these hundreds of years," she asks in amazement.

"Yes," the Guardian answers with a slight chuckle in his voice. *"Someday you will tell The Crow of the stones true function. Certain stones give me the ability to insert my consciousness to retrieve information from the surroundings. I have used so many stone with so much of my consciousness; I find I am unable to extract myself from this state I am in to once again become humanoid."*

He then tells the real reason we are asked here. *"There is an entity stranger than I involved with this world. It is so ancient and alien I had difficulty comprehending. I finally discerned its essence after a long and troublesome investigation."*

The Guardian pause momentarily.

We merely stare at each other in wonderment.

Then he continues: *"There is a sickness that is invading the entity, this world! For that is what this entity is. It is 'CAMELOT'!*

I cannot find the cause, nor do I have the solution. I am warning you it is here and ailing. If the cause is not found; if counter measures are not implemented, the entity - this world is doomed." The guardian pauses.

Abby asks hesitantly, "You have no idea at all as to what is causing the illness?"

CHAPTER 15 Secrets Abound

Meanwhile, back at Sir Jeres' castle.

"Dean," Jackie begins, "what you are seeing is not a dream!"

He looks at the Crow quizzically and questions Jackie.

"What I am to say to you must stay in this room," he explains to Dean and Jere. "There are some of us who are privy to the truth."

"You have our word on that, Jackie," Jere promises, "neither of us would break that trust."

"There are alternatives to this world," the Crow explains. "Where important decisions were made in the past and more than one reality was created," he finishes.

Both men seem confused.

"Because we live here in this world, it is our reality. But we can cross into other realities, other alternatives."

Dean is the first to recover. "Is that what I am experiencing," he asks?

"We believe so, Dean."

"So, someone from another world is coming into this one and asking for help," Jere put out to Jackie.

"Not coming into this world but corresponding into it," Jackie corrects.

"Can someone from another alternative survive in this one, or the other way around," Dean wonders? He is hoping against hope it can be done, for he has fallen hopelessly in love with Beth. He doesn't know why or how, but he knows he cannot live without her.

Jackie pauses, "Miss Abigail and Frank are from an alternative."

They give him a long, hard look.

"This is why we need secrecy here. We do not want invaders in our world."

They nod in agreement. Their oath is sacred.

"I am going to teach you the spell to open a portal into the other alternative. It is simple enough. What is important is the energy needed. You may have insufficient power in the other world to return, so be cautious," he intones.

Dean learns the words, and the thoughts involved to find his way, to have a focal point to move precisely between the alternatives. To focus on a person coordinates the move easier.

He agrees and understands, promising to use all caution when he cast the spell later that night. "Night for us is daytime there," he explains. "I do not want to frighten Beth with many people. She may think we are nothing but mere thieves."

"Very good," The Crow agrees. "And you will be immediately aware the energy level. If you are unsure, keep the portal open."

CHAPTER 16 Beth Discovered

Later that evening, in the quiet of his room, Dean cast his spell. He pictures the feel of Beth, her essence; he imagines her gentle tones. The portal forms and opens revealing a sleeping chamber of grand proportions. Upon a large, canopied bed lay a young woman sobbing.

"Beth," he whispers, hesitantly, hopefully.

"Who calls," she asks through the tears, sitting up.

"Tis I, Dean," is his shy answer.

She rises, glancing about, noticing the 'looking glass'.

He walks through, cognizant of the fact if the portal closes, he may be trapped.

They meet on her side. She slips nervously into his embrace. His arms en-wrap her to be sure she is real. She peers up at him, then pushes him away harshly.

"Why did you wait so long to come to me?" she demands.

"I thought you were a dream," he admits. He feels the energy sufficient to weave spells, but with her cradling in his arms again, he does not care if he is trapped forever. "Once I knew you were real, I needed help to locate you and transport to you," he explains. "Tis not a simple journey, but now that I have found you, come back to safety with me," he implores.

"I cannot! My family is in need. The brigands hold my two young sisters..."

A door opens.

"Beth," a voice calls, also feminine. "To whom do you speak?" she questions and enters unbidden.

"Mother, this is Dean, from through the 'looking- glass'."

She eyes him dubiously.

He takes the older woman's hand and gallantly kisses the back.

She giggles.

"Sir Dean," Beth begins, "Madeline, my mother and Queen of all 'Eyre-land."

"Queen?" He echoes. "Your Majesty," he intones with all formality, and a deep bow.

Then with a quick look at Beth, "my apologies Your Royal Highness. I did not ...!"

And with a look back to the Queen, "But a coincidence, my Mother is also named Madeline."

"It is fine," the older woman assures. "We are informal here. Madeline is a good name. It means 'tower' in the old tongue. Towers are strong and upright. Remember that." She instructs, to place him at ease. "As long as all is well, I shall depart to check on your father. I will leave you two alone. But, Sir Dean, the King does stand on formality when it comes to his daughter's honor and 'drawing and quartering' is still in vogue." A sly wink as she readies to take her leave.

"Oh, Mother," Beth says exasperated, "that was an old boyfriend." She looks at Dean and explains. "I was eight and he was an older man of ten."

Deans' face goes through a myriad of contortions not knowing how much is true and what is facetious.

Beth puts her hand upon his arm, "We are joking Dean."

He let out a breath he is not aware he is holding. "I am so relieved," he smiles. "It would not do for the King to 'draw and quarter' his future son-in-law," he pauses for effect, "Or be good for his future Grandchildren."

The Queen pauses in her exit, turns and with a wave says, "I know!" closing the door after her.

"At times, my mother reads the future," she explains.

He smiles, leads her to a chair and bids her sit. "Explain to me these bandits, my dear. What do they want and where do they go?"

"They heard stories of precious gems and jewels found lying upon the ground. To us, they are nothing, a nuisance. We dispose of them as harmful. Where the brigands come from, they think them rare and valuable," she concludes.

"Where could they get information like that in a closed society, unless..." he pauses for a moment, as if in an argument with himself. He finally resolves the internal struggle. "I notice your Mother walked in and out of the room. Is that the only way to leave," he asks her?

"How else could she leave; fly?" she inquires.

"Well, to tell the truth, yes," he says.

"We do have stories of magicians in fairy tales, but only one man could actually do magick.

He was a wizard from another land. He did simple tricks of conjuring and sleight of hand," she explains.

"What name did he give? Was there anything unusual about him, his appearance, maybe," he inquires.

"I do remember that he appeared quite old. I think he said his name was Sir Orson."

"I will inform my Father. Perhaps this 'Orson' might be the one known to us."

"What troubles do you have with the brigands that must be settled," he asks?

"I must give them extra gems to ensure my sisters safety. They will be here in the morning, so I have much work to do."

"Have no care, Dear Heart. I am here to help. Where do we find these gems?" he asks.

"In the fields," she replies.

Taking his arm, she escorts him through the opulence of the castle, past servants who bow, guards who salute with a wary eye, being sure their Princess is safe.

The couple walks together, *closerthanthis,* out of hand-carved doors trimmed with rosewood inlays. Into a large, rock-faced courtyard surrounded by guards with pikes, and a waiting carriage.

It is a conveyance of grand proportions, befitting a royal house. He waves the footman aside and hands the Princess up into an interior of teak wood and leathers; pillows and blankets. Four beautiful white stallions stand snuffling, impatiently stamping. The reins run up to two richly attired coachmen. Armed horseman adorned with helms and mail sit, a dozen each, front and back to escort their Princess.

Once the portcullis is raised it is a pleasant ride, over hills, by fields and passed gardens. Down through villages where the populace comes to bow and curtsy to their Princess. Grand homes and properties line avenues which he sees little of, as his eyes never are off Beth. After too short a ride, they stop alongside a freshly tilled field. Much involved, they pay little heed. The footman, with a loud throat clearing finally gets their attention.

"Dean, *Dean*! We have arrived," Beth giggles breathlessly.

Raising his head from where his lips pay homage to her pretty neck, he reluctantly lets go and the coachman gently hands the Princess down to his waiting arms.

Hand in hand they walk to the field.

She giggles as he kisses her palm.

Rolling up his sleeves he waves people back, then weaves a grand spell. Some slight gestures, a sentence; his hands flash again in the sunlight. More uttered words, sparks fly, a flash of light and...

...A giant sieve stands partway out of the soil. A final word, another hand flourish and the sieve moves through the soil separating stone from the dirt.

Farmers, clad in protective clothing pick through the piles looking for the gems. With heavy gloves they sort rock from stone and soon there are ample amounts cooling in pails.

Now a new problem arises; a farmer accuses Dean of being in with the outlaws.

"I assure you, I am not, Sir," he protests.

The farmer obstinately condemns, "only the brigands are capable of magicks."

Beth is quick to intervene. "Watch your tongue! Sir Dean is here to help."

But the man continues to shout, "Only the brigands can do magic!"

The populace crowds the couple. The Royal Guards stand ready.

"You do not trust your Princess' Judgment?" Dean asks. "You do not believe that someone can do good magick?" He is near to losing his temper, and it seems the crowd is about to become an angry mob.

The Guards intervene and with their horses push the crowd back.

She puts a hand on Dean's arm to show support but cautions him, "These are my subjects," she whispers. "I would not like them harmed."

He nods and smiles.

"Let me show you real magick," he says with a laugh.

Taking her hand in his, he kisses it. A small, clear bubble forms about the two of them, keeping the mob at bay. As he enlarges it, the people and the Royal Guard are pushed further back.

Then, a melody; strings soft and low spring from the surrounding trees. A drum beat, slow and empowering vibrates the ground. The mob looks down at the earth in wonderment. Music fills the air, horns echo with their airs; the song, rich and melodious. The people glance nervously around for the source, nearing a panic state, never having come up against anyone with such strange powers.

Dean slips his arm around Beth's waist, leading her in dance. Slowly, tenderly they turn and step together with the music and each other, gently spinning in cadence to their hearts. And with each turn, each step, they rise upon the air. First five feet, rising to ten, then twelve, and finally twenty feet; oblivious to all around them. They swirl, dip and dance, following the road back to the castle. Townspeople point and marvel at the sight of the couple on air! The coachman and guards chased breathlessly below, helpless to do more than worry for their princess. Wondering as to their punishments if something terrible should befall Her Royal Highness.

Breathless, the happy couple lands in the courtyard far from the maddening crowd.

They plan to meet again after the pirates visit. Beth cautions him, her sisters were at risk and it would not do to have it known the Royal Family has found a magickal ally. So, after several long goodbyes, Dean walks through the portal, looking back the whole time.

CHAPTER 17 Oh, Oh, Oh Diana

We had conversed at length with The Guardian and heard his thoughts on the situation. Whatever is poisoning the lakes is harming the entire planet.

Abby finally forgives me for the secret, making me promise to never hide important information again.

So, we investigate yet another lake where the fish are dying. Small animals also lie dead along the shore. I feel bad there is nothing I can do to stop it. It is getting scary.

"Those furrows cover the field next to the lake. It looks like someone took a plow and oxen and went berserk." Abby observes.

"You're right, but again there are no foot prints. This is strange, indeed," I mention. "And we find more of those stones. They are pretty and they have some type of magical ability as you have said but what can they be used for?"

"I think we should check back with Diana," Abby suggests. "May hap she has learned something of what is happening."

"Good idea," I agree as Abby opens the portal into her garage.

We walk onto the patio...

...And into the waiting countenance of Diana.

"Well, it's about time you two show up," she mumbles, nearly dropping her coffee cup. It seems there might be more than coffee in her drink. After a deep breath, "It is all real, isn't it?" A frightened and confused stare.

Abby sits and places her hand on Diana's arm. I guess to be told there are alternatives and other universes is one thing, but to then sit and hold an intelligent conversation with a crow and you are not the most intelligent one in the conversation; well I guess it is too much for her.

"Come inside," Abby suggests, "You can use my bed to rest. And then we will go investigate the lake."

She smiles up at Abby and stumbles off to the bedroom while I brew fresh coffee sans alcohol.

How easy was it for me to accept a talking, intelligent bird that was a wizard. Although I did have an edge, Jackie was in my mind. Eve was the same at accepting this, although she watched me for over twenty-five years do things that normal people could not accomplish.

Abby, from a world of wonderment; has a cat that communicates with her. So, it was an easy step for her to accept Jackie as a talking crow; and Alex was a no-brainer. Being married to Abby, anything is possible.

None of us knew any better to not believe. Diana is a scientist. She was taught to disbelieve everything unless there are believable truths; then still question. But when that mentality is shown alternative worlds, magicks and wizardry, and intelligent talking crows; a few screws are bound to bounce around a little.

I am sure after a little rest with her intelligence she will be fine.

I sit on the porch, the noise of the trucks and cars racing by grate upon my nerves as I watch the sun travel through this polluted stuff, we call air.

CHAPTER 18 The Longest Day

Dean waits, anxious. Hours later with great apprehension he focuses upon Beth. The portal opens into her bedchamber.

Crossing quickly, he enfolds her in his arms. They speak briefly of the pirates and their greed for gems.

"Do not worry, Dear Heart," he tells her. "Come back with me, meet my family and friends. We will find a way to rid your world of these scoundrels and save your sisters."

"Give me but a moment with my parents to ease their concern?" she begs of him.

Returning, he sees the anxiety in her eyes, the worry of the coming journey and the meeting of strangers. He takes her hand to calm her fears.

A smile from her lips is all the impetus he needs. Pulling her to him, they engage in a long, soulful kiss. Then, both out of breath and breathing hard they walk towards the portal and into...

...Deans' bedchambers.

It is a small room. Not opulent like hers. It is made for sleep.

"Why have you brought me here," she inquires with a slight smile.

Embarrassed that he did not think through the implications, he quickly recovers, grinning, insisting it was for her ease, to give her a moment to compose after traveling the portal.

"And also, to have another moment with you, alone, yes," he answers honestly. "To look at you and hold you and think how lucky I am to hold such a fantastic woman as yourself."

She peers up with amazement; "How can you say that? We have barely met," she insists. "Besides, all you see is a scared little girl that came running for help," she admits.

"*Shh*!" He quiets, a hand gently upon her very pretty lips; "you are wrong. I see a woman who needs help to save her family and friends and does whatever she thinks she has to do. I see a woman who is smart enough and brave enough to stand up to those bandits." He holds her in his arms, gazing down into her face. "What do I see? I see a woman with beautiful green eyes smiling up at me making me want to kiss her again and again."

Several minutes later when both have a chance to breathe and readjust their clothing they venture forth, hand in hand to his parents.

All eyes instantly fix upon the couple. Beth is pretty and one look tells they are much in love.

"Please," she whispers hurriedly, "Do not mention my being a princess?"

"Your wish is my command, dearest," he smiles.

Introductions go all around. His parents are taken with her. Additional refreshments are brought in.

His mother knows what has transpired as all Mothers do. She reaches out and grasps Beth's arm. "I understand that there is much you have been going through."

She holds her arm for a moment with a squeeze to show compassion. "We have invited members of our Wizard's Conclave to help you."

Beth nods, "Thank you, all," she says, confused at the strange surroundings.

"Call me Maddie," Deans' Mom offers. "It will make things simpler."

"A coincidence that my Mother is also named Madeline. But a conclave, you have no ruling family. No King or Queen," she wonders.

"No dear," Dean answers, "we have no royal families here. The Wizards' Conclave rules in place of a Royal House," he explains.

Beth looks askance.

"Well, that is not entirely true," Jere interjects. "As Dean mentioned, we do have the Wizards' Conclave as the ruling body. But we still do have royalty."

He explains that once upon a time a King ruled the country side. As the population grew, he needed advisors, some of whom were unscrupulous in their activities, overtaxing and threatening the population. "The old King had had enough. He threw all those advisors in the dungeon; picked his four most trusted friends and they devised the concept of the Conclave to run the kingdom. That Conclave rules in honesty and fairness right until this day." He finishes the story with this little bombshell. "That King who gave up the throne for the good of the Country was your

Great, Great Grandfather, so that makes you Prince Dean. We are still royalty." Jere jokes to Beth; "I hope that it does not make you look unfavorably upon us, knowing we have royal blood?"

"No! I would love him no matter what type blood runs in his veins," she smiles.

His parents stare as Dean takes Beth's hand.

They were filling plates with food when Jere mentions that Jackie will soon be in attendance.

"Where are Frank and Miss Abby," Dean asks.

"I am not sure, son. They still investigate for Sir Jackie, I believe."

That was the moment The Crow picked to appear.

"Sir Jackie," Jere says with a broad welcome, "so glad to see you."

Beth jumps back as The Crow flutters onto a chair back.

Maddie, who is sitting right next to Beth, grabs her hand in support.

"Do crows normally drop in around here? she asks concerned.

Maddie, stifling a giggle, answers first, "Just the magickal ones, dear."

Jere gets to his feet and takes matters in hand. "Miss Elizabeth, allow me to introduce you to one of the oldest and most honored of Wizards; Sir Jackie. Sir Jackie, The Lady Elizabeth," the introductions conclude, he sits back down.

Jackie hops to the table for a closer look. With his head at an odd angle he says, "Yes, Yes, as I thought."

Beth is panic stricken, "the bird talks?"

"Actually, Your Royal Highness, I do, I do very well," he comments as his feathers fluff and then calm.

"What," Jere states.

"*WHAT*!" Maddie echoes.

"How?" Beth began...

"Well at first I was not completely sure. But upon a closer look, I realize that the painting was you when you were somewhat younger," he says with a smile in his voice.

"Painting?" Beth asks.

"Yes, the oil hanging in your parents' parlor. You were quite young, I suppose, when it was done," he says thoughtfully.

And in explanation, "I was researching a problem several years ago and came across your family's realm in my travels. I met your parents and had several lengthy conversations. You and your sisters were away for a vacation, visiting your Mothers' Sister, I believe. Horseback riding and canoeing that they so enjoy. You went along to care for them since your Aunt was getting on in years. That was quite commendable of you."

Once everyone has calmed sufficiently, Beth relates story of the abductions of her sisters.

CHAPTER 19 The Royal Encounter

"Now," Jackie begins, looking around the room to collect his thoughts, "Those pirates are due back tomorrow, Princess?"

She nods, still taken aback with a talking crow.

"And the time difference is half a day between our realms," he asks, again she nods.

"So, if the three of us leave now, I can have a conversation with your parents, then rest in your realm and be refreshed for the meeting first thing your tomorrow morning," he states simply.

Jere argues about being left behind and is cut off with a quick wave of a wing.

"We are going to reconnoiter and gain an insight to the bandits. I am going because I am known there. Dean and the Princess are going because they must. When we need muscle, we will call you," Jackie explains.

Now Beth complains about being called princess.

The Crow squawks quietly and shakes his head.

The trip through the portal is an easy one and they walk in off the main throne room where the Royal Couple are conducting audiences. Beth gets her parents attention and with a hasty end to the session, Dean and Jackie enter.

Courtesies of the day are observed all around; Jackie and the couple reminisce over refreshments before getting down to work.

"So, what we must do Highness is follow them back from whence they come, find your daughters, make them safe and capture these 'Pirates'," Jackie finishes his explanation with a quick sip of his beverage.

The King glares with fire in his eyes.

"And what in Hells name do you think we have been doing since they showed up Sir Jackie," he says dripping sarcasm "sitting and quaking in our boots?" He rises and stomps to the Crow.

"I understand, Majesty," he starts, looking back up at the King without a tremble.

"NO – YOU - DON'T!" The king roars. "Since that first day I have had spies, thieves, beggars and loyal subjects trying to find where my daughters are. Anyone and everyone that I could ask, plead, pay, coerce or threaten I have called upon." He hurls his cup at the wall in frustration. It bounces off with a hollow, metallic twang and rolls unevenly across the floor. "I have had my entire Kingdom scurrying to find my daughters and bring down these outlaws! What can you do that I cannot?" he finishes, exasperated, a tremor in his voice.

The crow fidgets, moving from one claw to another.

"Old friend, if I may. I understand that you have been doing all that you can to find your daughters. The thing you do not understand is they are not on this world," He finishes quietly, explaining alternatives and where he and Dean are from.

"Not of This World? Those bastards are from another world entirely?" The King sits heavily back in his seat, trying to fathom the last statement.

"Let me explain in the easiest terms, but you must remember, this information is secret and must not be shared."

They solemnly agree.

The crow's wings open slightly as he begins. "We have found that there are many worlds like this one." Jackie states.

And after a brief explanation.

"So, as I understand it," the Queen voices, "They are from one world as you and Dean are from another?"

"That is correct, Highness," Jackie affirms.

"So that is why we could not locate their hideaway," the King reasons looking calmer. "I was to begin putting people in the dungeon again," he laughs, "If we could find it as we have not used it so long," he jests. "But how do they travel between here and there," he queries.

Dean takes over the explanation, looking from Beth to the King, "They have magickal powers, Sire. They open a doorway between the worlds and they walk in as easy as you walk from this room to the next."

"And what do you know of Magickal Powers young man," The King commands looking first to his daughter and then to Dean.

"I am a wizard, Sir. I deal with the Powers daily," he states with all sincerity.

"And you will be able to catch these bastards that my best men have not been able to even find," The king demands, his voice louder each word.

Dean stands and faces the King. "I will do my damnedest, *SIR*, to do what makes Beth safe and happy."

"Uh, Your Highness," Jackie interrupts, "we still lack much needed information, and may hap my young assistant would be best suited to listening rather than running his mouth."

Dean gives Jackie a dark look and Jackie winks.

"Might I prevail upon you to let Dean and the Princess move into another room where they may converse in quiet and may hap, he can gather additional evidence," he recommends.

"Well, we do need to capture these men and free my other daughters. But remember young man; that is my daughter you are with," the King states. "And those guards with you are for her protection," he cautions with a slight growl.

"Yes Sir, I am aware of that. I will treat her as the most precious thing in all the worlds," Dean answers as they leave the room.

"And you, Sir Jackie also remember that is my daughter he is with."

"Sir," Jackie caws with a small sigh, "I have known that young man since he was a suckling babe. He is well meaning and conscientious. He is loyal to a fault and your daughter will come to no harm when he is in attendance."

"You had best be right, Crow," The king mutters, his wife placing her hand upon his royal arm to calm him.

"What is your idea to find these pirates," he asks, finally calming enough to think.

"I will not be finding them," Jackie coolly informs the king.

"What?" he sputters, attempting to jump up again.

"They will be right here," Jackie reminds. "I will follow along and travel with them when they leave," he explains. "Once I find where they are and observe where your daughters are, it is a simple matter of making plans to capture them and return your daughters back to you."

"It seems the logical thing to do," the Queen states to her husband. "Why go running around when they will be here in the morning."

"Exactly right, Highness," Jackie reiterates. "Now if we can be off to sleep, I would like to be rested for the meeting," he suggests.

"Well, I will have a guard show you and young Dean to your rooms," the King says.

"A guard?" Jackie questions.

"Not for you Wizard," the King explains, "for that young man with you. I will take no chances of having either of them unattended in the same world together. I saw how they gaze at each other," he further intones, "Her Mother had that same look in her eyes the first night we met and I have not been able to get her off me since," he grins. She smacks him behind the throne as Jackie is escorted out of the hall.

CHAPTER 20 Down the Worm Hole

"So, what do we have to do," Diana asks? She seems better after a few hours of sleep.

We are transporting to the lake where I took the fish from. With all the equipment she packed, it might have been simpler to move the lake.

"Walk into that portal," Abby instructs. "We will be in the other world in moments."

With trepidation she walks into Camelot. It is a nice day, the air is warm and we did come in upwind, so the air is sweet.

Her face blanches when she turns and sees the fish afloat on the water. A deep breath, she slips on a mask and begins her investigation.

She plows right in, taking samples of everything, from everywhere. A soil sample here, a test tube of water from there. She pokes a fish with a stick and even dons heavy gloves to pick up a dead squirrel. The flies swarm, showing their displeasure at her disrupting their meal.

We make our way upstream to better air and fewer flies.

"So, what *are* we looking for," I ask.

"I don't know," she admits. "I was hoping to find pollutants dripping into the water or seeping into the ground. Something to contaminate the stream."

We investigate several new furrows.

Stooping for a closer look, a glimmer of liquid catches her attention so she takes a sample.

It is thick, stringy and sticky. But then, a glint of light off a stone partially buried in the dirt makes her look twice.

With forceps, Diana carefully extracts the stony specimen and holds it. It shimmers in the light.

"That looks similar to the stone Allain gave me the other day," I mention.

She reaches for it with her gloved hand and stops, "I don't think so," she comments. "This stone is giving off too much heat!"

"The stones we had were warm," I inform her.

Using a large rock as a table, "First we will check for radiation," she takes a Geiger counter, flicks switches, but the machine barely makes a noise. "Registering normal background radiation," she observes. Flicking another switch, "Now we take its temperature. Wow! Getting up to around 200 degrees Celsius and climbing."

She drops the stone into a beaker and pours in water, it sizzles and steams. Mixing it with a glass stirrer, she pauses before placing litmus paper into the beaker. The paper disintegrates.

"This is why you are having your problems," she states categorically. "These stones contain enough acid to turn the surrounding area hydrochloric!"

"Oh, come on," Abby says. "Some stones can cause this much damage in so short a period? We have fish dying in streams and lakes all around here."

"It is not solely the stones causing the contamination, but whatever is depositing the stones. Whatever is creating those furrows is spreading enough contamination around to pollute large areas." She pauses for a moment, looking at the sky. "Have you had rain recently?"

"We have rain most nights. Some of the wizards manipulate the clouds and put rain where it is needed at convenient intervals."

She appears surprised but quickly recovers, "that would explain it then. The rains wash the contaminants into the streams and lakes, thus cooling down the surrounding soils and rocks."

"But what creature could make these furrows and cause this damage," Abby asks. "We have never had this problem before."

She peers from Abby then back to the furrows and chuckles. "Look at one of the furrows and think small. If you still can't see it, think fishing and you will have your creature but let me have a few minutes to double check my hypothesis." She removes samples from the soil and root area and adds chemicals to the beakers. Checking those findings, she takes forceps and snips a piece of the root. Placing the sample onto a slide, she examines it under the microscope. I had one of those as a kid. It was neat checking the size of things through the magnification settings.

She fiddles with the knob and adjusts the light tray. She slaps her hands together in glee. "As I suspected, the samples here are similar to what we find for our common earthworm." She offers to show what she sees. I wave her off, not very interested to look at magnified worm pus. Abby also declines, reading my mind by the grimace on my face.

Diana explains, "I researched for a food supplement company many years ago. They wanted to increase yield of their crops by introducing earthworms into the fields. The theory was the worm, in its normal day to day living would furrow the field, aerating the soil, helping water and nutrients circulate on a quicker scale. It worked. The worms they used would dig deeper into the ground when it rained, unlike some species of worm that rise to the surface. By using a worm that digs deeper," she explains, "it helps bring water and nutrients further down, giving the roots a deeper base; thus, a bigger plant and higher yield."

"Do we have any idea what type of worm we are dealing with here," Abby asks with a concerned look.

"No! I would have to do further research to pin down the species and sub-species, if we can ever discern it to be a known type," she answers. She is partially occupied with calculations on a pad and her tape measure.

"So," I begin, "with the size of these furrows, these worms would have to be…"

"…12 to 14 inches in diameter and averaging 9 feet long," she finishes for me, showing us her calculations on the pad. She slowly rises from her crouch by the furrows.

I hear her joints creak as she lets out a low moan. Sympathizing, I offer my hand. With a smile and nod, she takes the proffered appendage and stands.

"I guess these creatures are not from around here," she queries with a slight smile.

"We have lived in Camelot for some years, I do think I would remember seeing ten-foot-long earthworms," I mention casually.

Abby smiles at me, "That reminds me of a comment you made a while back, Frankie, that sci-fi books would become text books,"

I return the smile, "Yes, didn't they cover this in "Dune" by Frank Herbert and, what's that other movie, out in the desert..." I try bringing the name to mind.

"*TREMORS?*" Diana replies without the slightest hesitation, "with Kevin Bacon and Fred Ward."

"That's the one," I say with a smile. "Tremors' is a favorite movie of mine."

"Don't go running off to make explosives," Abby quips. "We haven't heard of any human casualties from these things, yet."

"I don't think that they are harmful to people," Diana informs us. "Most worms do not have teeth. You would have to get right in front of one and then lay in its mouth. But then it would most likely spit you out again. I have enough samples. If I can have a place to work?" she queries.

We have used my Manor as a base of operation since it has more rooms. After our spouse's accident, we spent days together in my Castle, fighting depression and loneliness. Abby found her Manor was a constant reminder of Alex. Besides, the energy flow seemed better at my place. So, we pack the samples and the gear.

Abby smiles and we are...

...In my main hall.

Diana's face pales white as a sheet and I help her sit as two of my pages run over.

"Please pour some wine for the young lady," I instruct one page and of the other I bid to return with men to carry the equipment.

They move everything to a bedroom suite with room enough for a laboratory.

Diana calms after a sip of wine. I notice she would take a quick, sidelong glance at me when she thought me otherwise occupied. When I glance back, she will look away. I need to have a talk with Abby later concerning this. What is going on?

Diana is cautioned to keep the techno devices out of sight. Trusted friends know from whence we come, but we keep the general populous in the dark. She agrees and scampers off to play with her toys.

Most of the everyday running of the Castle is done by the overseers. But there are little chores we need to do personally.

And with those out of the way and all the other little things that crop up during a day it is time for a meal. I am starved. It takes much energy to investigate. And that energy needs to be paid for.

~<>~<>~<>~<>~<>~<>~<>~<>~<>~

Diana comes down to report just as Allain appears, always at dinner time. We have children that have that uncanny knack, nearly magickal in itself.

Introductions are made and with his magnetic personality and the many stories and adventures to tell; Diana's attention now focuses upon him. He offers to conduct her on a tour around the grounds after the meal.

The new surroundings seem to have no effect upon her appetite, though and she and Allain wander away shortly after coffee.

"It's funny to not feel Jackie inside my head," I tell Abby, now that we have a few minutes alone.

"Is he still in the Alternative with Dean?" She queries.

"According to Allain, he is," I answer. "Fighting brigands and chasing jewels thieves. It sounds a mite easier than hunting worms and healing the world."

"A crow would be better suited to hunting worms," she quips.

"True, but these worms are of a size to eat the Crow," I retort with a smile.

A faraway look clouds her eyes.

"What's troubling you?" I ask softly, taking her hand.

People use this room for meals and meetings. With a quick look around to be sure we cannot be overheard, a smile comes to her slowly and she squeezes my hand.

"I feel guilty of not thinking of Alex..." I see the pain cloud her eyes again. "You and I have a conversation, we joke, and I begin to enjoy life for a moment. It then hits me that Alex is gone, swept from my life forever and I am alone. I feel guilty," she gasps, wiping a tear from her cheek.

My eyes mist over, for a similar reason. I also feel guilt, but not quite for the same thing.

I give her hand a supportive squeeze. "I loved Eve and miss her terribly, but it is not our fault they are gone. It was an accident that we had no way to stop." I slowly shake my head. "But never think that you are alone, dear lady. I am here!" I squeeze her hand again to get her attention.

"Remember, always..."

I see a look in her eye as she starts to reply, but Allain and Diana choose that moment to return from their tour laughing and talking animatedly. So, I assume he is being the charmer that his profession bids him be.

I release Abby's hand to make room for the two to sit.

Diana gives Abby a look seeing my action.

"So, did you enjoy the tour of the grounds," Abby queries.

"Oh, most definitely, the landscaping is quite striking with the colors and contrasts most amazing," she answers.

"Thank you. Frankie and I designed it together this past year," she explains.

Abruptly Diana stands. "I must get back to run some additional tests." She turns to Allain. "Thank you for such a delightful evening. It is good that I am an older and wiser woman, or I should hold you to some of those promises," she laughs.

Allain takes her hand and lightly kisses it. "Wiser and beautiful, but never old," He smiles over her hand.

She giggles, heading for her lab.

Merlyn and Dagwood having returned from where ever they were command Allains' attention once again.

He smiles looking down at them, "Well come up on the bench, you do not think I would get on the floor with you?"

CHAPTER 21 Cold Feet, Warm Heart

"What am I doing," Rebekah screeches, slamming her cup onto her desk in frustration, sloshing tea. *"OH!"* She cries at the spill and attempts to clean it before it smears the page she is writing.

Kaye chooses that moment to enter, sees the distress on her friends' face, the mess on the table and moves to help.

"Miss Kaye," she asks tearfully, "Am I doing the right thing?"

Kaye smiles down at her, "In what dear?"

"Getting married; am I doing the right thing? Am I going to be happy; can I make him happy?" She stops to wipe tears from her eyes. "Do I even know what I want?"

She looks to the girl she has been thinking of as a daughter and senses this is a case of cold feet. If there were no doubts then there would be cause to worry. "Rebekah, have no care! Every woman has this same type of worry." She pauses a moment to formulate her next response. "Answer several questions honestly and we will see where it leads."

Rebekah nods through misty eyes.

"Do you love Jonathon?"

She gets a startled look, "Of course I love him, more than anything!"

Kaye nods.

"Does he love you?" she asks her young protégé.

Rebekah smiles shyly and nods again.

"Is he good to you?"

"Oh, yes, very good," is the quick answer.

"Does he make you smile and laugh? Does he make you feel special?" are the next questions.

She nods, laughingly.

"It is a very big step in your life. I think you will be very happy for many years to come. Jonathon is a hardworking and honest young man. I have known him since he was a babe," Kaye admits.

By now Rebekah is smiling so broadly her cheeks hurt.

"And what is more," Kaye finishes, "You are going to have many wonderful and beautiful children."

At that remark, Rebekah blushes red. She stands to tightly hug her friend.

"Thank you," she murmurs with teary eyes, "I think I should go to compose myself."

"Take all the time you need, dear," Kaye nods walking to her own desk. 'If only! That should be me with Merlin, er, Jackie, um…' she muses.

"Now I have forgotten what I was doing," Kaye states aloud to no one. "When will it be my turn for happiness?" Her mood grows melancholy as she sits pondering. A slight tremble courses through her body. Rebekah sweeps back into the room causing her to put those feelings aside, not wanting her friend sad, again.

A page knocks and enters with a message. "Miss Kaye! Miss Abigail and Sir Frank are in the main hall. They have a woman with them," he states.

They ask several questions as they follow to the main hall, but the lad has no other information.

"Do not worry yourself, Diana. You will be fine," I tell her. "These are all friends here."

"But some have swords and are wearing chain mail," she replies hesitantly.

"Those are the guards," Abby reassures. "Every castle has guards and guards require swords," she teases the poor woman.

Kaye and Rebekah choose that moment to enter. Introductions take but a moment and they quickly get down to work.

Rebekah stares at Diana, knowing she is from another world nearly as hard as Diana stares back. But the big question is still in the air.

"What is twelve inches across, eight to ten feet long and burrows in the earth?"

It sounds like an old joke from our world, with the punchline, 'I don't know, but here comes one now'.

Neither woman is familiar with this creature. When asked about the gems both girls shake their heads. I see a look pass between Kaye and Abby. And I get a look that says, 'not here or now!'

CHAPTER 22 Back to The Crow

Jackie has settled down for a long night. He realizes he will have to follow the bandits into their realm to track where they have hidden the two little girls. He sleeps fitfully, moving from claw to claw awaiting the dawn.

Beth too knows what needs to be done. She tosses and turns in anticipation, worried. If something goes wrong, they can be hurt or worse.

Her Fathers' health is also an issue, what with his worries over her two sisters, their realm in peril, she is afraid the stress will be too much for him. And then there is Dean, the love of her life; so willing to risk his life for her and her sisters.

Sleep eludes her.

Dawn comes none too soon.

After a hasty meal the three wait in a field.

Dean wants desperately to punish these villains. But she quietly reminds him he is merely to play the part of a field hand helping to carry the gems. Any premature trouble and the two little sisters could be lost.

"We do not want these men to think we have help," she reminds him with her sweet smile.

"But..." he begins.

"No back-talk Dean," Jackie orders. "Keep your anger in check and fade into the background."

"But..." he again starts.

"Dean," Beth enjoins, putting her fair hand on his arm. "Please stay calm, for me?"

She smiles sweetly at him.

All he can do is sigh and nod.

Jackie watches, shaking his head.

A moment later, "Be ready! I feel magick," he warns.

Three men walk out of the mist and up to the Princess.

"So, you brought help Princess," Hans asks.

"Help, no! This is my field manager. He is here to carry the stones," she answers meekly. "Their weight is great and I require help."

Hans roughly jerks the sack from Dean, reaches in and extracts two gems. He hands the satchel back to one of his cohorts. He weaves a spell to test the quality of the stones.

A big blackbird in a tree mimics his every movement.

He notices the crow and to one of his followers orders, "Kill that bird."

Beth stops him with a hand motion, "Why kill the helpless bird?"

"It mocks my every move; no bird mocks me."

"You cannot kill that bird," Beth states with finality. "They are sacred to us. If you expect gems, you must promise to never do that," she warns.

"Never do what," he asks sarcastically.

"To kill a mocking bird," she states.

With a slight bow and a small smirk, he promises, "I will honor that request."

With a head nod he motions his troupe back to the forest where a fog magickally swallows them.

Unobtrusively, Jackie follows; needing to see where the alternative leads so he can venture back later to free the two little Princesses. Fortunately, their magick is slow and inexperienced; he is unobserved as he poofs his way into the portal.

CHAPTER 23 The Peeping Crow

Later that afternoon Jackie asks for an audience with the royal family.

"Highness," he begins, "I will create a small opening into the kidnappers' realm so we can examine where your daughters are being held."

"I thought you went there to investigate?" the king asks.

"I did but could not get too close. It is farming country and a crow is open season. If an archer misses too often, it could arouse suspicion," he explains.

"Why can we not enter and retrieve my daughters? It sounds like the simplest plan?" the king queries.

"We cannot tell the repercussions of such an act. Other of your subjects may have been taken as further safe guards. The Baron may frown upon an invading force in his lands," he explains.

They gather around while Jackie starts the spell. Beth holds tightly to Dean's arm as an opening appears in the center of the main hall.

"This is one-way. We can see and hear, but they have no idea we are looking.

The scene coalesces in the common farm yard.

"I thought pirates had ships tied at anchor or were near water. These people are common farmers," the King intones with some surprise.

"And poor farmers at that," the Queen adds.

"None of our people live that badly, even in our worst years," Beth says quietly.

The King strokes his beard in thoughtful habit. They espy movement from behind a well. Two young people, a boy and girl carry a water bucket between them.

"That is Grace," the king panics, moving to a better vantage point. "But who is that miscreant with him?"

"They have children with them, these pirates?" the Queen asks.

"The young lad is Leif, son of Hans.

"I told you it would be easier and faster if you let me help carry the pail," Grace says, looking up at Leif.

"But I did not want you being hurt. These buckets are heavy," he cautions, smiling back.

"Silly! I am not some little girl. At home, I often help out in the kitchens when needed," she explains.

He opens a door and they enter a small cabin.

It is all they observe as there is no one else in the yard.

The window pops out of existence.

"She seems to be in good health and spirits," The Queen mentions. "And the young man seems to be mindful of her."

The King gives her such a look her crown might have melted had she been wearing it.

"I will hear no such talk as that," he demands. "I want my daughters out of there with all speed."

"Yes, friend," Jackie agrees. "Another day or so, as we need to make proper plans. We would not want to have the girls unduly harmed or other innocents hurt," he explains.

The Queen places her hand on the King's elbow to calm him. "He is right, my husband. We want no harm to come to those who are innocent."

Dean takes Beth's hand tightly and leads her away to a side chamber.

"Beth, my love," he whispers, "will you stay here the night or return with me?"

She smiles sweetly, "I must stay, dear, my family needs me and you are welcome to stay with me," she tempts.

"I do not think I am so welcome at your hearth!" He explains. "Your father smiles very little when he espies me with you."

"My father has little to smile about these days. With my sisters abducted, the Kingdom under attack and his health being poor, there is not much to make him happy," she states plainly. "These are things that he must concern himself with. Sit with him. May hap he will warm to you. Besides, you are to be his son-in-law?" she giggles as she kisses him again.

After another long and loving embrace, they return to the main room, flushed and excited from their encounter.

The King, upon seeing, frowns deeply.

She catches his expression, "Father! Why must you be so? Dean is here to help and protect."

"The young man can hardly help and protect when his one hand is always upon yours and his eyes are nowhere else but on you. Five bands of miscreants could attack before he would know," the king tosses back at her.

Dean releases Beth's hand and turns to face the king.

"Sir, I did swear that I would do whatever it takes to protect and defend your daughter and her family. I do not make oaths lightly. I would give my life willingly if I must," he smiles at Beth and continues. "And once your daughters are safely returned to the bosom of your family, I plan on abducting Beth: with your permission, of course," he finishes with a flourish and a bow.

The King sputters while the Queen smiles warmly and leads him away.

CHAPTER 24 Cave In

"Peter," his Da calls from the entrance to the mine. "Take Willow inside, she always wants to follow us. When she is older, maybe, but today is too dangerous."

Peter does as his Da asks, taking his sister in hand and leading her to his Ma in the cabin. He is named for his Da and nearing fourteen, Willow is six. Their family are miners and they have been digging rock for generations with many holes dug, a few even had ore.

Relatives died in the cave-ins if they weren't careful. His grandma used to help move rocks but she was killed last year after the ground shook and the cave collapsed, crushing her instantly. They tried to get to her but it was too late. Now, his Ma helps occasionally in the caves, too.

This mine is pulling ore but it is getting harder to dig. They tunneled a new shaft with scant timbers to shore the walls and ceiling.

Peter's job is the family garden for their food and feed for the animals. The milk goats and chickens for eggs help supplement their larder. He goes back to watering the beans. He draws bucketfuls of water from the stream which is fed by the cascading waterfall on the mountain by the mine. He is on the last row when the ground shakes hard, knocking him from his feet. That low rumble from the mine sounds ominous. A huge cloud screams from the entrance. Smoke and dust billow everywhere. His eyes sting and he chokes on the debris the cave-in spews. In his coughing fit he hears another scream.

"No! Please, *NO!*"

As he shakily gets to his feet, his Ma runs past shrieking for his Da. He grabs at her but she wrenches away, leaving him sprawling on the ground again with a mouthful of dirt and a handful of cloth from her skirt as the only reminder of the sight of abject terror he saw in her eyes.

He watches in horror as she runs into the dust cloud, forgetting all the lessons taught of the dangers of cave-ins. An aftershock trembles the ground again. His Ma manages a quick scream before the rocks crush her. He jumps back to avoid being crushed himself as a new cloud of dust vomits from the entrance. He lays there several moments, breathing hard, attempting to comprehend what happened. And then the tears come as he realizes the unthinkable.

His sister's scream brings him back to reality. Smoke curls from the cabin door. The tears in his eyes blur the flames; the roof glows.

"Willow! Willow, where are you?" He screams, racing for the door.

"Here in Ma's room," she coughs.

"Stay there, I will come get you."

He crawls in as his Grand Da taught him during a fire. The smoke is thick and foul smelling but the clear air is low near the floor. The dung used to seal up the cracks is already ablaze adding a sting to the air. He is lost, confused and can not find the bedroom door. "Willow, call out. I cannot see."

"Here Peter, over here." She cries weakly.

He follows her voice, finds his Ma's room; pulls Willow out and along. The heat burns their hands and knees, their clothing smolders. Bits of roof fall, flaming whatever is left to burn.

He tries following the wall, frantic. '*Where is the door? I need air.*' He hears his Ma's voice call, clear as day. Maybe she escaped the mine? Maybe she is alive? He pulls Willow desperately towards the voice, towards the door. A glimmer of light, a shadow; someone beckons it seemed.

And then they are falling through the opening, rolling into the yard away from the cabin, gulping great mouthfuls of clean, sweet air. He is beating at his sisters clothing, smothering the embers.

"Ma! Ma, where are you?"

The roof collapses; sprays of sparks rise dancing on the heat. He yanks Willow further from the danger, coughing and gagging on soot and smoke trying to get his breath.

He yells again expecting to see his Ma but they are alone.

"What happened, Willow? How did the fire start?" He asks, panic in his voice.

"When the ground trembled, the candles fell onto the curtains." She gasps and cries, remembering. "They burned so quick, Peter, I could not stop them. Where is Ma and Da?"

The look on her face is one of horror as he explains what happened, and that they are alone, with no place to live.

He holds her close as they watch their lives burn to the ground.

The next days are a blur as they comb the ashes for anything to salvage. A pot, kitchen pieces and an errant piece of clothing is all they find.

Willow is silent, barely cognizant of her surroundings. Several times he pulls her away from the mine afraid that rocks will fall and she will be injured. She seems not to care whether she lives or dies.

On the fourth day their water supply turns to a trickle and then stops. It had cascaded down the face of the mountain and along the stream bed by the cabin. But the earthquake caused it to go elsewhere.

With no family, no cabin and no water he decides to move on.

CHAPTER 25 The King's Demand

"Sir Jackie," King Edward directs, "two days have passed, you are taking entirely too long to resolve this. I want my daughter's home safely, and I mean to have them now!"

"Highness, I understand your concerns but you must have patience. We are as of yet unsure if there are any other of your subjects involved; either as hostages or as traitors," Jackie explains, hopping from claw to claw. "Let me assure you that the girls are quite safe," he explains. "They are learning as well as instructing."

The Queen is rightly concerned, "How do we know for sure, Sir Jackie?"

He harrumphs before speaking again, being perturbed and not used to being questioned. "I have been there myself to check on them."

CHAPTER 26 Trouble Comes Again

"It is not good news, is it Betta," Hans asks as she comes back to the cabin, her face ashen.

"No!" She says slumping into the chair by the fireplace. "All that we tried- failed. He died from the fever. We are being ravaged once again."

He goes to hold her, console her, to help ease the pain.

"What else can we do?" she laments.

"We do the best we can with what we have; we tough it out," he whispers, remembering what it cost when last the sickness ravaged the village. He holds her closer.

"If the sun warms a bit, we will open the cabins to air," she suggests, trying to bring hope.

Looking around, "Where are the girls," he queries.

"Anne is next door helping her friend Rose watch the little ones. She is very good with them and she adores Rose. And Grace is out to the barn with Leif and the others tending the livestock," Betta informs him.

"Do keep them away from the sick ones. It would do no good to have them come down with the fever," he half-whispers to her. "If they should sicken and die..." His voice trails off.

She nods, understanding; not saying what was nearly said.

"But," she reminds him, "Leif has been to most families, helping with the firewood and hauling water... they both were. Grace is helping with the laundry in some homes."

With that, Hans head comes up sharply, "You cannot let her do that anymore. She has much chance to catch the fever."

"I cannot stop her; she sees people that need help and she does what she can; her sister also." Betta pauses, her next words carefully chosen, "Are we sure their Father would not have helped, if we had first asked?"

Han's eyes focused on his wife, at first with a touch of anger and then upon a quick searching glance he stands confused, mulling over her words. He storms out.

The children's laughter fill the barn. The weather is warming, the smell of new life buds from the soil wafting upon the air. The young ones work in the barn starting the spring clean out. The old and dirty hays and rushes are being bundled to be burned in the giant bonfire that night.

Leif explains of the coming celebration to bid goodbye to the cold and snow and to herald in the spring with the hope for good crops. It will be a subdued festival. What, with the winter harsh, the supplies dwindling and friends dead from fever.

With Spring, the chance of the sickness leaving is greatly enhanced. He almost said life will be better once they barter the gemstones.

But it is her abduction and pain that his future will be built upon. He is regretful that she and her sister have been taken; even more contrite about the way he treated her that first night.

Since then he has found her funny, capable, intelligent, helpful; along with warm, encouraging and beautiful. While he is bossy, obnoxious and a bore. He hopes she has one more important trait - forgiveness!

They are alone in the tack room checking rigging's for the plows. The others work in the main barn and have been laughing on the antics of a silly old crow.

It acts drunk, flies around cawing at nothing then lands on a shoulder and pulls the hair, quick enough to not get caught. Erik stabbed at it with a pitchfork but he missed by a feather.

Grace holds reins to show Leif a wear spot that may cause trouble. She glances up as he laughs; recognizing what a loving man he is and touches the dimple upon his cheek.

He gazes down into smiling eyes, takes her hand; they fall into each other's embrace, kissing as only young, new lovers can; noses bumping, teeth banging, giggling. Upon hearing a sharp noise, a quick intake of breath they jump back from each other, embarrassed.

It is Inga; Leif's neighbor. His age, but seemingly so much wiser. A quick look at her grin, he knows she has seen. "It is about time you two," she sighs. "The tension since yesterday has been terrible thick."

She rounds on Leif, "I always thought that it would be you for me; but Grace is a much better match, she can handle you like the wild stallion you are." She grins at the Princess, "do not break him too much. What a waste for me," then runs from the room after a whispered "I will not tell." With a yell to the others, "Let us be home and supper. We are finished today and have much to celebrate tonight."

All the children run yelling and laughing from the barn. Leif and Grace walk sedately hand in hand to the well. He is exceptionally quiet and unsteady.

"Are you all right?" she asks concerned.

He gives a quick head shake and a wide smile, "Sure I am, my love," he whispers to her, "but a bit addled by your kiss!"

"Well if it is going to addle your head, I will be giving you no more of them," she threatens with a smile.

"You would not be able to find your way back home to me."

"Let me be lost forever in your kisses, then," he exclaims, as he grabs and kisses her with more practice and passion.

At the dinner table that night, the conversations center on the fever and the celebrations.

Anne speaks up, "I do not see why you cannot ask our Da for help and healers?"

Hans begins to answer but Betta speaks first, "Dear, I am sure your Da would be willing to come here with aid. He would then hang all the men folk and his army would use the woman in a way not able to be properly mentioned in earshot of you young'uns. All for abducting you two," she sighs deeply.

"But I do not see why?" Anne answers. "You have taken very good care of us as if we were your own daughters. You have not harmed us in any way and as for chores, we work harder at home than you have us do here."

"But you forget, young one; people do not like their children taken from them to be exchanged for precious stones," Hans jumps into the explanation. "And since it was my idea, it would be my neck stretched after your 'Da' does other unspeakable things to me," he finishes.

"I do not think he would be that harsh," Grace answers. "There would be a trial and everything would be sorted out. We would speak up for you. You thought you had no choice in what your options were. And those stones you prize and put much stock in, while to some are precious; to us they are bothersome pieces of rock we would have given you willingly to be rid of them."

Leif stares quizzically. She giggles, standing to move empty plates from the table to the wash bucket. "You still cannot discern what those stones truly are," she laughs with a quick grin to Anne.

"Those are not rare gems you harvest from the fields," Leif inquires also standing as he removes dishes to help Grace clear the table.

Hans and Betta both gape, astonished that their son would even consider to do 'women's' work'.

"No silly," Grace starts as she takes the plates he proffers and gives him a quick kiss.

She stops, realizing what she has done. Now, both red faced and grinning, "Those 'gem stones', if left in a large container break down and can be used as feed for plants. If we do not recover them from the field, they burn the soil, kill the crops and the area is useless for the season. We do use some for decorations. We cool them rapidly in water, first. When we do harvest them, we need to wear gloves and protective clothing, or we sicken and die horribly."

Hans peers down at his fingers worriedly and replies, "But they are the same stones our Nobility wears, it is what gives them their great wealth."

Anne, laughing, "To us they are naught but the excrement of 'The Creative Ones'; Holy, definitely, but valuable, not really." She leaves to go next door to help Rose with the children. The seven younger ones are a handful but Anne enjoys it and she cannot wait to tell her best friend about Grace, Leif, and the kiss.

Betta and Hans can not wait to talk to the two young people either about that same kiss.

The door closes behind Anne, "Leif?" his mother says with a questioning eye.

A protective arm goes around Grace's shoulder, an automatic response from him that neither parent fails to notice.

"It cannot be so," she cautions.

"Leif!" His father says in a more threatening tone, "She is daughter to a King! Look around and see what you offer her."

"Da, we have too little to offer, for sure, but I die without her," he laments.

Graces' gaze goes from Leif's loving face to his parents and back. She knows the look on his face and knows what he speaks is not only true but felt by her also. "Please kind Madam and Sir," she curtsies, "he has yet to offer naught but his heart and it is enough for me," she states in a whisper.

The parents stare at the young couple.

Hans starts to reply but Betta speaks up first, "Hans, you had not much else to promise me all those years ago. It has been hard, but the hearts are still promised and still big enough," she says as her eyes misted.

He pulls his wife to him in an embrace, "Yes, still big enough. We will do what we must," he promises.

The celebration that night is fun, but somber. An elderly man passes prior to the festivities. It makes the hope of Spring that much more important.

The treats made for the evening, the pastries and candies along with the drinks, though not plentiful, are much talked about and well received. The entertainment is all self-made and good. Grace is much surprised that Leif is in fine, clear voice when he sings an old tune of new spring loves.

After a hurried conference with her sister and a brief word to Betta; the two sisters sing a duet, which they had performed the previous year for their own home festival. They are also well received. Leif sits staring adoringly at Grace during the entire song.

All had a grand time.

Anne and Rose whisper around to their friends about the kiss bringing titters from the young ones. Leif and Grace take some ribbing, but some very worried looks come from the older men.

Several hasty meetings assembled that night, after the celebration with little resolved.

Things became decidedly worse the next morning when Leif comes down with the sickness.

His fever rages; his stomach and bowels purge all they have. The worst is; Grace refuses to leave his side. She is going to 'tend' him back to health and there is no denying her. If he is infectious well, so is she. There is no reason to expose anyone else. If she is to get the fever, she would already be ill.

They air an empty cabin and move Leif in, with Grace at his side.

A big argument rages about getting help.

"Hans," Betta pleads, "send to the Baron for healers! We cannot lose another child." The look in her eye is pitiful for him to see.

"Woman, the answer will be that of the last time," he states with certainty.

"But we must try," she cries, "he is our last child." With a slow nod he agrees. Alerting several friends to saddle horses, "We ride to the Baron for healers." Minutes later, three men ride *hell bent* for aid; Betta sits in her kitchen, somber, quiet, and afraid.

Anne, having heard the exchange from the back bedroom brews tea and politely offers it to the woman along with the honey jar. She smiles at the child, not realizing Anne had even been in the cabin.

"Thank you," she whispers, teary-eyed.

With a slight smile Anne states, "I am sorry but I overheard your conversation. You had other children?" she asks somberly.

Betta takes a sip from the sweetened tea and a deep, ragged breath, "last fall, this sickness ravaged the village. Many became ill, some died. Our young daughter was one of them."

Anne sees the tears forming in the woman's eyes and reaches out.

"She was a bit younger than you, as pretty with dark eyes and hair as you have."

"But was there not somewhere you could have gotten help, or healers?" Anne wonders aloud, gripping harder on the hand.

"You do not know the way of it," Betta says, with much vehemence. "The Baron refused to aid us. We were not important enough for him to waste healers on us. Friends died," she whispers. Then louder, "*my **daughter** died.*"

She stands quivering, not yet able to grieve for her child. "My *Catin* died because we were not important to someone!"

For months she has held back the tears and sorrow for her daughter because that is how she was raised; to be strong, be fearless, not cry or make a scene; but her daughter dead, her only son sick maybe dying, she has no resolve, no more strength. She can no longer hold back, and the floodgates open.

Anne, almost at an age to bear children of her own, feels the loss, feels her pain and with a sob, embraces Betta as if she were kin. Together they cry, they wail and with the pain purged, anger partially drained away; the loss, with an edge taken off, Betta gasped with the shock of who consoles her and pulls away quickly.

"What is the matter Miss Betta?" Anne asks, rocking back on her own heels.

"We did to your Ma what the illness did to me; ripped daughters from her bosom. It is not right," she laments. "You should be the one crying, not me. Yet you sit here consoling me, helping us..." her head drops in sorrow.

Anne realizes what Betta means. "Once it is explained, my Ma will understand and not hold it against you. You have only treated us as you would have your own kin."

She peers up at Betta, "If your Baron offers no assistance, aid me in getting home. My Ma will listen with a sympathetic ear."

Betta looks back at the girl, giving thought to what has been said.

"Talk to Sir Hans. We have healers and help waiting," Anne finishes.

"And what do you think your Da will do to my Hans?" Betta throws back.

"Maybe harsher than he should but he will still be fairer than your Baron. We have suffered no harm. Healers will be sent, then justice will be meted to be sure; but it will be no worse than it is, and my sister and I will do what we can to help," she is near tears of her own.

"Tears will not sway me child," Betta mentions.

"I cry not to sway you. I only think what all you went through watching Catin die. How Blessed I am to have two healthy and wonderful sisters and one nearly married.

"You have a sister to be wed?" Betta asks as she reaches her hand out to Anne's face.

"Yes! Grace! With your son Leif."

It is the older woman's turn to look shocked.

"My Da would not turn away family," she smiles.

The two sit talking and laughing and crying as a natural Mother and Daughter will.

The neighbors visit to bring food and get news. They all know, with no healers the fever has to run its course. But Leif is young and strong and has a good chance to survive. And Grace is a courageous nurse who will not give in to anything. Hans will survive, or else!

Just past dark, hooves are heard as three tired riders return. The healers are engaged helping the Baron's family, the Court and the merchants. They will be along in a ten-day, maybe.

Leif continues to hold his own, buoyed up by seeing Grace's lovely, determined face. Will he recover? Only time will tell.

With neighbors wanting to hear of the ride there are extra people for dinner. The talk is not kindly towards their Baron. If they could leave, they would and gladly; but with no one to barter with and nowhere else to go...

"Sirs, please?" Anne interrupts.

Hans stops his tirade, a snarl still upon his face from his earlier anger.

"Take me home Sir, please?" she begs. "My Da will help, I promise. We have healers and people that care."

He waves her to silence, "You do not know the ways of people child! They do nothing for free. You think your Da will come with healers? He will be here with soldiers, and swords." He slams his hand down sharply on the table. "They will take what little we have, use our women while we watch; then hang us all and burn whatever is left. This was what happened when I was a lad; it is the way of the world. The rich take what they want and leave little more than scraps for the rest."

He peers at his friends and then to Anne with a kinder smile. "I was once young and naïve like you. We came back from a hunt, a friend and I to find our men strung up, our women spread upon the grounds tied naked and disemboweled. The children were gone and the rest was nothing but ashes. My parents were among the dead and my siblings among the missing." The last said in a quieter voice, nearly a sob. A deep breath and, "That is how people help; themselves! How did you think people act?" he sneers.

"I am sorry for what happened and for your pain, but grown-ups act differently from my home," she tries to explain.

Hans partway up from his seat to make a point glowers at her, "Yes, you and your sister are kind and helpful. More helpful than we have a right to expect," he mentions, softening a bit. "But what makes you think your Kin will be helpful and forgiving?" he smirks.

"Because," Anne smiles, "They are who taught us!"

He sits down hard, looking at her.

His one friend comments, "May hap she is right? Even if we are severely punished for what we did, if our families are safe..." He breaks off.

"Even if we hang?" asks Hans.

"Even if we hang," his other friend agrees sadly.

The women sob thinking of what loneliness may be forthcoming.

They glance to each other as if deciding telepathically.

With a look to Anne, "Would you swear to do what you could to have help for our families?" Hans asks of her.

Somewhat taken aback by the intensity of the requests, she agrees solemnly.

"Then I will return you and Grace to your family, tonight," He promises.

Her eyes go wide as she shakes her head.

"What do you mean, *No*?" Betta demands. "He consented to return the two of you. What more could you want of us?"

"Grace will not leave Leif, nor would I expect her to. She is much in love with your son," looking towards Hans. "She will not leave him no matter what. She will see him healed and well."

"I will go alone and when I have said what I must to my family, once I convince my Da that no harm has been given you will come forth."

Hans nods once.

"I will go explain what we do," she decides.

Betta walks with her across the way.

Two sick neighbors were moved into the house. Grace thought it prudent that no one else should be exposed.

The sisters converse from a distance. Anne marvels at Grace's courage, risking illness and maybe death to help heal strangers.

Grace admires the poise Anne shows in convincing the villagers to ask for help.

They each enjoin the other to go carefully; Anne says she would explain all to the family. Taking up torches, now that full night has fallen, they make their way back to the cabin.

Neither notices the very large, black bird taking flight from the nearby tree, winging into a very eerie circle of light.

CHAPTER 27 The Whole Truth

"Young Highness," Jackie calls to the Princess as he poofs into a side chamber of the castle.

Beth looks up in puzzlement, forestalling her conversation with Dean. The Crow never uses the formal title, except in the presence of her family.

"Sir Jackie, May I help you?" she asks anxiously.

"Your sister Anne will be returning shortly," he explains.

"What of Grace, is she not also returning?" Beth worries. "Is she well? Is she all right?"

"She is nursing people during an epidemic and will remain until the crisis passes. Be assured she is well and happy," he partially explains. "Anne will explain the entirety of it. Be sure your Father listens to all before making rash decisions," he again cautions.

"What rash decisions?" Beth asks.

"The man who heads the Brigands, Hans is also returning here. He is risking his life to garner healers and aid for his village," the Crow informs them.

Dean feels her hand tighten in his, feels the tension build as Jackie relates the upcoming visit.

"Why would he now ask for our help? Does he understand that my Father will run him through on sight?" she throws back with restrained anger?

"He does, but comes anyway," he continues. "You must hold the guards in check and keep your Da from acting presumptuously until all is explained," The Crow declares. "Your sister trusts this man, believe me on this."

She looks to Dean. All he can do is shrug and nod towards Jackie. "I would believe him, dear," he smiles giving her hand a tighter hold. "His word is good."

"We have time yet," Jackie mentions and he sees Beth's shoulders relax a trifle.

"Engage the help of your mother," he suggests.

She nods and the couple walk to the Queen's side. Jackie poofs unobtrusively to the rafters, hopefully unneeded. Several minutes go by, conversations bandy back and forth between the couples and the King's advisors.

An argument ensues. The King's voice raises in anger as his face changes to all shades of reds and purples. He is trying to make a point for beheading Hans on sight.

Conversations cease as a portal coalesces at the end of the Hall. Guards spring to, steel rasps against scabbards as swords are drawn. The Royal Family rises to their feet, several people appear at the portal.

The King spies Hans immediately. "I want that man's head!" He demands, pointing.

Three guards jump as one wanting to be the first to give their king his wish.

"*Hold!*" The Queen's shout countermands that royal order. Everyone stops, never having heard the two disagree before.

The confusion gives Anne the moment she needs to move closer to Hans affording him some small measure of protection.

The King rounds on his wife with a scowl never before seen.

"What do you mean, *hold*?" he demands. "I want that snakes head and I want it now," he commands.

She takes hold of his sleeve and whispers, "Look who protects the one whose head you so want."

Upon turning and focusing, he sees Anne standing, unbidden and defiant between the man and the guards.

"Da, no!" she pleads, hands held up to stop the guards.

Beth and the Queen briefly confer with the King.

"Hold that man but harm him not," he commands. The King, much relieved that his daughter had shown up, unharmed, nearly smiles. But what of Grace? He was concerned, especially when he sees the portal close.

"Come daughter, speak with us in private," he orders as the guards force the man to his knees in the Court.

"No, Da," Anne stands adamant, "let us perform this ritual out in front of all the eyes that attend."

"There is little to discuss, daughter." He counters. "The man deserves to die and die horribly."

"Father, you know not what has transpired," she defends.

"Daughter, that animal has abducted two of the women I love. One of whom he still holds. There will be no discussions."

He stands in front of his daughter, towering over her but she does not back down. She is not intimidated by him as she once was.

He notices her new demeanor. "You have my permission to speak," he reluctantly acquiesces.

Anne, in a grownup pose she saw others use, begins the tale. Starting with her and Grace abducted by strange men coming at them through the mist in the gardens. Their fear of not knowing, at first, as to the why of it! Then, about the dark room they were initially locked in, and how Betta, Han's wife interceded on their behalf; talking of kindness and compassion. "She treated us as family instead of captives." Anne continues. "We did chores and helped in the village. We taught the children their letters, numbers and life as we know it. And we learned of their people and their ways."

The King relaxes, looking at ease as the tale unfolds. Anne goes on about the festival, "similar to the one we hold here every year; the singing, the fun times and the dancing. The sweet treats, good tasting but little in quantity being such a poor village. But they still tried to keep to their traditions; still trying to cling to hope!" She pauses a breath-length to control her emotions.

"Then the sickness struck again. Miss Betta told me of the Autumn before, when people sickened. Their friends, neighbors and family died. No help came from their Baron. And then to their horror, trying all they could on their own," Anne whispers, "they had to bury their own young daughter, Catin."

Hans head droops farther down as he kneels; the pain and sorrow washing over him again. Old wounds re-opening. Wishing he had died in place of his daughter. Struck dumb this young girl even knew what had transpired.

"Yes, Sir Hans," she continues misty-eyed. "Miss Betta told me of your misfortunes and all your village has suffered."

She turns to face her father again. Standing tall and defiant. "And Da, Grace is there with Hans's son Leif, nursing him through the same fever that took his little sister. She felt it was sensible after being so close to the young man. If she hadn't yet contracted the fever, she was probably immune with no reason to expose anyone else."

Then with a sly grin she finishes the tale, "She would not leave his side. They are much in love."

The King's face turns ashen. "Was that the lad we saw helping with the water?" he asks, not realizing Anne knew not of being spied upon.

Jackie takes that moment to flutter down from the rafters, "Yes Majesty, that is the same lad.

People jump back horrified, some reach for weapons, while others bless themselves to protect from the evil eye. A talking crow must be evil?

"So, there you are Sir Jackie! Have you been enjoying the show?" the King ask, sarcasm dripping from his voice?

"Yes, actually, and the best is yet to come," he chuckles, alighting on a chair back near the thrones, "let the man speak, Highness. You will find his story most interesting."

The King motions for Hans to be brought forward. The guards drag and slam him back to his knees in front of the thrones.

"Speak quickly man while you still have breath to use," The King commands.

Nervously, Hans gazes around, mouth working, trying to bring up saliva enough to speak.

"Get that man something to drink," the Queen softly orders. Two of the guards carry out the royal order, bringing wine.

A quick sip and then another, he begins, "Majesty, my life is forfeit for the wrong that I have done. I do not mind the punishment for me but please spare that of my family and village. Do not punish them for my greed and stupidity." He stammers and chokes as he speaks, another sip of wine helps. "It is of no consequence what happens to me, if my wife and son are safe." He says pleadingly to the King.

"As your very kind daughter informed you, we were denied help when most of our village was stricken with the fever that first time. The sickness raged, 27 villagers died, nine of them children, including my own, sweet Catin. She was not but ten years. Precious to me and much a bright spirit in our lives. Our Baron chased us away, telling no healers would come; that the deaths of our loved ones were of no consequence; no consequence," he repeats near tears. "This last time we went to ask aid he set the dogs on us."

He stops for another sip of wine, to compose himself. The King did a very un-kingly thing; had his conciliator bring a chair for Hans. With a hoarse thank you, he continues.

"We farmed for a Royal House once. I was a young man, my son barely walking. We were set upon by a drought, several ten-days with little rain. We took to traveling to the river with wagons and barrels to bring water to our village. Water for drinking, for the animals and extra to keep our crops alive.

The river was wide and deep but the King put guards. He wanted the water for his Castle, for his flower gardens and fountains. He was afraid that a few barrels might endanger his missing a bath. He threatened us with death if we were caught stealing his water."

Hans shudders before continuing. "Two of my friends took a chance and were caught. They were staked out naked to die of thirst in the hot sun next to the raging river. Their screams and cries carried far at first."

He takes another small sip, his hands shaking, remembering the scene.

"The guards caught a distraught young son attempting to free his Da. They ran the lad through, left him bleeding, writhing, crying just feet from where his Da begged for mercy for his child."

Hans wipes tears from his cheek before taking another sip.

"It took them all a long time to die," he whispers.

The King motions refills for them both.

With a murmur of thanks, another sip from the newly filled cup, "We moved from there immediately after. We had help as an old wizard stumbled upon our poor village. For aiding him regain his health, he taught us spells to facilitate our move to the Barony we serve. It is little better, this new place," he finishes the story with another sip of wine.

The King glances round the room; his eyes alight on Jackie who made a short bow, with wings out. "And these stories are true?" The King asks.

Jackie speaks up, "Sir, the last part about the dogs I can vouch for. I was there when the

Baron sic them. Hungry, mangy mutts they were, too. They would have ravaged anything they could get hold of."

Jackie turns towards Hans, "So where did you acquire the Magicks to open the portal?"

Still un-nerved, talking with a crow, he tries to answer, but stumbles over some words, "I followed the wizard and heard him mutter words before the portal opened. He wore a small stone that glistened whilst he spoke. Later, he wanted us to find similar stones."

"We brought many but he complained that none were suitable. We eventually found one in another of those portals. He switched his small one for the newer one, then vanished from the village." He thinks a moment on how to explain the rest.

"I stumbled across some small bits of stone as I searched in his cabin. A spark jumped when I picked up the largest shard," he finishes nervously.

"And you used it to open the portals and come through to this place?" Jackie asks.

Hans merely nods once.

"This wizard of yours, he had a name?" The King asks.

"He called himself, 'King Orson', Highness."

Jackie nods to Dean to confirm what he hears. He nods back.

"So, you were hesitant to ask for aid but had no compunction about abducting my daughters for ransom? This wizard helped with the abductions?" The King inquires.

"No, Sir. He had long gone," Hans answers.

"So how did you learn of this place and the stones?" Jackie asks.

"During one of the trips through what you call the portal; The wizard took me along to look for stones for his magick. We stumbled over those rocks but they were not good for him." Another pause, another sip of wine.

"I took one back and we traded it for supplies and got much in return. That was what gave me the idea of getting more," He states in a bit of a contrite voice.

"So, you thought these stones would help you finance your farms and help garner riches. Why did you not just come here and take them? Why abduct my daughters?" The King demands.

"We *saw* the swords of your armies! I did not want anyone getting hurt. I thought if I had some bargaining power, I could get gems without risking anyone. Besides, we could find no stones in the fields," Hans explains.

"Sir, I admit that what I did was wrong and I accept any punishment you deem. My life is in your hands. But please send healers to my village with swords. My people are suffering from the fever and the Baron may ride in to take whatever he can find thinking we are vulnerable."

The King glares down to the man, "I will think on it!" He motions to his guard, "Take him and his friends to the side chamber. See they get food and drink. Let nothing untoward happen." He dismisses them, with a nod to his daughters he rises to depart. Taking his Queen's hand, they stride into the small royal chamber, Sir Jackie fluttering at his shoulder.

As they settle in the room gathering refreshments the King asks, "Sir Jackie, how much of this story should we believe, and how much help should we give?"

Dean speaks up, "Majesty, we have healers that could be there post haste. As for the story, we can investigate its validity but I think the man would not risk making it up," he concludes, taking a sip from the wine glass Beth hands him with a smile.

"Da," Anne begins, "from what I learned from Miss Betta, it corroborates what you heard. If you try him in the courts, I will testify to force you to help Sir Hans and his village."

"Daughter, that will not be possible! The man is guilty and will be punished severely," The King demands vehemently.

Anne stands her ground, arguing "The law states I must speak truthfully. I will ask for leniency in his case," she states bravely.

"We will discuss this later," The King commands.

"We will discuss this now, Da! I am but a child but you did teach me right from wrong. And what was done to them is wrong." She stands looking up at him, so much like her mother, he shudders.

"Something must be done to help," The Queen agrees placing a quieting hand on the King's arm. "If they were our subjects Husband, what would you do?" she finishes.

He stops for a moment, sighs and sinks back in his chair. With a quick look around seeing that all that attend are Family and advisors.

"You do not understand; for the last ten-day or so, since my girls have been abducted, I had been frantic. I failed to protect them, my own daughters. ***In our own home***, they were taken." He wipes his hand across his eyes.

"I wanted to find the ones responsible, gut them slowly and place their squirming, impaled bodies on display for all to see. I wanted them to slowly suffer for what they did to my family." Overcome with emotion, he takes a calming breath.

"I only thought the worst of the perpetrators. Now I find that I am thwarted in my retribution! My youngest daughter shows compassion to her captors that I could not show, my future son-in-law offers the aid I did not think to offer. All I wanted to offer was a sword across the neck of each of the brigands!"

He continues to sit, coming to grips with what he must do as King, not what he wants to do as a father. Another deep breath to control his emotions. He thinks of the women in his life, knows he is out numbered and with a sigh, "What would you have me do?"

With the rescue effort beginning, Jackie shows Dean how to manipulate the portal to open in the village square. Healers and food supplies top the list.

Then the Crow goes in search of his royal friend, finding him in a small side chamber, alone and despondent. Alighting upon the table, the Crow magicks wine and cups for them both.

"What have I become, Sir Jackie?" he questions with a raised eyebrow. "A vengeful old fool; wanting no more than to lop off heads of people that displease me?" He takes a sip of his wine.

"Old friend," Jackie starts, "you reacted as any father would react where his daughters are threatened. Your saving grace is a loving and understanding family that held you in check until you came back to your good senses."

"So, what do I do? What they did was wrong and they deserve punishment. Is there no justice for what they did to my daughters?" he demanded, slamming his hand down upon the table top.

The Crow magicks the glasses back upright and restores all to what it had been.

"Sometimes Your Highness, justice is a legal form of revenge! No matter. It will take several days to sort out. Let nature take its course. We can resolve all without a lengthy trial. Take several days to learn of these new people. Talk to the healers and aides sent to the village. I think you will be surprised at what you learn," he suggests to his royal friend.

"I must take my leave but I think I have the proper punishment where all will be satisfied."

"Friend Jackie, I thank you for your help and your guidance."

"No thanks are needed old friend. I shall return soon." He poofs out leaving the King sitting, contemplating the changes coming to his realm and the hopes that his missing daughter is safe and secure.

CHAPTER 28 Meanwhile, Back at My Castle

After several days bouncing around the country-side hunting worm, I have this desire to go fishing. Actually, I need a few days home to relax and unwind. There are duties to perform and the complaints concerning '*Fido*' to clear. Nothing terrible, small grievances; livestock missing, some disappearing vegetables and some gallons of ale that got drank, er-drunk.

I will admit to and replace the vegetables and sheep but ale drinking dragons; I think not. Although, I will have a chat with Fido to make sure.

I also need to spend quality time in my woodwork shop. Abby's birthday is several months away and I am building an apothecary cabinet. It will be a long and arduous project, especially with no power tools and thirty drawers to lay out and cut. May hap if I get too far behind, I can ask the local craftsmen to help.

Abby has retreated to her workshop with jewelry to create for friends.

Diana stops by to reinforce her claim those worms need to be removed, and quickly. She is nervous, fidgety and seems to have an ulterior motive.

"What else is bothering you?" I ask, noticing her unease.

She hesitates, unsure of how to phrase her question. "How do you manage during these long and chilly nights?" she blurts. "I miss cuddling with my husband since he is gone. How do you cope and adapt?"

This wasn't the first time she has hinted around. I pour coffee from the pot atop my small wood stove. I burn my wood debris as a fire cheers up the space and keeps my coffee warm.

She has been looking over the plans for the apothecary project. With a complimentary nod she hands back the final drawing. "Nice design. Are you using it for spices or to hold hardware?" she wonders.

"Neither," I comment, "It is a birthday present for Abby to store her beads and stones. I will in-lay a sample of the contents of each drawer on its front," I finish, taking another sip of coffee.

She shakes her head, "What is this relationship between the two of you? You are always together, an almost couple but at night it is strictly different bedrooms."

I take a breath and another sip from the cup, stalling, before explaining my strange relationship.

"It is not that long since the tragedy of losing our spouses and I want her to have enough space to mourn. It was a terrible loss and we need to wait. I don't want to take advantage of the situation, or of her," I finish.

But she wasn't finished, "How did the two of you meet? I want the real story," she says. "I once caught part of a conversation between Alex and Abby through the back fence. I was down working my roses and I overheard Alex complain that she had never told him about you."

"I was ancient history," I inform her. "My wife wasn't told either since the subject never came up. Are there people in your life before you were married and did you tell your husband?" I toss the idea back at her.

"Well, there was no reason to tell him of the others. It was before we met," she defends.

"This is the same thing. We were introduced by mutual relatives. Abby lived across the country and we corresponded, finally becoming engaged, meeting and breaking up all in the course of a couple of years. We parted friends and went on with our lives separately. We didn't meet again until several years ago with Jackie's initial set of troubles. Does that satisfy your curiosity?" I query, taking another sip of coffee.

"So, what type of relationship do the two of you have? Just friends, like in a handshake goodnight or is there something else happening?" Sheepish of that line of questioning.

"I don't know what you are asking so I have little to say." I give her a sardonic smile, confused.

"I am trying to see if I have a chance to warm your bed in the future is what I am wondering?" She laughs nervously at giving such a blatant answer. "Boy, you are dense."

I nearly drop my coffee. It is not every day I get hit upon. I hem and haw, trying to think what answer to give and how to say it to not hurt her feelings.

"Uh, Diana," I start slowly, "you are a very attractive woman and I am flattered and appreciate the compliment. But I do have deep feelings for Abby. You are smart, witty and fun to be with but my feelings for her go back a long way. I often think that I made a mistake by letting her get away. I believe we would have had a fabulous life together all these years had we married. But, given this chance I will wait and see, not sure what her feelings are for me."

After a hesitant goodbye, she retreats back to her workspace in the manor with the attitude, 'nothing ventured, nothing gained'.

~<>~<>~<>~<>~<>~<>~<>~<>~<>~

Diana was startled when Jackie poofs in. She is still not used to people or crows, just popping in. This is a new enough environment for her.

"Miss Dee! Hope I did not scare you but very pleased to see you again," he greets warmly.

"I'll get used to this soon enough." She stutters. "But very nice to see you also. Can I help you with something?" she wonders.

"Yes; I saw those tests you ran on the incompatibility the worms have on our environment. I was wondering if checking samples from different environs will tell if they would be hospitable to other areas and environments?" he asks with an almost quizzical look.

"What are you ultimately looking to find out?" she asks point blank.

"If a person were to move from one place to another, could that new place be harmful to their health?" he wonders plainly.

"You mean as in moving from my earth to here?" she questions.

"Nearly along those lines, Miss Dee," he confirms.

"If all the samples are compatible then the creatures living in those conditions can survive," she states.

"How long would those tests take to run?" is Jackie's next question.

"They are simple enough for the answers you want and the results should be evident within a day," she responds. "Traveling would take most of the time," she muses.

Jackie's feathers fluff out, "Could we begin now? The traveling is the easy part," he mentions.

"We can begin whenever you are ready, Sir. It seems I don't have much else to do but work," she laments.

"All work and no play seems a bit boring, Miss Dee," he interjects.

"Yes, but unfortunately it is not much fun alone," she replies sadly, looking around to prove her point.

"Oh, and the other person you had in mind had someone else on their mind?" he mentions.

"Um, yes," she states with a slight head shake. "How can you be apart from someone for forty years and then think you could still be in love with that person?" She stops and stares at the crow for a moment before collecting the equipment.

"Oh! You mean Frank?" he chuckles, "I thought you meant Allain?"

"Isn't Allain a bit young for me?" she asks wistfully.

"He is nearly sixty in your years," Jackie explains. "So, I do not think him too young."

She gives him a double-take. "I thought him mid-twenties," she mentions, retrieving the last of her tools with a thoughtful look. "We can leave anytime you are ready."

"Now?" And a moment later they are on the outside by one of Franks' new gardens. "I will open a portal from here. We will be making three stops in all."

She nods in agreement as the portal coalesces and they walk into the first test site.

CHAPTER 29 Hook, Line and

It's nice to laze along the banks of my stream and try my luck with fish. The last several days have been hectic; searching for worms and detailing the apothecary cabinet. *Now* is for me. I don't care if I catch fish or not. Although Dagwood is here for me to feed him fish, not feed fish.

We sit several minutes; I have a nibble or two and so I had to re-bait my hook when one of Dagwood's ears goes to attention. Merlyn must be nearby. Anyone else warrants both ears.

Within moments, with a meow as greeting in my direction Merlyn is lying next to her mate. Abby, a moment behind briefly greets Dagwood and then she settles down upon the cushion I proffer.

"Strange seeing you out this way," I mention. "Last I heard you were locked away in your laboratory putting together your latest creations," I joke, using my best Karloff Imitation.

"Well, I was, but was interrupted by one of the cleaning girls who wanted to talk," she begins. "Actually, I should amend that as girl would be the wrong word since she is older than either of us." Abby smiles nervously. "She mentioned a conversation overheard this morning." A quick cautious smile. "You should be aware of who is around when you have discussions. The staff overhears many things and some come tell me the most tantalizing tidbits."

I stare at her with a concerned look, trying to think back to a conversation I would have wanted to keep secret. The only person I had any real chat with was Diana. But I said nothing ... Ah! I see where this is leading.

"So, what was so upsetting or secret that your stool pigeon said to you?" I query.

"She told me our friend Diana came *on* to you," she blurts out.

"So, there is something wrong in that?" I ask. "I am a reasonably good-looking man, somewhat charming, more than a bit entertaining, funny, a good cook, handy to have around and I am house broken. The one bad quality, I have a dragon that isn't quite house-broken," I joke. "So, what's the problem?"

"You turned her down," the amazement plainly evident in her voice.

"Um, yeah! She isn't really my type," I explain. "Diana is a nice person; pretty on the eyes, great personality with nice chrysanthemums and all but not my type. Too cerebral; analyzes everything," I say with a slight shiver.

"Oh! So, what is your type, exactly?" she asks coyly.

"Well, someone a bit younger than me with an eye for creativity; a bit of a sense of humor helps, too. Most importantly she needs to like cats and dragons. Dee would start to sneeze every time Fido came near. Very distracting when I am trying to put the moves on," I joke.

She holds her hand up, stopping my patter.

"Why?" she asks; her face going serious.

"Why what?" I return.

"Why all the secrecy? You should have said something." She pauses a moment, trying to get the words right in her head. "It's obvious that you are talking about me, so why didn't you just say something?" Her demeanor goes from one of impatience to one of near anger.

I take her hand in mine, "I was waiting; I didn't want to rush you, take advantage of you. I thought when you were ready...," I answer. "The other day I nearly told you, but you began lamenting that Alex was gone and I didn't want to cause you more pain. Then Dee and Allain came in and the moment was lost," I sigh.

"Maybe it is as much my fault?" she interrupts. "I should have said something sooner. This was mostly Alex fault anyway. If he hadn't tried to bring the technology into Camelot, he and Eve would still be here. You are suffering and it has nothing to do with what you or Eve have done." She stops, a tear rolls down her cheek and she shudders.

"Okay, Okay," I whisper to her. "It's no ones' fault. It is something that happened."

She is much closer, my arm wraps around her shoulder to comfort as I will often do, to comfort the both of us. I feel her warmth as she snuggles, as if a chill takes her and it feels right, somehow. I look down at her, she look up at me, she smiles and we kiss.

Nothing spectacular in and of itself but it does feel good, feels right. A tear slowly rolls down my cheek as my emotions catch up to me. My other hand raises to caress her face and feel the tears upon her cheek, as well. We sit together for a while, unmoving, yet moved; holding each other.

I guess it is spectacular after all! Though I was to discover all was not that great; some damned fish took my bait, again.

CHAPTER 30 Comparing Gems

That evening we meet Beth. She and Dean poof in to ask our help.

I think her a warm and friendly person. You can tell they are in love.

Additional help is needed to heal villagers in Han's realm. Several more have died from the fever.

"Maybe you should ask Miss Kaye." Abby suggests. "She is a healer and familiar with various sicknesses."

Liking that idea, we all poof to Jackie's main hall to share a snack; it seems all we do around Camelot is eat.

After a warm greeting, the Crow's first question is about the investigation. Reports of larger animals succumbing to this strange illness prove it is moving up the food chain.

While we discuss the findings, Kaye asks Abby about fixing the clasp on her necklace. It would pop open and she is afraid it will become lost.

Beth gasps upon seeing it. "That stone Miss Kaye, from where did it come?"

Abby turns to me and I answer, "It was found in a field in a furrow. Allain gave me several samples. We think they may have magickal energy to them. Why?" I query eagerly.

She pulls one from her bodice, nearly identical.

"We get these from the 'Creative Ones", she explains. "I call Them to the fields and They till the soils from below. Their dance leaves stones which if not handled correctly can cause burns, sickness; can even cause plants and small animals to die," she explains. We sort those stones wearing protective gloves, then drop them into earthen containers to let them break down. The heat they generate disintegrates them. Once the residual powder cools, we use it back on the plants in small quantities to help promote growth."

"Like fertilizer?" I ask.

She thinks I speak a foreign tongue. "If rapidly cooled in water, they change into these gem type stone," she finishes.

"What do these Creative Ones look like?" Abby asks?

Beth glances around for a moment, seizes upon a sausage link and with her hands gestures to something much bigger and much longer.

"But how could you have found those stones here?" she asks a very good question.

"Allain told me he found these stones in furrows right outside your property, Dean," I relate.

"That seems highly unlikely. If we are from two totally different lands how could the stones be in your fields, unless you have a similar creature?" Beth observes.

I look to Abby, "Could these creatures have come through a portal we opened?" I ask.

"Could it have been when Dean and Beth first found each other, talking across the alternatives? Didn't you say you saw a portal and it appeared to be partially buried in the sand?" Abby mentions.

I nod.

Beth chimes in with, "The looking glass I saw was a portal?" She thinks for a moment. "It was buried part way in the ground. The worms could have entered," she surmises.

"Beth," I ask, "how many of these creatures inhabit your lands?"

She stops to give it some thought. I guess no one ever had reason to ask that question. "We have many 'bands' of them. I call Them to a field and a 'band' attends. They dance the soil, churning the dirt, making it ready for planting. But to how many bands, we have never had reason to count?" she answers.

"You call them?" Abby repeats part of Beth's statement as a question.

"Yes! As the oldest of the Daughters, I am *"The Princess of the Bountiful Harvest,"* she admits.

Jackie interrupts the conversation with a reminder we had many sick and possibly dying people that need looking after. He wants me to tag along, placing a thought into my head about a possible run in with the Baron who rules the lands, badly.

LH and I will be happy to help especially if it keeps me nearer to Abby.

With an agreeable nod we walk through the portal to find ourselves in a very poor looking village square. Healers are dispersed to check on the inhabitants. Beth and Abby look to find Grace.

Later, Abby fills in the story for me. "The King's middle daughter Grace fell in love with her kidnappers' son."

I laugh, "There will be fireworks when the King discovers that. Abducting children is not something you do to endear yourself to the parents."

The healers work their magicks; and they do use magick. Whenever I walk passed, the hairs on my arms raise. Others of us transport supplies across the alternatives. Several of the Manors' kitchens, including my own help with the foods.

Clothing, bedding and other supplies are much appreciated by the villagers. They sleep in comfort and with full bellies for the first time in many ten-days I was told.

CHAPTER 31 The Hunt

We walk another of the many fields searching, hunting worm. Landholders are alerted to the dangers of the invasion and this particular farmer reported strange occurrences. So, we walk this one, searching.

Abby bellows, "Will you call your Dragon off?"

I take a quick gander; Fido flits in the field wanting to play with Merlyn. The dragon will drop down, snout even with the felines, snort air at her and flick his tongue planting a little kiss upon the cats' nose. Then bounds back up into the air again.

Merlyn will screech and hiss, not hurt but annoyed. She won't attack since she does like him. But he is still a young, playful and very impressionable dragon; wanting to have fun and explore.

This field is adjacent to Sir Jeres' lands and the farmer has let it go fallow. So large, wild grasses sprout, to be plowed for the spring planting. Bushes cluster around blooming colorful flowers to attract bees and butterflies for better pollination.

It isn't fun, fighting our way through over growth is difficult and exacting work. The brambles and stickers will pull and pinch and the vines will grab and trip at every step. But we do try to enjoy it.

Our relationship has been changing since our conversation by the lake. We know the feelings we share, making the future brighter. We banter about which of us is the better cook.

Abby makes dispersion on a few of my dishes; while I remind her about a turkey she had cooked during a snow storm. While it was delicious, she had forgotten to remove the plastic bag of giblets from the neck cavity. Not catastrophic but enough to tease her with.

She is reminding me of a dessert I had baked, forgetting the sugar. Needless to say, the pumpkin pies were inedible.

We meander the field separated by several hundred feet. I am near the tree line looking for furrows in the dirt. Abby call and points towards the bushes. I can't quite hear but maybe she sees something in the trees.

I take several steps, then see what she saw.

Everything now moves in slow motion. LH vibrates a warning as a large gray blur growls and moves fast at me from my left. As I turn to defend, there is a vicious snarl as I am hit on my right shoulder by another gray form. Strong, sharp teeth snap into my arm, waves of pain hurtle through my body. LH, in my left hand swings down at the first blur.

"Damn, *Wolves*!" I shriek.

LH connects with the head of that first wolf with such ferocity the impact split its skull wide open dropping the beast immediately. LH again swings; another animal backs away uttering a low-pitched rumble.

I hadn't realized I was screaming until Fido appears; grabs the wolf on my shoulder, rendering it to pieces.

I go down under the weight of yet another beast on my back. I struggle, fighting back to my feet almost; LH swinging wildly.

Abby grabs two of the beasts with her powers and tosses them into the trees, their bodies shatter upon impact.

Another wolf grabs the back of my leg trying to wrench it off; while yet another is atop Fido slashing one of his wings.

The screams of terror may have been from him or me, I don't know.

Jackie, feeling my panic along our link, poofs in; instantly assesses the situation, freezing the pack in mid-stride with a wave of a wing.

Other than the slight ringing in my ears and the pounding of my heart there is a sudden and deathly silence.

I remember little after that.

I am in agony; my arm ripped and blood drips. My side throbs as pain shoots down my hip and leg.

Abby screams.

I finally realize my situation and my body does the first smart thing that morning, it collapses.

CHAPTER 32 Time to Heal

It is quiet when I next open my eyes to see the familiar surroundings of my room.

I sense the pain from Fido. Not intense but more of a dull throb. I try to sit up when two things stop me. One, the pain shooting through my body and two; Abby's arm across my chest holding me down. She is next to me and senses my awakening.

I turn my head, muscles scream at me all the way. She is so pretty with the flood of relief running in her face. Purrs from the two felines atop my legs bring them to my attention. I see the bandages and feel their pain through my empathic abilities.

Jackie poofs in, hearing me.

Fido sends a tired message of love. I return the feeling in kind, adding that he is to stay where he is since the room is nowhere near large enough. And it is filling with visitors as word spreads that I have regained consciousness.

Ana brings coffee. John, our manager stands aside to let Allain and Diane into the room. Soon twenty people have filed in, all with concerned looks, a few women weep.

I think someone has died.

"Tha- th," my voice won't work. A squeak was the best I can do. A quick thought to Jackie and...

"Frank will heal much quicker with all your kind thoughts and healing energies," he relays to our friends. "He wants to thank you all!"

I take a sip of the coffee to help soothe my throat, while Abby pushes cushions behind me so I can sit up with less discomfort.

"The cats?" I croak. I clear my throat again, "what happened? Are they all right?" Still hoarse and raspy.

Abby answers as the felines sit looking at me. "They attacked the wolf that grabbed your arm; otherwise it may have ripped off." She has a tremble in her voice. "They will heal well and fine."

I nod and try to say 'thank you', but the words stick in my throat.

Jackie chimes in, "Frank says 'Thanks."

"Save your voice and think thoughts to me. In the meanwhile, we will relay what happened yesterday."

'*Yesterday?*' I question to Jackie.

His head bobs, "Yesterday!" he answers, aloud. "You have been out thirty hours. The farmer apologizes. Had he realized you were investigating; he would have warned you of the wolves."

He pauses a moment to glare at me. "Why did you not poof out or freeze the wolves?"

I shoot thoughts back to him and he verbalizes, "You did not think fast enough. Understandable!" His head bobs up and down and feathers fluff out in sympathy for our pains.

"Fido took out two of the beasts before being attacked. Abby grabbed the two she saw and disposed of them. You and LH smashed the skull of one and splintered the rib cage of another. When I heard your scream, I poofed in and froze the rest. They are now residing deep in the forest up on a mountain." He stops to regain his breath and sips coffee.

"And how is Fido?" I squeak.

Abby takes over, "His wing was slashed. That is what worried us most. Because of his tough hide, he has only some minor cuts and bruises." Her face is still pale from the stress, worries and healings. "I had to go back through several of the 'Pern' [8]novels until we found what they did to save a dragon' wing." She smiles reminding me of my quip. 'How sci-fi books are becoming our text books', "and now medical books as well", she vocalizes.

"We used a sheet as a membrane to paste his wing onto. We used a bit of our Earth technology to deaden his pain since we had no 'numb weed[3],' she goes on to explain. "The wing was in tatters and we are holding it together with a tapioca mixture used like glue. It is sticky and will not harm his metabolism."

I try to alter my position to ease the pains and be comfortable.

"Go slow, dear," she reminds. "You are held together with bindings and prayers and are ripped apart inside. It takes time to heal all those little pieces."

I try settling easier.

"Kaye and I have done the majority of the healing on you and Fido. But you will need another day lying here before you can move around. Your arm is ripped when the wolf grabbed and wrenched it. There is a little muscle damage but that will heal. We pushed the skin

8PERN – A world created by sci-fi fantasy genius Anne McCaffrey. [3] NUMB WEED A plant where the sap is a powerful topical anesthetic it can be used straight from the plant or boiled sown into a salve or medicinal cream which, when smeared on wounds, kills all feeling.

together and wrapped it with bandages while we fused and healed you."

"Your hip and side took some damage and contusions when one wolf knocked you to the ground. Its weight and sharp claws tore the skin. Another wolf grabbed the back of your leg tearing that apart." She stops to take a ragged breath. "You have some muscle damage, but again most was superficial. With all the attacks, you came out rather lucky. We think that although you didn't put a protective barrier up, your mind automatically protected the vital parts of your body. You will need assistance walking since the leg will take longer to heal," she assesses. "Maybe LH can do double duty for you?" she jokes.

Jackie jumps in while I sip coffee. "We understand that you are grateful and thankful for everything. I will be back later to check up on you. While it will be a while before you can show your gratitude to Abby. I will just take verbal thanks." He caws a laugh and poofs out.

The rest of our friends have drifted out returning to their duties. I am sure Allain works a song about the wolf attack. He might make Fido and the felines the heroes of this one.

I turn to look at Abby; tears brim her eyes. Her hand finds mine and she grasps it with a sense of terror. Then, I realize I may have been killed.

She sees the color drain from my face as the shock finally hits home.

"Frankie," she whispers, "I didn't know what was going on. Merlyn yelled 'wolf', in my head; then, all hell broke loose as Dagwood pounced on one. The wolf threw him off but it gained Merlyn enough time to get its attention."

"I saw two attack you and I grabbed at them. In my panic I heaved them towards the forest, breaking the back of one and the other shredded to pieces." She takes a breath and shudders. "When you collapsed there was blood everywhere. I couldn't sense how badly you were hurt or if you were still alive."

She settles carefully on the bed to not add to my discomfiture. "Then Jackie poofed in, froze the rest of the tribe and transported us here. He was the one that brought Kaye and Rebekah in with herbs and bandages. Cook and Ana gathered what was needed to help Fido." She pauses, a smile upon her face. "They were afraid of him at first but learned he was as gentle as a pussycat even though he was in so much pain."

"We spent hours healing you," she continues with a catch in her voice. "I was afraid that you wouldn't make it."

I put my good arm around her shoulder and pull her close. Her body warmth helps a little.

She gives a quick look to Merlyn and then a look to me with an unspoken question on her lips.

"What?" I whisper, just loud enough for her to hear.

"Merlyn can hear you in her mind, and you can communicate with her the same way," she accuses in a jealous tone.

"A little bit," I try to explain. "Feelings mostly," I confess hoarsely.

"Well, it was clear enough for her to tell me to get under the blanket with you," She exclaims.

"Body heat," I whisper with a grin and a wink. "I'm cold!"

The cats move around until we are comfortable. I lay on my left side and Abby slides with her back to my front. I put my bandaged arm around her bare waist and sigh.

I hear, “No Merlyn, you don’t have to translate that sigh.”

The felines settle around our legs, adding their warmth and comfort.

I give her a little hug and kiss the back of her neck. It is the only part I can reach without hurting myself.

“I love you too, Frankie. Now get rest and heal,” she orders pleasantly.

“Yes, dear,” I agree and drift off to sleep, hurt but healing and very contented.

CHAPTER 33 The Universal Cure

I awake, alone; disappointed, at first. But after examining the situation I realize that it means I am healing or she would have left someone to watch over me.

A squawk and a flash remind me of my forever 'bird-watcher, Jackie.

"Well, good morning. Frank," he greets warmly. "I see we are doing much better."

I return the greeting and explore all my moving parts; aches, pains, but nothing I can't bear and LH by my side if a problem occurs. '*I guess it all works*', I think to him.

Another mind-contact opens in the front of my brain. Fido with his joy of not being in pain and his wing nearly healed. The frame was removed earlier today but the wing is still stiff and sore. I feel for him, his wanting to fly and not being able. He is tied so he won't try. I see his thought of what holds him; it would be easy enough for him to break free, but he is smart enough to wait.

It bothers me they had to restrain him but I see the logic. He would not do well in a barn, but under the stars unfettered, he might try to fly prematurely. They were unsure of his intelligence, so they tied him.

Please wait, friend, I send to him. *Let me see when they think you can use the wing. Just be cautious about re-injuring yourself.*

I hear a 'meow' as the door opens, Abby and the two felines enter with everyone jumping for the bed.

Abby eyes me critically, "are you feeling all right?"

"Sore, stiff with a little bit of lonely tossed in," I lament.

"Well, I do have things to do. We both can't lounge around here for days on end. Someone needs to work," she jokes.

"We do have that trial soon," Jackie reminds, "and we must attend."

I look to Abby, "will I be well enough to travel?"

"We will do Reiki today and that will heal you sufficiently," she pronounces.

I sigh, also eager to fly the coop so to speak. "What of Fido?" I ask. "When will his chain come off?"

"Well, it's not really a chain," she begins. "I asked Merlyn to communicate that he shouldn't fly until we think him well enough." She pauses trying to choose her next words most carefully. "We didn't want him harming himself or us by mistake. We used a twine instead of chain," she finishes.

I smile.

"What?" her eyebrow shoots up in a question.

"Fido is smarter than you think. He could break free at any time but decided to humor you."

She smiles at that thought.

"He understands you are helping him and promises not to fly until you tell him he can," I smirk. "He also thanks you and the others for caring for him."

Kaye knocks and enters the open door having heard the conversation. "Tell Fido he is quite welcome," she mentions putting a small satchel she carries down on the table. "That dragon is a very good patient. Better than some," and eyes me in a jovial manner.

"Since you all seem to have everything under control, I will depart." The Crow announces. "Do be careful," he winks, and with a quiet caw, poofs out.

"And how is our patient today?" Kaye inquires.

"He seems to be in better spirits, Miss Kaye," Abby answers, standing right over me; talking as if I am not here or can't answer for myself.

"Let us relax and prepare for the last healing," Kaye suggests.

Abby maneuvers the pillows so I can lay flat against the pallet.

Kaye pulls the bed coverings off with no regard as to whether or not I am even decent. She finds I wear nothing as a covering to bed.

It seems as if social nudity is an acceptable practice here. Cloth is hand-made and clothes are hand fitted and sown while others are handed down. Communal baths are used and bathing suits for swimming are unheard of. Most of the smaller children run around in the altogether because it saves on cloth as bruised skin heals and washes easier. Abby and I have seen each other nude before, if just in passing to the washroom.

After the attack, my clothes were torn and needed to be cut away to facilitate the cleansing of the wounds. So, there is nothing that hadn't already been seen.

I have received Abby's Reiki healing before. With her, it is a simple touch as she did with the burn on my wrist because that was all the healing I required.

But this is different. Her energies are already depleted with keeping me alive, plus healing the wounds of Merlyn and Dagwood. And then her help with Fido. She hasn't enough energy left to heal a fly.

All she can do is watch Kaye do the Reiki and offer me moral support.

It is complicated. Each stone, and there are several, need to be put in the proper spot along my body with the proper hand movements and words. I will pay strict attention to what is going on around me.

It is disconcerting, lying there exposed this way. But Abby takes my hand and I feel my spirit quiet.

Kaye holds her arms wide as if to hug the air. I see the gem on her necklace sparkle and glitter. A soothing contentment seems to take hold of her entire being.

She has laid out the stones along the table and now she turns towards them. I hear some words, as if a prayer and she reaches for the first stone. It is fiery red. She carefully places it upon the bed between my legs, just above the knees.

I feel more at ease.

She speaks as if to the air around us, a voice of authority; *"to link the soul to this physical world, to anchor it here amidst our plane. To calm and dissolve tensions of your troubled and pained spirit."* She places her hands palms downward. The warmth and power courses through that region of my body.

She reaches back without a glance, feeling where the next gem lay. I hear Abby whisper, 'Tourmaline', naming the stone seemingly in a semi-trance state herself.

That stone sits upon my abdomen below the navel. She makes motions with her hands and the stone takes on a luster all its own. I feel as if it is melting into the skin.

"To rejuvenate the spirit and revitalize your energies," she intones. *"To realign creativity and raw emotion, I invoke the power of the stone!"*

Several muscles twitch, but the stone stays as if glued there, a part of my being. A sense of energy flood into me. Goose bumps rise all along my stomach.

She places the next stone. It sits above the navel at my solar plexus. It glows a pretty yellow. With her hands open flat above it, the glow deepens and it pulses once.

"To rejuvenate your being, to enhance and anchor your persona, to aid your spirit to a pacific temperament, I ask of thee!"

My body relaxes. I think I will ooze from the bed. It is a glorious feeling. I lose focus; reality fades as my body absorbs the energies of the stones.

The next one is familiar; Emerald and it settles upon my chest.

I am becoming one with the universe.

"You heart grows and strengthens; you love without fear. You revel in the peace of the world and the understanding of the people around you," Kaye prays.

I feel a slight pressure as Abby tightens her grip on my hand.

The next stone is arranged on my throat. I sense a touch of green; Aqua marine comes to mind.

As Kaye moves her hands to it, I hear the cry of the world, the anguish and the pain as well as the chittering of birds, the wings of the insects and the sigh of the breeze swaying the trees. Smelling lavender; I feel the purple pervade my senses; raising my consciousness to soaring heights.

"This heals your spirit, allows it to sing out to the world, a song heard above all others. It will redirect the energies, bring peace and harmony to those near and dear," she intones.

I see Opal settling upon my brow; at the third eye. My skull opens; energies flow directly into my being. From a distance I hear a voice, *"KNOW THYSELF*!

"Bring your being into reality in the physical plane and the metaphysical world. Know others in their deepest personalities; resonate with those you love."

I smell Basil, as if I am a child again in my mothers' kitchen as she tears the leaves, bringing alive the oils and flavors of this healing herb.

All runs through me at once; I float in the warmth of the sea of life, no fear of drowning, no fear of death; the fantastic feeling of being, of one with eternity.

And I feel rather than see the last stone she places upon the bed at the crown of my head. A crystal; clear, transparent as glass but filled to the nth degree.

I see the worlds, the universe, the darkening of space bright enough to appear lit. The vast emptiness, so filled with mass and power it overflows, spilling into other universes, other alternatives. Beings that transgress realities and space-time; all in one and one in all and then - total blackness!

CHAPTER 34 Back to Reality

I open my eyes several seconds or hours later, I can't tell. The room is empty, except for the felines. Dagwood down across one leg and Merlyn sprawled across my chest, her head on a par with mine. She appears to wink as if sharing some grand joke of universal appeal.

Abby enters moments later summoned by Merlyn.

I am trying different muscles and joints to check my mobility. My mind is also assimilating what all I feel. It was an enormous excursion, the likes of which I need time to decipher.

Abby's smile brings me back to this reality. "I see you are feeling better," she mentions. "Kaye would have stayed but she experienced something that never happened before. She got lost in the healing." Sitting on the edge of the bed, Abby takes my hand in hers. "She said that it carried her along, almost as if you were guiding the spirits, the energies and the reality of it all. Would you care to elaborate?"

She seems more concerned than I think she should be. "Kaye termed it as being orgasmic in feeling." Her eyebrow rises up in consternation. Hearing her describe it in that vein, makes me think back and realize that it was how I felt it. Not in the sexual sense, but in the realm of feelings, the inner glow of it all. The enormity of the experience transcends anything that I have ever encountered. I grip her hand firmly.

"All I can tell you dearest is that it was an indescribable journey." I hesitate, trying to get the wording correct. "Nothing sexual; possibly it was sensual but in an entirely different connotation of feelings; simply auto-erotic. There was no sense of anyone else but not the loneliness we all experience in our lives either. I was alone, yet one with everything and everyone." I sit back to recover from the explanation. "You did notice the stone on Kaye's necklace?" I ask. "It glowed every so often during Reiki. She would reach up and it sparkled as if lit from within."

She nods that she was aware. "It seems that there is magick in many different stones in these worlds. We will have to investigate thoroughly. I, in the mean while..." With a slight smile, she tips her head down giving me the opportunity to thoroughly kiss her. It is a nice finish to a wonderful day. A meow intrudes upon the moment. I think I hear Merlyn mention, '*Get a room, already!*' I nearly pull a muscle trying to turn to where she has sat by the pillow. "This is my room," I tell her, aloud, smiling. Which causes Abby to glance askance at me knowing of what I speak, but also wondering how much of Merlyns' telepathic ability she will have to share? We both break out in laughter.

By now I am chomping at the bit to get out and about with many things to be accomplished. Beginning my tantrum, Abby advises that another quiet night can only do me good. She kisses me again, promising that if I am very good, she will gladly spend time and keep company with me. It takes all of two seconds for me to agree. I hear a smirk from the hall as Kaye knocks on the almost opened door.

"So, I see you are almost healed," she states. "You took much energy from me but I felt invigorated rather than depleted after the session. I tried to sleep but found it near impossible. I spent the last several hours catching up on works that I would normally need a full day to accomplish." Her head goes on an upward tilt, as if struck by a sudden thought. "It seems as if you healed you and me, instead of me being the healer." She glances at Merlyn as if confirming her statement.

Another knock on the door brings the conversation to a hasty close. Dean and the Princess Beth hesitate until they see Abby wave them in.

"No," Beth offers, "Don't get up."

Little does she realize how fortunate she is by stating that, since I haven't been up to dress since being healed. I see the laugh being held back on Abby and Kaye's faces.

I nod at the new guests, "Dean, Princess Beth..."

She forestalls my next comments, "Please, drop the formalities. I enjoy being just Beth, Deans' future wife," she sighs. "In my home it is all so stuffy." She laughs, as if picturing an event past.

Kaye nods to the newcomers and then turns to me. "I assure that Fido will be well enough tomorrow for the search," she says. "I am heading down to do his final healing."

"Fido?" Beth echoes with a quizzical look.

"Ah, Yes," Dean chimes in with a secretive type smile. "You wouldn't know about Fido, dearest. He is Sir Frank's friend and a dragon."

A slight grin as Beth's hand rises to her mouth. "A Dragon?"

"Yes dear. Quite harmless I understand unless you are an attacking wolf! He is improving? So very great to hear."

"You have a dragon?" she repeats with a slight hesitation almost as if afraid to say the word.

"Um, yes, he is a great friend and my savior. He was able to get a few wolves before they got to him," I admit. "If not for him, I might not have made it out alive."

"C-can we go meet him?" is her next question.

I give a look to Kaye. "You are the healer, Miss Kaye. Do you think Fido is up to a royal visit?" I wink to show it is a joke.

"I am sure that it can be arranged," Kaye answers with a quick bow to me and then to Beth.

"Now cut that out!" We all break out laughing as Beth yells, but she has seen the humor in it.

"Kaye, why don't you escort these young folks down to Fido?" Abby suggests. "Perhaps they can help with the final healing."

"And tomorrow we can talk of calling your Magickal Ones home to your realm, Beth." She finishes.

"That would be a pleasure, Miss Abby." Beth answers with a slight bow and a smile. She can also throw subtle jokes.

I settle back on the pallet, allowing Merlyn and Dagwood to settle around me. I can feel the vibration of their contented purrs.

I reach over to grasp Abby's hand and remember smiling up at her...

CHAPTER 35 Contentment

I awake before I even realize I have been asleep. Fido's joy has filled my senses and brings me out of my slumber. He is free to fly, hunt and search. I am ecstatic and caution him to not put much strain on that newly healed wing. I don't want him to re-injure it.

I glance around and realize the morning sun is streaming in the windows, the felines are nowhere to be felt or seen but I feel Abby's breath against the back of my neck.

She stirs; her arm drapes across my bare thigh. I reach and squeeze her hand lightly. She wakes, a sound of surprise in that first waking breath to remember where she is and, with whom; then a slight squeeze down my arm and a return pressure on my hand. I hear a small contented sigh and then a slight snore as she dozes back off again. I am moments behind her.

And I awake again to Jackie squawking in my head wondering if I am planning to spend the rest of my life in bed. I feel Abby's breath on my neck, her arm on my hip and for a moment consider it. But, alas! Duty calls. I acknowledge the wake-up and return the greetings. Abby rolls onto her back, still half asleep. The cats, who have returned and lay across our legs meow that they are disturbed by the noise and movement.

I turn to find Merlyn sitting by Abby with one paw on her shoulder attempting to rouse her. On she sleeps with a contented smile lighting up that cute face. I lean in and kiss those inviting lips. For a moment nothing, then a loud Meow from Merlyn as Abby's arms encircle my neck and that little good morning peck becomes so much more. But after a minute with a lessening of the pressure of the arms and a quiet sigh – "I guess we need to be places?" she says sorrowfully.

I sigh and let her rise.

She saunters off across the hall to her rooms not worrying who might be about to see her, sans clothing. I don't mind the view watching her walk away.

CHAPTER 36 On the Road Again

We need to get moving having slept a good part of the morning away. Once we are ready, Abby poofs us to Jackie's main hall with time enough for a quick repast.

Diana huddles with Allain as he fills her in on some of the local gossip, flavor and circumstances. An attempt to ease her adaptation to the new surroundings and maybe entice her to stay; this situation will bear watching. We get a wave and a nod as we walk to Jackie's table.

Cook is with Kaye finalizing the details for Rebekah's wedding. As we sit Abby gently pokes me in the side gaining my attention.

"Ow?" I grimace, grabbing my ribs and feigning major injury, garnering me a light slap on the shoulder. It feels different somehow now that we are a real couple, not just friends; but more. Not officially lovers; in love, but not lovers if you see what I mean. It feels right! With a smile to her, "What, Dear," I grab her hand much more to hold it than to stop her from slapping me again.

"Could you create a cake for the Hand-fasting?" Her smile tells me she already knows the answer and is egging me along.

I sit for a moment thinking up designs, "I could! Nothing as elaborate as Kaye's birthday cake; simple, yet elegant for the occasion. Do you have any suggestions?"

"Maybe create something in bone white, with purple ribbon accents, a bow and flowers.

Maybe several round cakes, cascading in size placed to form a staircase to show life's journey?"

Her ideas flow and it helps my creative juices. I draw cakes placed to form two grand staircases. I will put two figures atop one cake. The cakes will come around, cascade down to meet in the middle at the bottom. But I also have an idea with a touch of whimsy involved.

Abby has motioned to Cook to come by and excitedly explains what we plan. I hand her the drawings with a list of supplies and extras needed. It is a daunting task but Cook, in her own inimitable way simply smiles and nods.

"We have to be at the Castle for that trial but I will stop by to help lay it all out," I assure her. I don't say I would obtain some of the supplies during a quick trip back to earth.

It seems several couples are planning on 'tying the knot' soon. I am wondering if I am part of that number. If so, it will be the 'icing on the cake', so to speak. I will have to talk to Abby to see if her intentions towards me are honorable. In any case these will be busy days. With all the little items out of the way we can talk worms with the crow.

I relay the conversation I have had with Beth of removing the creatures from Camelot. His concern is that we may have to lure them all through the soil contaminating more property along the way.

"If we can find them and transport them out from their current location, it will save much of the properties and cut down on contaminating more lands." He advises.

"We are already working on that. Fido and the Felines are out on a search for them.

Diana walks over. She thinks a problem may be forth coming.

"What type of problem?" Abby questions as we sit to eat.

"It may come down to the Planet moving into a point of 'opposite energy' that it might not be able to recover. It then dies taking most of the plant forms and all of the animal life with it," she explains, "including humans!" Then pauses for the enormity to sink in. "There is not enough time for living organisms to adapt to the change. Some plants can rebound and survive which is what evolution is all about. But the humans, blessed with their long-life cycles have no chance to evolve sufficiently to maintain a presence here. We need to rid this planet of those worms," she cautions.

Abby tells her it needs to be postponed while we go to that trial. "Depending upon the outcome we should be taking care of the worms post-haste".

She receives a quizzical look from the scientist.

"You think these worms come from Beth's world?" Diana asks, taking a sip of water.

"It is a good assumption," I suggest and after explaining the situation she thinks so, too.

Then she mentions the soil samples she took for Jackie, some of which were familiar.

"What do you mean?" I ask.

She explains that they had traveled to several worlds checking the compatibility; to see if others could live comfortably in different alternatives.

"So, after running the samples, several seemed similar to the first samples you gave me;

the acidic ones anyway. They were still different enough from all the other samples I ran."

"What do you mean different?" I query.

"I know what the samples are for here in Camelot and the Brigands world; plus, the place Jackie said you and he explored were all compatible. So, anyone from Camelot or the brigands' world could live in the place you found. But there may be difficulty in a person adapting from Beth's world to here or visa-versa."

"Dean and Beth will not be too happy with hearing that," Abby mentions. "They have planned on being married and raising a family."

"They can still do that," Diana explains, "They cannot make a permanent move. Frequent visits back to their parents' homes will help tremendously," she finishes. "I wonder if I could move here, also," she says wistfully.

~<>~<>~<>~<>~<>~<>~<>~<>~<>~

We finish our meeting with Jackie and after coffee, poof back to our main hall with Diana to go over her findings.

John approaches timidly. He is our overseer, in charge of all the grounds, handling the gardens, fields and other farms. He is familiar with every leaf and blade of grass. I introduce him to Diana, but something is bothering him.

"Miss Abby, Frank," he begins, "I believe we may have a problem. One of the old trees looks to be dying and it bothers me so. Old trees die but this one feels different. That is a silly statement, is it not?" He asks perplexed and confused?

"Is the tree nearby?" Abby questions. "Perhaps we can go and look?"

"It is out near the workshop between the two Manor Houses, Miss Abby."

Being an easy walk, we investigate.

Diana joins us in an inborn sense of curiosity. We stop in front of our communal workshop and he points to the 'old willow'. *The Willow* that drew us to this property to begin with. It is looking yellow and ragged, seeming to sag. My heart thumps; the tree does not look good.

Abby's hand finds mine as we stand looking at what the Guardian has named *Camelot*. We both shiver right down to our very cores.

Diana takes samples from the tree and the surrounding area, promising a report post-haste. She feels there is something special in that willow.

I thank John for alerting us and we will do what we can. We stand for several minutes. Abby seems immersed in a type of trance. Her hand will grip mine then loosen and grip again, in a silent cadence. She shakes her head, "We need to talk to the Guardian again and soon."

The trial is the next morning for us, but first thing in the afternoon in Beth's alternative. We head off to sleep early. Abby still uses her personal suite in my Manor House. I guess it will take time to get to the one bedroom-stage.

CHAPTER 37 Hans the Pirate

After a restless sleep with only Dagwood for company, (No offense Dags.) I awake to Abby shaking my shoulder impatiently awaiting my company. Regretfully she expects me to join her rather than the other way 'round. (sigh!)

"We should visit the village first," Abby proposes as I finish popping into my boots. "I am hoping the people have healed? Then maybe we can find information concerning this man Hans," she finishes.

We meet Sir Jere and Madeline in the town square. They are organizing the last of the supplies.

"How have the villagers fared?" Abby wonders after our salutations are complete.

"Pretty well," Madeline replies. "Sorrowfully, we lost two others. We tried everything but they didn't respond."

"Do we have enough armed men in the event of an attack by the Baron?" I query. I had sent a squad of my own men to bolster the ranks of the estates. Not that we need armies in Camelot. But men like weapons, and training uses energies that may otherwise be used for dangerous or nefarious deeds.

"We have seen nothing of the Baron," Jere assures. "Several scouts have messaging stones to keep us apprised of his movements."

I nod at the good news.

"Is there anything else?" he further inquires.

"We do want to know of Hans," I admit. "The hearing is today and there is little we have heard of this incident."

Madeline interrupts, "I could take you to him. Jackie asked that everyone here pack their belongings in the event of attack."

We walk through a village of ramshackle buildings and run-down homes. With being in a rush earlier to help the people, we didn't notice how 'ghetto' this place is. Villages such as this on Camelot are razed and rebuilt being deemed uninhabitable. Madeline introduces us and leaves to continue her duties.

We have a quiet conversation over refreshments. Betta and Hans appear to be a nice couple put into horrible situations. We learn much of their lives, their loves and their sorrows.

I will have to talk to Jackie to find a way to fairly mete out justice.

CHAPTER 38 The Royal Courts

We assemble in the King's Great Hall. Jackie fills me in on the abductions, including Orsons' influence. The rest we know.

Having never been in front of a King's court before where the defendants could be hung, drawn and quartered and then punished severely I don't know what to expect. But with Jackie involved it is sure to be a spectacle.

There is Pomp to the proceedings as I expected. The Court Guard dressed in regal attire marches stiffly to the throne and bangs a very ornate staff on the floor; a call to attention. The sound of the staff resonates through the room garnering all attention.

LH shivers in my hand. I whisper I would never use him in that way and the shivering stops.

"HERE YE! HERE YE! HIS ROYAL HIGHNESS; KING EDWARD OF EYREAND AND HER ROYAL HIGHNESS, QUEEN MADELINE! ALL PAY HOMAGE TO THE ROYAL COUPLE."

Everyone bows or curtsies, including me. I wasn't sure of the protocols involved but with guards in attendance, all with sharp swords it is not something I want to lose my head over.

The Royal couple enter, dressed in regal attire; from the crowns down to the purple robes and scepters. They stride to their thrones hand in hand. A chill en-wraps me, a thought this is the precursor to proceedings in modern day Britain. The King takes a sip of wine. "Bring in the accused," he commands.

Guards drag three men to the front of the thrones and slam them to their knees. They are scared and shaken but not too ill-used.

The King's Magistrate demands, "Who speaks for this group?"

One man meekly lifts his head, "I do."

I feel a quick thought from Jackie in my head, 'that is Hans, Leif's Father.

I send back we had visited him in the village.

Meanwhile, the charges are read and a rather lengthy list it is: abductions of Royal Personage, theft, menacing, and on and on.

"How do you plead?" the Magistrate demands.

"Guilty," Hans answers in a quivering whisper.

"Speak up man," The King orders in an irritable manner.

"*Guilty*," he repeats in a louder tone.

"***Father***!" The voice comes from the end of the hall. Grace steps out, Leif by her side, trembling, barely recovered from his fever.

"Not now daughter," the king calls.

She walks purposely to the thrones, half dragging Leif with her.

Two guards follow at a respectful distance, hands on pommels if trouble occurs.

"Father, I want you to stop these proceedings now, please. These people have suffered enough."

"There must be punishment for what has transpired," The King commands, rising.

"Yes Da. There must be punishments, but we cannot punish the Baron."

Now Anne walks out to stand with her sister. "Da, you heard the tale. These people have been ill-used by their Baron and have been punished enough. Even our poorest farmers have kinder treatment and live better. Is there not something that can be done that will settle all people's feelings and not cause harm and hurt?"

The King looks upon his two daughters, sees how they have grown and matured. He pauses.

Jackie chooses that moment to poof in with much smoke, flash and theatrics. People back away, fearing again the curse of the evil eye.

"Your Highness, excuse the interruption but I believe I may have the solution to the trouble," he says with a flourish of wings, alighting upon the chair back. "If we could retire to the smaller chambers with the main participants and their spouses, we can clear all this in a short period."

"*CROW*, you had best be right." The king demands. Having some trust in the bird, he relents, withdrawing to a small, side court.

"Begin, Sir Jackie," the King commands as we all resettle, "and this better be good!"

"Your Highness, what better way to punish these men but to make them pay back the equivalent of what they took. Your Daughters were not unduly harmed by the ordeal, if anything they are even more charming and mature." He caws once and bows regally to both the young ladies. "Move the villagers upon new lands, have them work and tithe to you until you are satisfied, meanwhile under your benevolent hand."

"And what lands *do I have* that I can move them onto? Where do I put them to hold and punish but still let them repay what they owe?" The King remarks with a twinge of anger building.

"Well, I could gift you those lands except that I do not own them. Actually no one owns the land," Jackie admits. "Sir Frank and I stumbled across the area while on expedition. The lands are uninhabited. You could banish their entire village there with no trouble." He flutters his wings as he turns to look up at the King. "The amount of energies are too little to perform magick. The land is pristine, water for living and irrigation is near as is a forest for timbers and rocks in abundance. All in all, a great area and would add handsomely to the size of your kingdom."

"Having to build from scratch sounds like very much work to me," the King remarks.

Hans, whose head picks up upon hearing 'pristine farmlands', motions for the King's attention.

"Your Highness, we never minded hard work, it is only ill treatment we bristle under. We would willingly do whatever you command in repayment for the help and kindness you have already shown us and the healing of my son. I am heart fully sorry for the pain your family suffered. It is a credit to your teachings, the actions of your daughters in trying to help those who thought to ill-treat them.

The King nods at Hans and then peers at Jackie, "I decree banishment to these lands with no Magickal energy should be punishment enough." The king announces.

"Every spring and fall visit them to account to what they owe," Jackie suggests.

The Princess Anne seems pleased with the arrangement and the King goes along with all of it to keep his family happy. His anger has abated somewhat upon realizing how his daughters have matured.

"With your permission, Highness," Jackie

interrupts, "we will move the people to their village to pack their personal items. We will be happy to facilitate the move."

The King waves The Crow away to do what needs to be done.

A disturbance at the side of the room catches the King's attention. Leif and Grace are having a minor disagreement. The lad is explaining that he must make the move with his village. His expertise is with the livestock and he is much needed.

She is at first upset but looking deeper into his eyes she knows he is right and will go with him; much to the disappointment of her parents.

Her father calls after her, "Grace, do you understand what you do?"

"I am going to where I must, with Leif. It is to be our home." She answers innocently.

The Kings eyes go wide with rage; the Queen has an inkling of what the young folks feel for each other and takes her husband aside for a quiet conversation.

At first, his shoulders go rigid in defiance, then after another word or so in his ear they sag in acceptance as he sits back in his chair.

Abby and I stand nearby with Jackie organizing the trip to the new lands.

"Grace," the Queen calls, "You and your young man will attend?" it is more of a command than a request.

"Grace," The King begins, "these people are being exiled to a strange, fierce land. There is nothing there, it is barren and desolate. They will not care that your Da is Royal. You must work; there are no servants for you."

"Yes Father," she answers, "but

the land is not barren. It will be filled with love." She smiles at Leif, taking his hand in reassurance. He stands next to her, nervous, unsure how to act in the presence of a King, let alone the Father of the girl he loves.

The Queen catches his eye, "be not afraid, Leif. We want what makes our daughter happy but we must be sure. Say what is in your heart. Talk to us as her parents not as a King and Queen," she smiles at the last.

He nods, "I do not know how it came to be, but one moment we were arguing over the proper way to curry the horse and the next I was thunder-struck by her intelligence, her beauty and caring demeanor. I knew I could not live if we had to part." He holds back a sigh.

"Then I fell with fever and wanted her away. I feared she would sicken, catch the fever and suffer horribly. No matter what I said she would not leave my side." He pauses and quietly, "I would give my life for her, always and forever."

You can hear the passion. The King sits mesmerized.

I listened also to his fervent words and know it be the truth. I 'sent' to Jackie about his sincerity.

"Your Highness," The Crow begins, "what better way to be sure the villagers will be honest with you than to make some of them family," he quips. "Frank, do we have those communication stones?"

He knew we do. He had Abby tune them and give me them; though I had no idea for what reason.

With the Queen and Leif each holding a stone, the Crow explains the use in communicating across vast distances or short spaces.

They are wrapped in leathers and as they open and hold the crystals on bare flesh, they learn the true workings of the stones.

Leif sees in the Queen's mind the love and affection she holds for her family and subjects, the sincerity in which she speaks.

The Queen reads the love, fierce loyalty and compassion Leif has.

I take the stones from each with my gloved hands as to not intrude upon their thoughts and re-wrap them.

It is rapidly decided to allow the young couple to have their desire. Anne and Beth both come to give their congratulations. There are plans afoot for a double wedding as Jere and Madeline converse with the Royal couple.

As we take our leave, the story of the royal family of Camelot begins and how that King abdicated. Of course, that has much to do with there being wizard powers involved.

I open the portal and Abby and I travel back home, hand in hand.

CHAPTER 39 The Perfect Idea

We awake early the next morning, anticipating the coming celebration. Abby walks across the hall to her suite to dress. I will give her a few days before suggesting she move some of her personal belongings in here.

We stride into our great room to the clamor and bustle we are becoming used to. People meet, speak, eat and enjoy the start of each new day with us. Dean and his lovely future bride Beth, sit awaiting our presence. No one needs an invitation to join us at our tables. Our Manor is open to all; friends and friends of friends. We enjoy people enjoying our meals.

After a warm greeting and piling plates with food we sit and relax.

I watch in amazement as Dean eats. The quantities of food that boy puts away... I get full just watching.

After the meal the discussion commences to moving the worms. Fido is engaged in the hunt for them from aloft while the felines search the lands from below.

"Do they hibernate," Abby questions, "or go dormant for any period?"

"I hope nothing killed them," is my big concern. "That mass of bodies decaying in the ground can contaminate large areas and we won't find them until it is too late."

"Have we spotted places where they have been?" Dean inquires, taking another bite of a sausage.

With a thought from Merlyn, Abby conveys that the felines will update us.

"It would facilitate the search if Fido can communicate directly with the cats. They can coordinate the hunt better," I lament.

A double take from Abby brings, "Merlyn says that it is a great idea and they will cooperate."

"Yeah, Fido 'sent' that they can share pictures. That should speed the hunt along," I surmise.

"Not to change the subject but do you not have a hand-fasting today?" Beth wonders.

With a quick look to Dean I ask, "You both will be there? Your names are on the list of invitees."

"Um-er, well, I was not sure Beth would enjoy attending since she is new here," he tries piteously to explain.

The two women give him *The Look.* You know the one; where the eyebrow goes upward, the mouth goes downward and the head goes askance? That *Look*!

"It is short notice Beth," Abby mentions, "But I am sure you can throw something together from your wardrobe? We have a half-day."

"Well, I-um guess we could leave now?" Dean offers. "We can get you home and you can change and get back here quickly."

Evidently, Dean does not understand how things are done but before I offer my advice, Abby steps in. "Grab what you need Beth; and Dean, you bring her back to your Manor so she can get ready along with your Mother and two sisters. It will give them time to get better acquainted.

Beth's face lights up thinking the suggestion brilliant.

I shoot Dean a tight smile and a knowing nod.

He sighs thinking he is off the hook; little does he realize…

"And Beth, if Dean does something like this again, smack him in the back of the head," she teases.

We also need to get moving with much to accomplish.

Abby is going to her Manor to dress; I am due at Jackie's kitchens to put the finishing touches on the cakes.

Beth hugs Abby, thanking her for the advice. We both poof to our destinations.

CHAPTER 40 Having Your Cake...

I materialize behind Jackie's kitchens. The gardener, crouching, planting herbs, startles at my sudden appearance. He loses his balance and topples backwards into the spearmint. Their fragrant scent wafts pleasantly throughout the gardens. It takes a second for him to recognize me and smile.

"Good thing I was not working with the spiny succulents," he jokes.

It takes a moment to realize he means the cactus. "Yes, good thing, sorry;" I offer my hand to help him to his feet. He stares down at his grimy hand pulling it back. I grab it, "A little good, clean, dirt never hurt anyone," pulling him upright.

I walk into the kitchens...

...and into apparent bedlam.

Pots simmer, breads bake, every open fire has a spit turning or grills with vegetables steaming, people scurry to and fro with Cook in the middle of it all smiling. She smiles ever wider eyeing me enter her domain. She loves her job; normal meals are a joy but special occasions are the challenge. And cooking for several hundred people is a challenge she loves.

In the front corner of the room the cakes stand ready for finishing and arrangement. The pastry chef, Olivia hurries over as she sees me.

"Do you like them, Sir Frank?" she asks with a huge smile. "We followed your instructions the best we could."

“They look perfect,” I admit. “Now let’s get them all in the proper order.”

“We waited so you could apply your magic to the display,” she states.

“Well, we place this single eight-sided cake so, facing forward with the replicas of the happy couple atop it. We will position these two larger round cakes, one to each side and slightly behind. The rest will cascade down and around until we come to this smallest one.” I position them the way I want, largest to smallest while Olivia places the couple on the cake.

She brings out the other smaller figures I had had them construct. Images of the happy couple in differing postures and positions which I place on the other cakes to depict them climbing to the top. A whimsical depiction of their climb to happiness. Olivia installs little handrails to further give the appearance of the cakes being a stairway. And with that done, the last little cake in place, we step back and ‘viola’!

Cook has walked up behind me, “Brilliant. It’s the shape of a heart. Very clever, indeed,” she congratulates.

Jackie poofs in at my request bringing Kaye. They both marvel at the simplicity and the grandeur of the sweet treat. Olivia and I finish with ribbons and well-placed flowers, both real and sugar throughout the arrangement. The kitchen staff watches in awe as it all came delightfully together.

“Very well done, Frank,” Jackie commends; “very well done, indeed.”

“Thank you, but the credit needs to go to Olivia and her staff and of course, to Cook for her help in this endeavor,” I suggest. “It is a simple design but the way it is carried out is all the kitchen and pastry staff." Kaye turns to Olivia and Cook, "Nice job, both of you. Is everything else prepared?" she curiously asks.

"Definitely, Miss Kaye," Cook answers with a proud smile. "Everything is perfect!"

"As always Cook, as always." she smiles. And then looking to Jackie, "if you could poof us back to my office where I was in an important meeting. You can help me solve a little problem that has arisen." She gives a quick nod to the Crow. "I was talking to the parents of the bride and groom when you so spuriously magicked me away. I am sure they are worried as to where I have gone."

We walk from the kitchen to get out of the way of the staff. "What type of problem is there, Kaye," I question.

As a faithful companion of Jackie, I am often in these discussions about his household. It gives me insight to the proper way to run a castle.

"They are upset with the amount of people, the refreshments and entertainment. They are simple, quiet people with little means and they worry how they will pay for this lavish spectacle?" she explains.

"Did you mention what this is all worth," Jackie queries.

"No, of course I never dreamt the question would even have come up," She admits.

"They approached me and I said I would discuss it with the Master to resolve the issue." She is looking back and forth between me and my shoulder where Jackie perches.

"They are proud, hard-working people," he says with the head bobbing and fidgeting from claw to claw. "I should have realized they would take exception to this."

"Maybe I can solve this problem judiciously? Where are they?" I ask.

"They are in my office all pacing around in a state of fright. They will wear my floor out soon. I told them we would work it all out but they are small holdings and are afraid this will ruin them for decades to come," she finishes with concern.

One thing I have learned early on, Jackie and Kaye truly love the people that work for them, both in the Manor, proper and in the farms and fields. And they have real concern over holdings of their friends. It makes me feel good thinking I have those same warm feelings for the people on my staff. "I believe I have a solution to this," I advise as we poof into the hall outside Kaye's office.

We are barely in the room when Rebekah's Dad nods a greeting and addresses the Crow, "Sir Jackie, we should be grateful and this is a bit late to address the issue but I am afraid I will be in debt for several lifetimes."

Jonathon's Father also jumps in, "we do not want to seem ungrateful, Sir Jackie, Miss Kaye, but we never expected this many people. The cost will be immense!"

Both families lament the price of the affair. They had expected to pay for their children's hand-fasting, a simple ceremony, a few friends and neighbors… but not the spectacle going on.

"Excuse me," I try interrupting, raising my hands. "Excuse *ME*," I repeat louder trying again to gain attention in all the commotion and get a word in. *"Let me say something!"* I yell to be heard over the complaining and lamenting of cost.

Several people jump, a woman gasps and the young boy, Arthur I believe, starts to quietly sob. His Grand-mum picks him up with an evil look in my direction.

I give her a weak smile and shrug.

"There will be no cost to either of the 'Happy Couples' families," I declare.

"Wait," the one man says; he seems to be the eldest of all. "We do not want charity! We can pay," he states proudly.

"No!" I forestall him with a wave of my hand. "Let me finish." I send Merlyn a feeling I need her and Abby here, afraid of an argument I may not win. I sense the cat smile in my head.

"Sir Jackie, Miss Kaye," I begin formally. "Miss Abby and I would love the pleasure to make this our treat. We will incur the entire costs." I smile all around, thinking this has solved the problem and everyone will be happy.

The explosion begins again, even louder. They still consider it charity and will not accept it.

Jackie quietly drops into my mind with the question why.

'Rebekah did save Abby's life in the Black Dragon's Manor House. It is worth everything and more to do this. A least we can begin to show our appreciation to the families,' I send.

Jackie caws loudly for quiet. And "Go on and explain your reasoning for this action."

I turn to Rebekah's parents, "Your daughter risked her life to save my friend, Miss Abby. It is the least that we could do to begin paying back a debt that we owe. We will not let you spend one farthing on this party! And as for Jonathon, he gave us all the help in establishing our holdings, so we owe him a debt of gratitude also."

They are beginning anew to argue when Abby and Merlyn poof into the small space, causing the argument to stop, 'mid-lament'.

"Miss Abby," I begin formally, "the parents of Rebekah and Jonathon are arguing over the payment of this celebration. I informed them we will pay for the festivities; as a small token for her saving you from the Black Dragon. They feel the need to continue the argument."

Abby leans back upon Kaye's desk assessing the situation. She looks each parent in the eye and with a wide grin, "You must let us do this for them! There is no real way to ever pay back the heroic act she did. This small token is something we must do," she indicates. And so there will be no argument from anyone, "but I do understand your feelings." She pauses for a moment to be sure of everyone's attention; "Here is what I propose. Work out with Miss Kaye what you expected to pay for the hand-fasting and we will cover the additional costs."

"That sounds fair to me," I interrupt, "and to make sure, if I hear one complaint, I will send Fido to visit your farms," I joke.

"You think some little dog would deter us from actions," one man comments. I think it was Rebekah's brother Brandon.

"No," Abby interjects, "Fido is his friend and a dragon," she laughs. "He might not harm you but picture a twelve-foot dragon sitting in your yard."

"*WOW! A DRAGON,*" I hear the exclamation from the little lad, Arthur. "Can I pet him?"

It is all that is needed to break the resistance. Hands are shook, hugs are given and glad tidings are enjoyed by all.

"And later when we need advice and counseling on farm matters and livestock, you'll agree to come help," Abby suggests.

That further closes the deal. Now they feel as if they are contributing something.

I pick up Arthur, so much reminding me of my Grandchildren. He is shy and scared at first, "C-can I really meet the d-dr-dragon," he hesitantly wonders.

"Sure, you can," I promise. "I will talk to Fido. Maybe you can even sit on him."

His eyes light up and his grin goes from ear to ear. "*Wow*!" he cries.

With all that settled we return to what we had been doing, preparing for a hand-fasting. Arthur goes back to his Grandma, I walk into the hallway, then poof back to my bed chambers to dress for the celebration.

I hear a quick thought from Jackie, *"Nice work: diplomacy! They save face because they pay what they thought they should. They help you and Miss Abigail in your farming endeavors. That was how they would have paid for the ceremony in their farm house; barter and coins they amassed for the occasion."* There is a slight hesitation, *"but how are you going to pay me for all the festivities, tonight,"* he jokes.

"Well," I shoot back at him along the same mind link, *"I did save your 'tail' once. And there is all the coffee and London broil from my world. Then there is saving Camelot from a mad Wizard..."*

I tick off several other favors before realizing that the link has been broken. Though, I imagine him on the perch in his great room, laughing and cawing loudly. Abby poofs into the room and I explain the conversation. We are still laughing as we materialize in Jackie's gardens, hand in hand for the spectacle.

CHAPTER 41 The Spectacle

And it is some spectacle!

I see why the families panicked when they saw the appurtenances. I am having second thoughts myself!

The fields abutting the gardens are set with tents, tables, chairs. The servers for food and drink are spaced about the perimeter of the fields ready to assist the celebrants with adjoining cooking stations with meats and fish turning and roasting, adding the wondrous smells of food intermixed with the aroma of the flowers. Throngs of people mingle, laugh, drink and enjoy the musicians.

A large tent sits at the end of the field with an altar. I ask Abby, "A religious service?"

"You don't attend the local rites. They are based on the Wicca. They celebrate the four seasons. Some have local ceremonies for the full and new moons and of course Beltane, which is our Halloween," she explains. "So, it will be a hand-fasting rather than a wedding. This is a Matriarchy where a Priestess presides. Several Priestess travel the lands, all under the benevolence of 'The Priestess' who is the head of the Sect. They lead the larger ceremonies as well the hand fasts, deaths and others.

Kaye makes her way through the crowds with Jackie perching upon her shoulder. "Thanks for solving the cost issue with the families," she says. "We were not going to charge them more than a nominal amount. But then the conversation got out of hand. After you all left, I continued the discussion with them. I suggested they could tithe a bit more in their share of the crops over the next few harvests and if they had coin, they could give it to the couple for their future," she further adds. "They like those suggestions and will work out the tithe with Sir Henry and happily went on their way."

Sir Jere and his wife Madeline walk over, drinks in their hands to join the conversation. They are accompanied by a strange woman swathed in robes with the cowl pulled up around her face.

Madeline takes the lead and introduces us to the Priestess Vanessa.

We exchange greetings. She is taken aback when The Crow greets her most warmly in English. The look of horror upon her face shows that she is new to this part of the world. Chagrined, I jump in, "Sister, it seems that no one explained that this crow is Sir Jackie and Master of this House."

She stops the hand movements, as if warding the evils away. "No, I was not so informed. My apologies, Sir Jackie," she whispers hoarsely. Her voice has a mid-European accent, sending a shiver down my spine. And with a look at Abby it has done the same to her. The fur on both felines seems to rise. I guess we watch one too many 1940's vampire movies with Bela Lugosi.

She gives Merlyn one quick glance and to Abby, "We must talk later, Miss Abby. Much can be learned by both with dialog."

Madeline interjects. "Sister Vanessa will preside over the rites this day."

The priestess pulls her cowl tighter as if to protect her skin from the sun and with a nod, proceeds to the altar.

We spend several minutes with Sirs Albert and James and their wives, Eleanor and Maria respectively. They have questions pertaining to the investigation and even though it has been just over a ten day since we have begun, they are pleased with our progress finding the cause for the dying fish and animals.

Has it only been that long since Kaye's birthday celebration? It surely seems several lifetimes.

We give them the reports, but ten-foot-long worm like creatures, even in the lands of wizardry still seems preposterous. I assure both men that the threat is real and very much a danger. Not so much a threat of physical harm from the worms, personally but their chemistry make-up disrupting the balance of the ecosystem.

Suddenly, Albert is not listening; his attention focuses on an event unfolding behind me. The crowd quiets except for a few mutterings, a question and a surprise gasp. All I hear from Albert is a four-letter expletive, "*Damn*!"

Then his face brightens, "Excuse me, my parents have arrived." And he dashes off.

Kaye's eyes grow wide and Jackie fidgets and caws nervously on her shoulder.

"Were not his parents invited and expected?" Abby wonders to both Kaye and The Crow.

"Albert's Mother is *The Priestess*," Kaye explains and then pauses, considering her next words.

Jackie interrupts and takes over the dialog, "They are both very aged," he continues, "When the Wizard Orson was being banished to the other alternative, they were both infants we think. No one is sure of their ages and they seldom venture out as of late, even for the important gatherings."

Albert reappears with his parents flanking him.

Jackie speaks first, "Priestess Victoria; welcome to my humble dwelling and be warmed, and welcome to you also, Sir Albert." He bobs and bounces from claw to claw showing much social etiquette.

"So, the stories are true," the Priestess remarks. "You are a crow, Sir Merlin!"

"A crow yes, Good Mistress," using the honorific, "but Merlin no longer. I am Jackie," he pauses a moment longer to allow the information to be absorbed. "If not for my friends, here, Miss Abigail and Frank I would not be here, nor would I have survived the experience."

A soft meow.

"I did not forget you, Merlyn but was making your introduction solo for honors to you. This feline is Merlyn, an all-important member of my friend's family and her mate, Dagwood.

We act formally during the introductions. Victoria glances down briefly at the two felines, "Yes, definitely," and to Abby, "very interesting company you keep Miss Abigail," taking her hand. At that moment, a slight nod of knowing. "Ah! Now I see," as if opening up Abby's entire life in one touch.

Chairs appear and the couple sits while I am increasingly uncomfortable stretching my hand in greeting.

"Come, Frank - with no title, I do not bite young men anymore," she teases. She lightly grasps my hand, "Yes, very modest and unassuming; yet honorable and faithful to your friends and those in need, to a fault. The makings of a fine Knight of the realm."

She appears to be of great age now that I had a moment to analyze. Her hand has the feel of antiquity, an almost fragile impression.

Sir Albert, Sr. appears years younger. But I imagine the powers a Priestess uses would take their toll upon the body. Jackie keeps reminding us the use of power must be paid for. And I feel those powers. The hairs on my arms rise and bristle. I see the pain in her eyes and the desperation; and then feel – something – strange, almost as if...

Her eyes catch mine, momentarily – "Ah, and a sensitive, I think, Frank- with no title," she labors with the words. "You will be most useful later I believe."

"Mother," Albert Jr. chides, "Rest. Why did you venture out? Why subject yourself to the commotion and the energies here," he wonders respectfully.

And there is commotion. Quite a crowd has gathered around our little group. Priestess Vanessa has come to stand by the aged Mother.

"Such a concerned child you are, Albert," his mother commends. He blushes at being called a child.

"Mother, I am almost 500, no longer a child," he reminds her.

"Always my child," she whispers in a ragged voice. And then louder, "*All* are *my* children!" Her feeble arm swings wide to encompass the entire congregation. "Much is coming. I need to be here to warn, shield," she takes a labored breath. "Joy, quickly followed by sorrow; danger, and it must happen to save all!"

Her eyes move from Kaye to Abby and back to Kaye; "What happens, will happen. It must! Sacrifices have been and are to be made. But you will know." That last directed to me.

She sips at the goblet of wine Vanessa proffers.

"Is all in readiness Sister," she asks Vanessa?

"Yes Mother, it is," is the respectful reply.

"Bring the happy couple so we may make fast that which will bring the joy." She stands aided by her husband and shuffles to the altar. A murmur travels through the throng as they realize who will perform the rite.

The Priestess waits.

Upon hearing of the honor being bestowed upon them, the couple is both pleased and scared as they timidly approach the Altar tent.

"Come, come, my children; we have not all day. Events must be, for others to be fulfilled." She glances to Jonathon who appears as if he will turn and run. He sees Rebekah's fear, grips her hand all the tighter, then guides her to the tent.

"Love conquers much; remember that," the Priestess whispers. And with a hand under Rebekah's chin, she slowly raises the girls head up 'til their eyes met. "Let me look at you daughter." Fear evident in the bride's eyes. "Calm yourself, child. I am here for more than this, though you are a large part." The old woman lets go the chin and sits back, weary. "I heard of your visit to the Black Dragon's lair to save a friend. That alone would bring me here. But you then saved the lives of several people at great risk to yourself. *No*, I know you did not do it alone." She smiles as a Mother would to a daughter and with a nod continues.

"And there is much you shall learn and do, yet. She takes the couple's hands and with their help, stands. She raises wide her arms and beckons to all, a deep breath, a sigh, "Come, be welcome and comforted here," she intones in a larger voice than a woman of her age should have. "Let us gather and help 'Hand-fast' this special couple." She moves her arms as if to hug the entire congregation.

"Divine Mother, I ask thee of thy blessings on this couple and in this gathering; Bless their joining as long as they live in love. And to each, may there be health, joy, love and fertility."

She turns to pray to each point of the compass. First the East, then South, West and North, each in kind; asking the blessings from each element they rule; air, fire, water and finally, Camelot herself.

I stand in awe, watching as the life and energies drain away from this amazing lady. Stepping back, I tug Abby's arm to follow. Jackie flutters his wings as I send to him, *"Something is not right."* I whisper also to Abby, *"She is dying before our eyes."*

Abby stares unbelieving at me and Jackie casts his doubt down our link. And to both again, *"She is using all her life force to stay alive to finish this service, but I cannot say why."*

We watch as she continues, "We honor the four points as we honor the four seasons, knowing love has the same cycle. Spring is the blossoming, the blooming of the love. becoming familiar and growing into each other's lives." She stops to steady herself against the chair before going on again. "The summer brings the strength of commitment, the active time of loving and living."

"Autumn is for the cooling of ardor's intensity, but knowing of your partner completely." A slight smile and then, "Finally the winter of loves' cycle. There is an ending, a parting and sorrow…" she stops a moment, almost as if to let that sink in. I think I see a tear glisten, then brushed away with a slight hand movement as if to show it of no consequence. "… But Love remains as we will love again in the spring of the next plane of existence, after the unfolding." She pauses, "It is custom to ask if both and each come willingly to this joining but by your smiles and the tightness of your handclasp, there is no need."

"It is also custom to ask, *who giveth this woman*? But by your heroics to save your friends, Rebekah, none can speak for you. None can give you, but you."

And lastly, "it is also custom to ask if any object to this joining. By the smiles upon the faces of family and friends and the joy I feel flooding these gardens, there is no need!"

"The couple has words they wrote to share with each other and all of you, Jonathon, you may begin."

Shyly, he gazes down and takes Rebekah's hands in his, "my love, I come to you with my hands out to give to thee wanting to share my life. I promise to be always for thee, always with thee. I further pledge my Heart, for you to hold; my Trust for you to believe in; my Spirit, for you to enliven. We shall be forever one in love, in spirit and in life, now and through the beyond. Always do I love thee, Miss Rebekah," he stares deep into her eyes, each word a symbol of his vast love. His eyes moisten with tears.

Abby's hand finds mine; I hear a sigh as I feel a slight squeeze.

Rebekah reaches up, brushes a tear from her lovers' cheek. "A tear to show your love for me? An offering I give freely in return for all the same reasons. I pledge to bring to you only tears of joy. I pledge a happy home to be content in. I ask the Goddess for long life to love you all the longer." She grasps his hand and with tears flowing freely, "I also will give thee respect as you giveth me. Thank you, my love, from the bottom of my heart!"

"Now that you have professed your love and intentions to one another," Victoria takes the vine from Vanessa and begins binding their two right hands together, one atop the other. "I bind thee with this vine as a symbol of your joining in all endeavors of life; even if this vine be poison."

She lets the words and meaning sink in. Several of the crowd gasp murmured concerns.

"I see that neither pull away nor flinch. Your love and strength in each other be strong through any adversity. You will have many a test in life, I hope that this be the hardest."

"You have rings," The Priestess states.

A slight nod from Jonathon to Little Arthur, he, trembling in fear of this great lady, holds aloft the cushion where the rings are pinned.

The Priestess with a kind smile bends and touches him on the cheek, "Stand straight and grow strong," she intones. The lad didn't bat an eye, calmed by her touch he announces in a wondrous whispering tone, "I am going to pet a dragon today!"

Some in the crowd gasp at the boys' impertinence; Rebekah turns, "Hush boy!"

The Priestess, still smiling mentions, "I would wish also to pet a dragon. But, alas, I shall not be here then." She then encourages, "Good job, Arthur," as she takes the rings and holds them aloft, as high as she can with trembling arms.

"To the Goddess I beg of thee; please bless these rings and wearers of each?" she prays. "As you wish to be one with each other united in Love; take of these bits of metal and bind thee to each other as a sign of your commitment."

Clumsily, they each slide the rings upon each other's fingers.

The Priestess continues, "We are ever-changing but with this, you are now and forever bound together. As the Goddess has brought two together, she sees as one, so say I in the name of the Goddess!" With her diminishing energy, arms shaking from fatigue she places her palms close and touches each on their heads, declaring, *"BLESSED BE!"*

She sits heavily and with a smile orders, "Well, kiss her already."

He, being the good man he is, obeys his Priestess and to the cheering of the crowd, the happy couple kiss.

I watch as Victoria sags heavily upon the cushions, a glass of wine placed at her lips by Vanessa. Albert, Sr. walks solemnly to her side, gently kisses her cheek, whispering a question.

Her head slowly shakes as she replies. His head comes up and his body stiffens.

The crowd has followed the newlyweds into the field for the first toast. Then the music starts, the bards sing the traditional tunes while many of the crowd dance merrily.

We walk to the altar to see if we can help. Victoria is feeble, drained. The ceremony has taken much from that grand lady.

Jackie poofs in feeling my consternation.

"Mistress," he begins, "Would not my humble abode be a more fitting place for you to rest?"

"It be a long rest I am to have," she states cryptically. Albert takes her hand as Albert the Younger and his wife approach, confusion etched upon their faces.

One look tells them what is happening.

Young Albert pleads at those assembled, "You are healers, is there nothing you can do for my Mother? Is there nothing to be done for the Priestess?" He is near to tears. His father stops him with a slow shake of the head.

Abby leans forward intending to lend energy but is waved off by Vanessa.

The Priestess, very weak motions to Kaye. The sounds behind me change, quieting. With a glance I see the crowd drifting back sensing that some great event is unfolding. In ones and two's, they return, drawn by the power and energy slowly waning from this great woman.

Kaye leans in taking the old Priestess' hand; smiles come to both faces, understanding what must be done. The Priestess' craggy face brightens, "I am at peace with this," loud enough to be heard by those near.

She draws her other hand up to Kaye's head and in her commanding tone exalts, "By the Goddess, I pass on my power to thee, Priestess Kathleen!" She takes a struggled breath and then continues. "There is much coming; all be strong! I am but dust!"

A quick nod to her son and his wife. She reaches for her husbands' hand; "I love you as the first day we met," she whispers. Her head sags; a beatific smile frames her face as she exhales her last breath.

The crowd gasps; this moment of history truly profound and etches forever in their memories. Vanessa turns to Kaye and offers, "As I did for The Mother, I will do for you!"

Kaye is taken aback, not understanding what is to be done, what will her duties be; nothing in life has prepared her for such a momentous event. *She* is *the Priestess*!

Vanessa smiles and nods, "I will help thee, Mother."

Those words fill her with a sense of calm.

Vanessa holds her hands aloft to quiet the crowd, "The New Mother will speak!" And whispers to her, "Take a breath, what must be said, will be said."

Kaye stands a moment; a vision of Victoria smiling enters her thoughts, which helps her stand taller. She faces the crowd and the newly hand-fasted couple with a serene composure while the congregation openly weeps.

With raised hands, "Our beloved Priestess has passed to a new and better place," she tells the quieting crowds. "This life is the illusion! The real, great adventure begins at our last breath." She pauses, a small tear crosses her cheek; a tear for what she lost and gained as the Priestess.

And then gentle words to Albert Sr. A hug to young Albert Jr. and Eleanor to help ease their sorrows.

Several men gently lift the worldly remains of Victoria and solemnly walk off.

Kaye whispers to Vanessa, some quick words spoken that I over-hear, "Why me? Would not you be better suited for this?"

A quick shake of the head tells Kaye that she never aspired for the job. "I have not the fortitude nor power to do what must be done," she advises. "I have knowledge that will help, when you need it. I am here to serve you, Mother!"

She nods her head in respect. "And for this last time, I go to help my friend Victoria cross to her new being. I bid your permission, Dear Mother."

Taken aback, struggling for words and thoughts Kaye simply nods her consent. And then in a panic, screeches, "What shall I do?" But she stands alone.

Jackie wings to alight upon her shoulder.

She shrugs, "I do not know what to do?"

He squawks quietly fluttering his wings to get a better perch, "Do what you do best, dear. Be yourself."

"But I have never been anything before, *now* I am *The Priestess*," she states.

"Kaye," he reassures, "You have always been someone, especially to me and your friends. Now you are *that* someone to all of Camelot!" His wing flings out to encompass the entire congregation.

She quiets at those words, stiffens her resolve and begins to be what she was destined to be; 'The Priestess'.

She gathers her skirts and descends the altar stairs to the waiting crowd. First to the new couple, she takes their hands and whispers, "It is fine. This is a joyous day for you. Victoria honored your union with her very essence. You both are truly blessed."

She turns to the waiting throngs, "I know not what is to be, but we will survive and prosper. The Goddess has shown me the way!"

The crowds cheer and the partying continues through the afternoon.

There was one not-so-slight disruption. As evening approaches, the rustling of wings almost as leather upon leather and the whirring colors of the dragon's eyes as he alights near the crowded fields. On-lookers back away, frightened by his sudden appearance, intimidated by his size. But one little body, legs pumping fast heads straight for Fido.

I notice and alert my friend of his new acquaintance. The dragons' enormous head turns, moving down closer to the sphere of this little admirer. Fido's eyes whirl all the quicker in excitement. Arthur stops short, cautious, as realizing the mammoth proportions of his target.

"It is all right," I soothe. "Fido is more than happy to make your acquaintance."

The boy's little eyes widen, taken with the beauty and the wonder of the dragon. He peers up at that giant face and asks, "ca-can I pet him?"

I point towards Fido, "Ask him!"

Arthur' eyes grow wider still as he stammers, "Ma-may I please sir? Pet you?"

Fido moves his head closer in anticipation. I take the boy's hand. The crowd watches as the possibility of the disaster that may take place. I re-assure the tyke that Fido loves attention and show right where to scratch. In and around the eye mounds; the best enjoyment for any dragon.

He reaches up and with hesitant movement,

scratches where I instruct. The look on both their faces is pure pleasure.

"Fido asks you to move a bit to the left," I say.

"You can hear him?" Arthur asks in amazement.

"I hear him in my mind. It is how we communicate."

For the next several minutes the boy and the dragon have the time of their lives as Arthur scratches in and around Fido's eyes whilst the crowd stands bemused but alert in the event something goes extremely wrong.

Arthur drops his arm in fatigue. Fido tilts his enormous head to better look at his new, little friend, winks once at me and darts his tongue out to kiss the boys' cheek. The hand, which moments ago scratched the dragon, goes to his own surprised face where Fido has kissed him, one friend to another.

"Are you sure?" I ask. I see the slight nod and feel the smile. Turning to the lad, "Would you like to sit astride the Dragon?"

He gawks, first to Fido and then up at me, "May I, please?" he gasps in a breathless utterance. His legs already carrying him forward.

"Your friend offered. Even I have never sat a-Dragon," I confess.

I lift and place him in the spot behind the head, in a cleft used for centuries on Pern to fight thread.

I mutter a quick thank you to Miss Anne for helping make this boy's life something to remember.

He sits for a moment, then lies down with arms as wide a hug as a little boy can. These two will be friends for life.

The crowd cheers. Arthur's parents who stand by with their hearts in their throats breathe again amid the back slapping and hand-shaking, I am proud to say a practice I brought to Camelot.

The music begins anew and the people enjoy the delicious foods and drinks. Arthur is swept away to his dinner. I send a quiet thank you to Fido who was surprised. He thanks me for all the love and attention and with a slight sense of sorrow, leaps awing to vanish into the darkness.

Abby and I return to our table with friends to enjoy the festivities.

I am in the middle of explaining to her the help I have given Jonathon and how it is more of a mixing of my words and his feelings; and how it also equates to what my feelings are for her.

I am engrossed to where I have nominally noticed the noise, or lack of it. The music has stopped, the dancers are taking their seats and the conversations mute to near complete silence.

I jerk my head up at a slight chuckle from Jackie along our mind-link. With a nudge from Abby I realize they are eagerly anticipating my addition to the party. A large table in front of the happy couple sits empty and ready for the cakes.

Abby's hand in mine we move forward; all eyes upon me. After the excitement of what we produced for Kaye's birthday cake with the replica of the castle, they are eager to see how we will out-do that. I hope they will not be disappointed.

We bid the couple to join us.

Seeing the slight apprehension in my face, "You can do this, Frankie," Abby whispers. Her smile touches me deep inside, gives me the confidence to poof the cakes here without them toppling. It will be a feather in my cap, so to speak.

All eyes upon me, the crowd eagerly awaits in hushed expectation. Rebekah and Jonathon stand at the table.

People crowd around.

"If you will help me, please…" I call loudly. "On the count of three! *One*," A few people begin to count. "*Two*!" More people join in. "*THREE*!"

The cakes drop gently to the table, the icings and fondants sparkling in the setting sun. Then, as everyone finishes gasping at the spectacle, they see the heart shape the cakes make which causes 'oohs and aahs'. The whimsical depiction of the couple climbing upon the cakes is another layer in this dessert. White and purple candles materialize around the tableau and light with a flash adding pizzazz to the presentation.

Then, as the people regain their breath, I yell, "*BEHOLD!*" And with a wave of my hand one hundred beautiful white doves take flight from under the tables fluttering to the skies, feathers glistening in the suns' final rays as they hoist purple and white ribbons. Abby clasps my hand all the harder as an initial sigh from the crowd becomes a wild cheer.

Rebekah hugs me as thanks for the beautiful design. I remind her to thank Cook and Olivia for the sweet treat. Abby hugs Jonathon because he looks as if he needs one.

A knife is proffered and the newlyweds do the tradition of cutting and feeding each other cake as an omen for continued prosperity.

It was a traumatic day, having the person who presides over your Hand-fasting to pass immediately after the ceremony.

Abby and I sit holding hands, occasionally a quiet sob escaping from one of us as we remember our own weddings and the spouses we lost. And so, we manage through the evening.

CHAPTER 42 Fanciful

I awake the next morning, alone. Abby thinks it wise we should sleep apart for a while longer; something about feeling vulnerable. I don't know if she is talking for herself, or me.

She walks in to my bed chamber as I finish dressing.

"Good morning," she says shyly, as if she fears what I might think after last night.

"Good morning, yourself," I answer. "I hope that you slept well, though we do need to talk. I do understand, more than you realize how you feel, and appreciate your caution. But it does get lonely with only Dagwood and LH to keep me company." I hear a 'meow' from atop my bed. "No offense, Dags, but I do need someone a bit warmer. You do have Merlyn when you feel lonely," I quip. "Besides, Abby gives better hugs than you do."

She glances at Dagwood and then "We will talk on it tonight, after we retire." I guess she needs re-assurance of my true feelings.

"Should we head down for breakfast?" I ask, thinking of all the things that need to be accomplished and also how empty my stomach feels.

She reaches out her hand and mine slides easily into hers. I wrap an arm around her shoulder and give her a quick hug as she replies, "Yeah, I'm hungry. With all the food last night I barely ate."

"What with the wedding and the Priestess passing, the entire night didn't go as planned," I remind. "And we have to find and move those worms."

We are already heading down the stairs to the main hall when I hear from Fido. Helped by all the felines, they pinpoint where the creatures are at the moment. And by the look on Abby's face and how Merlyn is reacting, they are getting the same information.

"We will have to contact Beth and Dean," She suggests.

An hour later, that loving couple poofs into the main hall and after proper greetings we get down to the business at hand.

"So, to where would you have me call the "Creative Ones?" Beth inquires.

"We will herd them to your lands so we can start there. Do you have a particular field that needs tilling?" I ask, getting things moving.

"Well we can start near the Castle," she begins, turning to Dean with a smile and hand on his arm, "Dear, do you remember that first field we worked with the crystals."

He returns the smile and nods, "When we are ready, I will open the portal."

We spend the next several hours traveling portals to maneuver the worms for the big move.

The Royal House is alerted and awaits us in the field.

Salutations made; Grace and Anne come to stand behind their older sister.

With the approval of the King I open a portal to the worms.

Beth grasps the gemstone from her necklace, a sparkle surges as she chants the rite of 'Princess of the Bountiful Harvest'. Raising one hand in the air, the other wraps around the glistening gem, she exclaims,

"Lumbricus Terrestris! I call; please attend this field and magic weave. For in your spirit, we do most believe. Please honor this humble request and bless us with a bountiful harvest!"

I feel the magicks course round us, the hairs on my arms once again rise. The ground trembles with action. Worms from far and wide attend. Not just the ones from Camelot, but the local ones heed the call. Her two sisters fall under the spell. They stand, swaying, in a trance, adding to the power. It takes several minutes but the last of the Blessed Creatures return through the portal to their home.

Now Diana could consider this being a 'wormhole'.

As I chuckle to myself about my witticism, I catch a thought from Fido. He has searched me out but lost interest when the first portal closed. Now with the new activity and this portal open, he senses my location and went 'between' to be with me. He alights with joy in his whirring eyes, for a moment anyway.

Something changes dramatically! I feel eager anticipation and surprise. I hear an unexpected squeal from Princess Anne. She stands with her one hand on her forehead and the other pointing to Fido.

A tearing pain rips my skull apart, as if a piece of me is gouged out with a swiftness that leaves me dizzy, dismayed and sick to my stomach. A forlorn loneliness engulfs me, devastates me. Fido is gone from my consciousness. I can no longer feel his presence. He is lost to me. My mind reels and if not for Abby grabbing me, I would have fallen flat on my face.

The sense of loss is so overwhelming I cry out. I no longer want to live. Screams echo through the loneliness of my mind.

Jackie comes flying into my brain with a caw so loud it deafens me momentarily. So great is my loss I nearly take him into a depression such as we have never had. He stops me from wanting to die.

An incredulous look sweeps across Anne's face. "*Oh, Fanciful*!" She shouts and crumples to one knee. Leif and Grace grab her before she can topple and hurt herself. Anne shakes off the helping hands and with a deep breath begins an unsteady walk towards my dragon. Her Parents are frantic. The guards surround her, slowing her progress but she breaks through them, not to be denied.

The Dragon rears upon his back legs trumpeting a warning. Anne stops, throws her hands in the air with the command; "Leave me!"

She continues onward unmindful of the crowd that has gathered.

She whispers, "His name is Fanciful!"

You can feel the love between the two.

He crouches, allowing her to rub by his eye. It whirls in delight, changing colors as she scratches. With her arms wrapped around his neck he settles onto the ground, comfortably placing his huge head softly upon her lap.

Coming out from her reverie she waves me to attend.

"Fanciful said 'thank you for all you have done', helping him find me." She gives an adoring look at her dragon. "I don't quite understand any of this but I see what is in his mind and heart as well as his seeing into mine. I have never felt so complete. I've never sensed how lonely I was before now!" She pauses, overcome with the emotions of feeling true love. "It is a joy I could never have imagined!"

Having recovered from the emotions of Fido leaving, I reach one last time to scratch him by the eye. "Tell Fanciful he is quite welcome and I enjoyed our days together," I admit. I feel a brief intrusion on my mind, a brief thought of thanks and then silence in there. If not for Jackie in my mind, I do believe I would have never recovered my senses.

Aloud, "Sir Frank," Anne relates, "If you are ever in trouble, think '*HELP*' to us and we will be there."

I smile and then realize we were surrounded by the King's entire guard, all with swords drawn.

"Help!" I call jokingly.

She assures her family that Fanciful is a safe companion and protector. The guards reluctantly put up their swords.

I catch one quick thankful thought from Jackie that the Dragon will be staying in this alternative, "and no more to be trampling in my herb garden!"

With a slight smile I turn to Princess Anne and Fanciful, bow and proclaim, "Princess, you and Fanciful are always welcome at my estate!"

I mentally stick out my tongue to Jackie and hear a quiet squawk in my head. I can't help but tease him, although he did poof to my aid the moment he felt the panic when the dragon left my mind.

CHAPTER 43 The Bad News

"I received a message from Jackie," turning to Abby as we climbed from my bed, our bed. "The services for Priestess Victoria will be tomorrow. We are invited to attend," I repeat to her. "Well, you are invited and I am allowed to tag along, according to Jackie," I laugh. "I think that is an off-handed slight for me inviting Princess Anne and Fanciful to visit here whenever they have a mind to!"

"Did he mention when?" Abby inquires.

"No, he will discuss it later when he sees us."

Abby has moved some of her things into the suite. And last night, after actually sharing a bed since the wolf attack, we discuss what the future will hold for us. What we both expect from the relationship and from each other.

It was a heart-felt talk with lamentations of the tragedy of our spouses and then, letting the hurt go and embracing the future.

I admitted that I love her and thought that maybe I have never stopped loving her from the beginning.

She assesses her own mental state. Something along the lines she 'must be crazy to get hooked up with an old wizard like me'. But she said it with kindness.

I partially agree with her; she was crazy. How many sane people have intelligent, two-way conversations with a feline?

She gently reminds me I have a walking stick I talk to and hear from and didn't I just give up a relationship with a smart dragon?

The rest of the conversation goes along those lines with an occasional kiss and small hug. We agree not to rush things. To let it slowly grow into the 'something wonderful stage'. We will do what comes naturally, as it seems right. After a tender, soulful kiss good-night we cuddle and I sleep most soundly for the first time in a long time.

And now we are on our way to the main hall for breakfast.

Several families have approached us to settle and farm parcels of our land. This is all new to us as how to proceed and whom to choose. There are interviews set for later this morning.

We don't need to attend, as John, our over-seer will handle the meetings, proper. But we do want to learn the procedure, so we will sit in.

Continuing on to our table, acknowledging various friends and workers along the way, Merlyn and Dagwood bound ahead knowing someone will be there to feed them.

LH lies dormant in my hand, and on that rare occasion would send a slight shiver or large jolt as a warning of impending danger. Thankfully, he has been quiet as of late.

Maybe I will look into setting up a woodworking shop of my own? We can cut trees and mill lumber for many projects. I can help out when I have free hours or when I am bored.

We don't need it for the income. Virtually all we use to survive, we have. There are cattle and other livestock raised for food and barter. Some many acres of lands are planted with fruit trees and crops for our own use with the overflow used for additional services.

Then there are all the little things that Abby and I do for the friends and neighbors in Camelot that leave us on the plus side of bartering. And with a little research from our Earth I established breeding ponds for various types of fish and mollusks. So, we can harvest catfish, trout, brim and crappie to supplement the diet of the Manor.

I have additionally co-opted with Jackie to find lands near the oceans to start the same process with saltwater fish. Clams and oysters will be seeded in beds along the shores for easy harvest. Flounder, fluke and sea bass, along with other salt water delectable can also be farmed. So financially, we are, what most people would say as, 'well-off.

But we still need to look to the future. We have family and friends on old earth that will want to move here. In our travels back for visits we note that the current political scene may soon be in chaos so we need to be ready for it.

We enjoy a leisurely meal, solve simple problems tossed our way and chat with our staff before they head out for their chores.

Diana joins us. We have moved her, part, parcel and laboratory to Abby's for added space and privacy. She has a lab in the woods to monitor the healing of Camelot. She also sets the standards used in our fish farms to keep them safe and healthy.

But the look on her face says there is a problem. She sits dejectedly as I pour coffee. With a sad look at me and a slow shake of her head it seems she is about to announce the 'end of the world'.

She is.

"The planet is not healing quickly enough." She takes a sip from the mug. "I analyzed the original waters and soils from where the worms first came through and the numbers are still dismal to say the least."

"Well," Abby reminds, "the worms have just left here. Give it time to heal."

"It doesn't make much difference," Diana cites. "That area has not had worm sign for a ten-day, as you would call it. There is no catalyst to help speed the regeneration of the area. The lands need to get back to where they were before the worms."

She pauses, looking for the proper words to give the importance of what she will next tell us. "The Willow is beginning to drop leaves!" She lets out a long sigh.

"Is there something that we could plant or sprinkle to help speed the healing," I ask, concerned. "Spreading lime on certain soils helps promote growth. Can't we do something similar?"

"The acid soil was an example to give you a frame of reference to see the problem." She stops and plays with her food chasing sausage across the plate, not looking hungry. "It appears the worms spread a type of virus, something that is completely innocuous in their own lands but quite harmful here." She throws the fork down hard enough for several other diners to look askance at her.

"It may take years for this world to heal properly but in the meanwhile the soils will continue to change. The plants can eventually adapt along with the smaller life forms. It is about the people that I worry." She sits back to let those facts sink into our nonscientific brain pans.

"Even after analyzing the worms I still have no understanding of what is happening. The changes are on a molecular level, almost as if the DNA is changing," she finishes with a sigh.

"We need to keep this quiet, for a while, anyway," Abby suggests. "See what Jackie's thoughts are and then bring it up the Conclave to find solutions."

"I will alert him," I offer.

"Tomorrow is the rite for The Priestess. May hap after that we can have a meeting?" Abby wonders.

"Jackie will inform us when the Conclave can meet," I relay after a quick commune with The Crow.

"Not to change the subject," Diana begins, "But have either of you seen Allain?"

I glance at Abby as she shakes her head.

"He's been back a few days, but I lost track of him yesterday during the wedding," Diana states.

"I saw him briefly at the feast and expected to hear him sing," Abby explains, "but after Victoria passed..." She let the statement hang there.

"Yes," Diana admits, "He was my escort for the event, but left me in the lurch. I have been worried about him ever since."

"He has been alone for so long, perhaps he got side tracked by duties..." I trail off, trying to make a feeble excuse for him.

"I understand all that," Diana placates, "but I have grown fond of the man and hope that he has not come to harm."

We both promise to keep an eye out for him.

CHAPTER 44 A New Beginning for Some

We meet John as we walk down to his office.

"There are two families to interview this morning," he informs us. "A large established group, 'The Clive's, and a smaller family, 'The Bakers'."

I spy both families sitting on benches in the hall. As we enter his office, he steps aside to allow me his chair behind the desk. I motion for him to sit.

"This is your office and you are conducting the interviews. We are here to observe. We want to be able to question and find what to look for in a family should we ever need to do this on our own," I inform him.

"Let's meet with the Clive group first," Abby suggests. "They have several small children who could become fidgety during a long wait."

From the door I motion for the Clive's.

As they stand, I see the facial expression of the Baker's older daughter. She appears crestfallen, as if she has lost her best friend. I wave the Clive's in and bid John to go ahead without me. I walk back into the hall.

The Bakers' seem a quiet, nondescript family. Tom and Sarah-Jane are the parents of two daughters and a son. The youngest daughter appears to be two or three, the boy nine.

The one that intrigues me though is the older girl. I think her fourteen and there is something about the look on her face with the red hair and freckles...

I sit down on the bench vacated by the other family.

"Sir, I am sorry, sir," Tom apologizes.

"For what Tom?" I ask nonchalant.

He stammers, hems and haws until the girl speaks up.

"Because of me and how I am," she pauses.

Her mother pinches her thigh.

"Sir, I mean," she finishes, though I think the word, 'Sir' doesn't come automatically like it does from others.

"What way are you... um?" I let that hang a moment.

"Deborah! My name, I mean, um, Sir." She smiles, remembering to use the honorific. "But most people call me 'Debbie."

"What way are you, *Debbie*?" I emphasizes her name. "You don't look any different; no horns, no wings," I tease.

"Well," a pause and she gapes up at me with those blue eyes. "Sir, I can be a bit hard to handle and outspoken so my Ma and Da remind me."

"And be outspoken, how?" I press her. "You mean the deep sigh and the outlandish frown upon your face when I asked the Clive's first for the interview?"

The parents sit with their heads down and Debbie seems to hesitate.

"It is because there is no room left, Sir." The little boy chimes in. It seems as if we have two outspoken children in this family.

I sit up straighter and wave the lad over to me. He looks up at his Ma. She sits with the look of horror and disgrace etched on her face. An almost swallowed expletive is whispered by his Da.

The lad hesitates as he makes his way across the hall. I watch him come. He seems well kept. His clothes are neat and clean for a boy his age. A patch or two on his britches and shirt, but well mended. His brown hair is long and the bangs keep falling into his eyes to where he continually brushes them away.

"So, what is your name?" I ask.

"It is John... Sir," he replies and smiles as he realizes he remembered to say, 'Sir'.

"Well John, what do you think of your sisters' outspokenness? No, don't look back to your family! You tell me what you think." I reach out and take one of his hands in mine to hold him still.

"Well Sir, Da says it will get her in trouble someday. That she ought to think first," he answers intelligently for such a young boy.

"Well is she a bad person, a bad sister?" I question.

"Oh, no, sir. She helps out watching me and Souzie; that is our baby sister. And she helps Ma with the chores and she reads to us when we can get a book," he admits shyly, as if thinking he may have said too much.

"She likes to read?" I ask.

"Oh, yes, Sir. Any chance she gets," he continues. "Except once in a while she forgets to do a chore or two because of reading. Da says it is where she gets her outspoken ways from."

"And your Da, he is a good man," I ask delighting in the way the boy is so fierce and honest in his telling.

"Yes, Sir," his big eyes turn bigger as they come up to meet mine. "Ma says he almost never drinks anything too strong and he almost never tans our hides for doing something we should not ought to, except for little Souzie since she is so little. And Ma is thinking Debbie is getting to big to swish over his knee. But he knows the plants and is good with the horses and such and I help where I can." The lad slows and runs out of steam.

My page Robert runs by; startled at seeing me here in the hall, he bows. I bid him bring back refreshments; with a 'Yes, Sir', he runs off.

"Wow," Little John exclaims. "He runs fast. He is your son?"

"No!" I laugh slightly. "He is Robert, a page; he runs errands for me," I explain.

"This is *your Castle?*" little John asks, a look of uncertainty crosses his young face; thinking he may have said too much.

I nod, "what do you mean, 'not enough room," I wonder.

Robert, with another young lad return with refreshments for all. Drinks, cakes, cookies and meats piled on trays. I motion to pass the food amongst the family. I take two cookies and hand John one.

His eyes went as big as saucers when he saw the size of the treat. He takes a quick bite as he sees me take one.

"Go on son, tell me what you meant."

"Well, Sir," he mumbles through the bits of cookie, "My sister said the land is only for a large family. That the castle would only want a family that could plant lots of seeds and have many animals. And we are not such a big family anymore since we came here after my Ma's family had the accident and all died.

He sobs and I see a slight tear form on his cheek. Sarah Jane's head rises, shock registering upon her face.

"Can you tell me what happened," I ask solemnly.

He sniffles and nods, screwing up the courage to begin, "There was a fierce storm that day, Sir. I was terrible scared with the noise of the thunder and the lightning flying across the skies." He stammers with the telling and remembering.

I hand him a mug with juice. He takes a sip and continues.

"It was real dark in the day and we were in the fields behind our house. We ran for the cellar when the twister came but Granny and they could not get out of the big house quick enough." He is sobbing with a hiccup thrown in. I pick him up and place him on my knee.

His Da, Tom finishes the story. "The storm blew in quick enough where we barely made it to our cellar. Sarah's family was in the big house. It had a cellar but the twister ran right over the house. There was no way to get to them or even get help," he finishes with a shrug and a shiver.

"So, you left the area because it hurt too much to stay?" I ask.

"No," Tom begins.

Sarah Jane jumps back in. "We did not have enough family left to work the land and we were asked to leave." The bitterness is evident.

Tom chimes back, "It was explained that the size of the property needed a large family to run it and they were sorry and they would help us re-settle in another place. They had no other plots for us." He stops to breathe and get his emotions under control. "I understood, really I did. We had lost eight family members but we needed to move so another family could come in and plant and rebuild." He pauses again to sip juice.

I motion for Robert to pour wine for us. Tom gives me a slight, crooked grin as he puts down the juice for the grape.

"So, after burying our family we packed up and came this way. We traveled until the provisions ran low.

I hold up my hand to stop him. "So, you have been traveling for several ten-day?" I question. Sarah nods.

I glance down at the boy on my knee, so reminiscent of one of my own grandsons. "Well John, what do you think we should do?"

The door behind me squeaks and I feel Abby at my shoulder. I know she has heard most, if not the entire conversation. His eyes widen and I see the start of a shrug. "I think that we need to live someplace but that other family also needs a place to live and they have more children so they should get the one place you have." His voice goes lower at each word knowing he will have no home again for a while.

"Do you think your Ma would like a nice home and garden around here," I ask. He nods and his smile grows wide.

I smile up at Abby.

She says, "That little house with all those chicken coops... the one near Judith and Alistair? With the stream where a young boy can swim and fish? The one with the four bedrooms."

"Yeah, and it has the nicest trees for climbing. Do you think it would be suitable for this family to make it a home?" I inquire.

I see the look on their faces, one of hope.

"Well," Abby says thoughtfully, playing along with me. "It will take scant days to clean up and get ready. But I guess they can sleep in their wagon a couple nights?" she suggests.

"As long as the wolves and bears do not eat them," I joke. I see the look of horror on the two children's faces.

"I guess they could sleep in the Castle and take their meals here while we help them clean and get settled?" Abby offers. "Maybe Debbie can help with chores, a bit of dusting and straightening of the maps and books in the library," she mentions casually.

With the reference of books, Debbie's head comes 'round and up from where it was down when she thought she was in trouble... "B-books," she asks in a stammer.

"Why, yes," Abby answers. "Can you read?"

"Some, but I am learning. I love places where books can take me," she finishes in a whisper.

She realizes Abby and I were teasing about the wild animals; that we aren't the ogres she thought we were. Then she pauses, her head rises, the eyes wide open, "I can have my own room?" She finally counted bedrooms in her head.

"And we will help you with your reading," Abby promises.

I turn to Tom, "It will take a couple of days to clean but with your and Sarah Jane's help it should be smooth. We will go out later today and look at the land. And tomorrow, you and our overseer, John will figure how many acres you will need." I watch their reactions and expressions on their faces along with the body language. It is all of wonder and thankfulness and relief that their journey is at an end.

Sarah Jane sobs, Tom stands to shake mine and Abby's hands. Abby hugs him, instead.

John hugs me with a shy smile. It is then I realize how much I am missing my own grandchildren.

I look over to Debbie as she stands and curtsies. “Here! None of that now,” I order. I have never had a person curtsy to me before.

Souzie, awake from her nap toddles over wanting to be picked up. Abby’s eyes brim when the little girl reaches up and calls, “Grammy,” offering her a bite of the cookie in her little hand.

I didn’t think Abby would ever turn the baby back to Sarah Jane.

I ask Robert to show them to the main hall and then later to where they will stay.

CHAPTER 45 A Sad Goodbye

We awake early. It is the day of the rite for the Late Priestess, Victoria.

We gather mid-morning in the Blessed Area of Sir Arthur the Senior manor house yard. It is a large, quiet yard with trees and stones. Many stones have names carved and etched upon them, remembrances of loved ones that have preceded those of us here.

A space has been set aside for Victoria.

It seems more garden than cemetery with flowers and bushes overgrowing the area; well-maintained, but no straight lines anywhere. I feel my spirit quiet and I sigh.

Vanessa readies the implements upon an altar, nervous to begin this service for her beloved friend.

I feel a tap upon my shoulder. Arthur, Jr. motions for me to follow.

"If you could help in carrying Mother out to her resting spot?" His red eyes brim and he takes a deep breath to gather control. "She genuinely loved to sit here and reflect. She would spend hours explaining ideas to relatives, even to those still alive!"

He sighs and his head droops to his chest. I hug him; trying to help him through such a traumatic experience. I know what it is like to lose a Mom.

"I will be honored. She seemed to be an amazing woman and I am sorry I did not get the chance to become better acquainted."

Several others have also been asked to help. No magicks here, just reverently bear the remains to the garden.

Her body has been lovingly swathed in a tapestry with scenes depicting manor life, her life.

As I move to position, Jackie poofs upon my shoulder. His condolences again voiced to both Arthur's and the remainder of her family.

As one, we bend to pick up Victoria. Arthur, Sr. leads the procession to her special place.

We lay her reverently upon a small platform by the altar and I return to stand by Abby. Funny, I think she would have been heavier.

Vanessa, with the Athame in her hand, "All are welcome, those of goodhearted spirits. All are welcome. Come and join, Blessed Be!"

And she begins the walk to close the circle to start the rite. Abby enlightens me, teaching me of the services and rites of Wicca, what different color candles mean, praying to the four points of the compass, the knives and water cup.

Vanessa reaches to retrieve a flower bulb. As she fights back tears, she recalls how much Victoria loved all the colors and fragrances; an errant tear slips down her cheek.

"Our tears will cleanse the soils. Our heavy hearts will plant the seed. Our spirits will invigorate and germinate the very essence of what we need. The memories of how she lived, the little things done day by day will guide us through life. As a bulb will be planted anew to grow again so will she renew our lives by remembering what she stood for, the love and compassion she showed and then to follow her example."

"We mourn, not for her passing since the physical body temporarily houses who we are but we mourn for ourselves; because we will miss her."

Quiet settles as we absorb the message. Then several family members and friends walk forward to speak.

The more I hear the closer I feel to her spirit. Having met just once has a philosophical effect on me. Those few touches of her hand remembered and I find myself walking forward.

"I did not know Miss Victoria well, but listening to you all speak of her and the profound effect she has upon your lives; what she means to you, I feel compelled..."

"There are those days to remember,
With us always in her debt.
She helped, prayed and forgave,
Never judging our lives, and yet
She guided our day to day efforts
Always making time to take part
With a kind word, a pat, a hug,
She touched each and everyone's heart
She reached through to our emotions
Unburdened our life's heavy load.
She offered a shoulder to lean upon
And a smile for our hard, dusty road!
If this is all she is remembered for;
That she helped ease our long-troubled day –
She can rejoice and slumber most peacefully,
For we know, 'She did pass our way'!"

I emerge from a trance. My spirit lifts while smiles beam around me. As I walk back to Abby, I hear a whisper, almost as a breeze through the trees; 'Thank you Frank with no title!'

We finish the rite. Sir Arthur has a favorite willow sapling to be planted near his wife's head. Many other bulbs and herbs we plant around where she will lie.

Finally, still wrapped in her tapestry, she is laid to rest with her plants covering as if a blanket.

Priestess Kaye, her movements unsure, her voice quivers as she tries to speak, keeping her emotions in check. She is burying a life-long friend, a mentor. Much of what she has learned of life was at the knee of the Priestess. Now, she must lay that friend to rest, console a husband, children and friends.

She stops to take a breath, wiping a tear away. "We are here to return our dear Sister, our friend back to whence she came; to the bosom of our Mother, *Camelot.* And soon they will be one."

"Victoria trod a long and winding road down the path she had chosen; a wife, a Mother, Grandmother, friend and *The Priestess*. It has been a life of joy, of tears; disappointments and successes."

"Helping those she encountered, giving her all in each instance. She could do no less! We bid you Sister, a warm hug for all that you did accomplish. And we feel that you are still amongst us. We hear your laughter when the breeze waifs among the branches and your encouragements when the birds chatter and sing. We feel your love and spirit in the warm sun. May our Mother welcome you back with arms wide open; may your days be fruitful and happy. Until we meet again in the unfolding, know you are missed and loved by us all." She has to stop, to sob. A deep breath before going on.

"I will try to follow your example and live up to what standards you set. Please forgive me now, since I do not think anyone can fill your footsteps." She sags at the last, drained of emotion.

Jackie flies, back-winging as he alights softly upon her shoulder, whispering to her.

I was not privy to those words, but her face did brighten.

She throws her arms wide, smiles and pronounces, "Blessed Be!"

A brief moment of silence, then Jackie announces, "Sir Arthur has refreshments in the hall for all who would like to partake.

As many of the attendees filter inside, Abby hangs back. She grabs my arm. The look upon her face saying something troubles her.

I turn and take her hand.

"It is time, I think," she admits.

"For what?"

"To bury our dead and began life anew." A small tear forms in the corner of her eye. "Alex, Eve, and Baby are gone. We never had a memorial, a funeral, nothing to mark their passing. We aren't sure what happened." She takes a deep breath to help control her emotions. "We didn't want to admit that they were truly gone."

"I think you are right. It is time to say good-bye. Kaye will be busy with her new role as The Priestess, so find when she can help us do this. May hap we can find stones to place in a common area of *our* properties and use that for a burial ground?"

Smiling. "I don't think it is quite that simple." Taking a breath, arranging thoughts in her head, "we need to consecrate an area. We need a place for us and our friends who may need a final resting place. Maybe tomorrow we walk the grounds and find that place?" A sad smile crosses her lips as she awaits my reaction.

I nod an approval. "Somewhere we can sit, relax; a place of quietness and solitude," I offer.

She nods, and hand in hand we walk to the hall. "Let's join the others to help ease a bit of pain in all of us," she whispers, charged with emotion.

A quick conversation with Kaye and Vanessa to explain our plan. I will tell Jackie when and where to meet us.

Now we sit with friends amidst laughter and tears. We toast the living and remember the departed. It is a memorial I am sure Victoria would have highly approved. We shed tears for those friends passed but not forgotten.

Such a shame she never got to pet Fido!

CHAPTER 46 I Never Promised You a Rose Garden

We rise early the next morning both sleeping better, sharing the same bed. It may also have something to do with putting restless spirits at ease. As we sit enjoying our meal in the great hall, Debbie stops to thank us for the chance to help out in the manor.

"Most of the books and maps are neatly arranged and dusted," she informs.

"Anything there that you might like to read?" Abby inquires. We have been collecting local books since coming to Camelot and building our Manors. We have had help from the other wizards and scribes.

"Well, yes and some that I could read to Souzie and John", she admits.

"Take one for yourself and one to read to your family. Keep them in good condition and as you finish and return one you may take another."

The smile on her face is payment enough.

"Tell us If you have any trouble. We have a school starting soon. You and your brother are welcome to attend," Abby mentions.

"I hope my Da will let me, we have much to do around the new farm," she worries.

"We will talk to your parents and make the arrangements. We would like all you young folk to attend." She waits to gauge Debbie's enthusiasm to the idea.

A smile lights her face like that of neon lights on Broadway. She thanks us and floats out towards the library.

We have another, secret library in the bed chambers. Books we can not share with but a few friends. Editions of health books, agriculture and manufacturing, references we may need to peruse in a hurry. We also brought along some of our favorite authors so not to feel too lonely.

We finish breakfast, do the last little things we need to be doing to keep the Manor Houses running in tip top condition. Most of the everyday situations are handled by our competent staff but certain items do need our approval. I hand the last of the missives to a page to run them where they need to go.

The pages are our telephones of the era. Young children of our staff and farmers who run errands, bring refreshments, deliver messages, and help out where ever and whenever they can. They are paid with coin, meals and sometimes a room and clothing. Robert seems attached to me. He is nearing fourteen and makes it his mission to tag along whenever I am in the Manor. He is John's son so that may have something to do with it. He also helps out the younger pages and keeps them in line.

You do get used to seeing the same familiar faces.

Abby and I walk out to our common workshop, the one we constructed when the four of us moved to Camelot. We have stayed away since the accident; many bad memories haunt us but it is a starting point in our search for grounds to consecrate.

We find nice sites, but the one Abby decides upon sits a little higher than the rest. A view of the Willow on one side balanced by the view of the lake on the other make it an ideal spot. Several older trees overspread the field offering shade. Other areas lie open to the sky. She thinks it a perfect place.

I agree.

We need to choose a spot to bury the memories of Eve, Alex and Baby. As we over-walk the land an out-cropping of stone off in the corner catches my attention. We wander over to get a better perspective of the spot.

She point out places to plant flowers, bulbs, even a small tree while I examine rocks to see where we can carve a small memorial plaque.

It is surreal to even contemplate this. The sun shines brightly giving a sense of well-being to the day. The breezes gently blow fragrances of flowers in bloom. A sense of contentment settles over our spirits and minds almost as if someone was guiding us in our decision.

Jackie senses my thoughts and rattles our link catching my attention. I show him where we are and he and Kaye poof in.

After a brief inspection they concur that it is a proper place. Near enough to make accessible for the families to visit or attend services, yet enough off the beaten path to not interfere or be interfered with. Kaye will contact Vanessa to set up the ceremonies of the consecration of our gardens.

CHAPTER 47 Peter's Travels

Using one goat as a pack animal, Peter and Willow move westward looking for a new place to settle.

Heeding his Grand Da's warning about adults finding and sending them to workhouses; they avoid everyone they can. He has harvested vegetables from the gardens but cabbage, onions and carrots will make for a thin soup. Adding an occasional rabbit or possum will make for a heartier meal.

For such a young boy he has learned well the lessons of survival. Willow has still not spoken, just an occasional nod or shake of the head. Her eyes are almost always cloudy with tears.

They follow the small trails and the back ways, avoiding people. They camp in the woods near small ponds finding natural food supplies and creating shelters as they can.

After almost a ten day they stumble across an old cabin. The door sags, the walls have holes but the roof seems solid and dry. They clean it, repair what they can and he goes to reconnoiter for supplies.

There are tracks of rabbits, turkeys; while geese and ducks swim the stream. Upon further investigation he finds a farm worked by a young couple. Large plantings of crops along with goats, chickens and sheep fill the lands. He will return at dusk to see what opportunities he can find.

He is down to the last of their supplies. Stealing is bad but not contacting others fearing the work houses is his main fear. He will barter without letting the farm couple know.

Over the next several evenings he cautiously visits his new neighbor to weed and hoe. He repairs leather bindings and straps, collects chicken eggs in a basket, all in stealth mode. In return he takes a few beans, an onion, a cabbage, an egg. Added to the little he traps gets them through. He has seed and starts a garden growing. A small spade along with two buckets found on the property helps.

In less than a year he will be 14 and old enough to hold property. He can go back to his Da's mine and fix the water source. Until then they need to live hidden from authority.

Late one day, sitting quietly in a dark corner of the neighbors barn, the owner enters, unexpectedly. Peter, distracted checking leathers, freezes. Did the man see him? Peter sits perfectly still, trying to not even breathe. It is nip and tuck.

The farmer replaces the tools on the rack and has a cursory glance around the barn. A few steps in, he stops. A voice from outside, a female voice calls. The farmer returns the call that he is coming, turns, closing the door behind him.

Peter, drenched in a sop sweat decides to be more careful. And for the next several days, caution is his middle name.

Until, on a bright, sunny afternoon; preoccupied with the troubles of the coming Autumn, he is not watching the path he treads. One of his water-filled buckets bangs against something rigid. He stumbles; then tumbles down the embankment nose to nose, knee to knee and hip to hip with...

...someone.

She had been sitting with her back against a tree engrossed in reading her book.

"Oof! What! OH!" the pails go one way; they go the other, water splashes everywhere. She screams, he yells as they plunge, rolling; hip to hip, shoulder to shoulder, finally landing in a heap. The sudden stop puts them face to face.

Both lay a moment checking to see if they are hurt. Collecting his thoughts, he gets his wind back and wonders what happened.

"Who are you?"

"Why are you here?"

"What happened?"

All the questions thrown into the air at once from them both as they disentangle and sit up. Finally, helping each other they climb to their feet, not hurt, but bumped, bruised and embarrassed.

As he readjusts his clothing, "I am sorry. I did not see you there." His apology is automatic as his Ma had taught him. "No one has ever sat there in the path before."

"I was reading and that is not a path, it is barely a trail," she mentions as she retrieves her book checking for damage. "It is a comfortable out of the way spot. Why are you here? No one lives around these parts." She is satisfied that no harm has come to the book. She peers back up to him. "Who are you?"

"My name is Peter and we live in that small cabin. Who are you?"

My name is Deborah and no one lives in that little shack." She smiles, looking amazed. "It is falling down. Did your folks fix it up?"

"No, I did. It is but my sister Willow and me."

"You are too young to be living alone. Is she your older sister?"

"I am not too young," he argues fiercely. "I am nearing four-teen and we are doing fine." He has retrieved one pail and bangs the dirt from it.

"Thankfully my book is not damaged. It is from a friend and quite valuable." However, she reaches over, picks up the other pail and turns it to shake out the debris.

He reaches to take it from her.

She pulls away, "At least let me help bring new water. It was my fault you tripped."

"I do not need help!"

"Oh! Let me help. Do not be so stubborn. How old is your sister?"

He relents, swallows a smile and replies, "She will soon be seven."

"Where are your folks? You did not run away, did you?"

"NO!" He stops a moment, takes a breath, recalling the events of that day. "They were killed in a cave-in with my Grand Da." He stops, not wanting to say too much to this stranger. Not wanting to re-live that horrible moment, again.

"That's terrible!" Deborah cries. "What happened?" She asks, putting her hand on his shoulder in kindness.

She seems nice, harmless, someone that can be a friend. He so needs someone to talk with. He gulps and goes on with the tale.

"The ground shook, it caused the mine to collapse. My Ma ran in trying to save them."

He stammers, trying to fight back tears. "And there was another trembler. The rest of the rocks slid down, crushing her, swallowing her."

He is having trouble seeing as his eyes blur. "The quaking ground knocked over a candle in our home. The curtains caught fire and the cabin burned down."

He is sobbing a little, trying not to. Trying to be strong in front of this stranger, this girl.

"Willow was trapped. I crawled in; the smoke was thick and I had trouble finding her. Then I had to drag her back out. We somehow made it to the door as the roof fell sending fire and embers over everything." A sob escapes him, tears run down his dusty cheeks, leaving a trail.

She stares, horror-struck. Where she had first seen a clumsy little boy, now he grew up right before her eyes.

"Was there not a wizard or land holder who would have aided you?" She wonders.

"NO!" He vehemently barks, and then, "My Grand Da said to trust no one in authority when you need help. Said all they want is to use people, to take my sister and use her - send me to a work house for years and then toss us away as though moldy bread."

She looks askance at him. "That does not happen. I know two wonderful wizards, friends that would help..."

"*NO!* I do not want help. They will separate us and put us in work houses or for Willow, something even worse." He snatches the pail back from her and storms off into the forest, towards the stream.

She follows along, quiet, letting him simmer and cool. The same as she does when a horse is frightened and runs. You give it lead, and it cools down becoming approachable again. She knows she can talk some sense into him.

Peter kneels to fill the first pail. She bends to fill the other.

He reaches to stop her and then closes his mouth. His Ma has taught him manners and he remembers them. He also thinks a friend may be nice.

They walk slowly back towards his shack.

"So, what do you do for food?"

"I brought some supplies from the old home. I will travel back to bring chickens and another goat," he explains.

"What do you do for the rest of it?"

"Well," he stammers, working on how to explain.

"You steal it? Is that what you do?" She accuses.

"I do not steal. I barter from the farmer near here. He does not know it," sheepish at that pronouncement. "I need to not be found out. They will take Willow away and use her. I cannot let that happen. She is much too young."

"How can you barter without Sir Alistair or Miss Judith knowing," she wonders.

"I weed his crops at night. Fix a fence or two. I take his worn or broken leathers and re-do them here and return them. I will collect eggs and leave them in the basket, taking only one or two." He finishes his explanation.

"Why did you not stay where you were? You could have built a small place there, with your garden and animals?"

He stops, put down his pail. His shoulders slump. He gives her a quick look, a small tear forms in his eye.

"Our water came down by the mine. When the ground trembled, the rocks caved in, the water stopped. And Willow kept wandering to the mine to get to our Ma. She does not understand. I could not stay there knowing..." He stops as a sob escapes his throat, "...Ma and Da were lying some little ways down the tunnel." She put her pail down and hugs him. A tear in her eye. He breaks down sobbing. After a moment, he pushes her off, then thinks for a minute. "Sorry! I did not mean... I have not cried... I..." He bends, picking up both pails to beat a hasty retreat to the cabin. Embarrassed that someone - a girl, has seen him cry.

She catches up to him and with her hand on his shoulder, stops him. "It is all right," she whispers. "I understand."

He turns to face her. "You do not understand, you could not know how I feel!"

"I do," she repeats. "My grandma, along with several other relatives died in a twister. Their house fell in on them. We had to move because the holder said the property needed a bigger family and then threw us off. So, I know a little of what you are feeling." A small tear runs down her cheek remembering.

"See! Just as my Grand Da said. Use you and throw you away. Soon I am old enough to have my own place. I will have a big farm and will help those that need it."

All this as they travel the final yards to the shack. Willow, hearing the noise of the discussion stands in the doorway, worriedly waiting, wondering what has happened. She is troubled when she sees the stranger with her brother. With nowhere to run and hide she stands her ground ready to fight if needed.

"Willow, this is Deborah. We met along the trail. She is helping to carry the water."

Willow gives a defiant look noticing that he carries both pails. "No need to fret," he assures her. "She will not tell on us."

"Will you?" He wonders with an anxious look to Deborah. "You need to promise not to tell anyone." He begins to dole water to the plants.

"Promise!"

She nods in compliance and takes the other pail inside, looking around at the shabbiness of the shack. She finds a rag and washes Willow who fights, sputters and complains.

"Oh, hush!" Deborah commands. "I wash up my little brother and sister every day. But we use hot water." Willow calms and lets the older girl continue.

"Are these the only clothes you have?" eyeing the ripped and dirty dress the young girl is wearing.

"Most of our things went up in the fire," she whispers to Deborah.

Peter, hearing his sister finally speak since that terrible day, races inside.

Willow is wrapped in Deborah arms, sobbing and crying; trying to tell everything that has happened. Trying to explain everything all at once.

She let Willow cry, knowing it will help the pain, some. It is what Miss Abby told her in the library when she had broken down, explaining about her family and her pain. The older woman held her; said crying helps but only time heals. Then she mentions 'there is never enough time'. A small tear ran down Miss Abby's cheek that day, too.

So, she let Willow cry as she had cried in Miss Abby's arms. It did help some.

She looks over to Peter. He is holding back tears, and puts an arm out to wrap around his shoulder, hugging him. The three cry together.

She sighs and pulls away. "I need to go home and do chores afore my Da whips my tail again," she tells them. "Can I come back to visit?"

"Only if you promise to not tell."

"I promise. May hap I can bring a few things."

Willows' face brightens thinking someone will help without sending her to a work house.

Peter agrees. Deborah gives them both a quick hug before running off.

"Is she gonna come back to help us?" Willow queries, pouring some of the water into the soup.

"I guess." He answers, a strange little smile on his lips.

Deborah speeds home, thoughts running faster than she does. Thoughts of her Grand Da, her Aunt and Uncles, cousins; all dying in that twister. Then the thoughts of little Willow, barely any food or clothes, her Ma and Da dead. No one to watch out for her but her brother Peter. And Peter; she slows her pace. A smile, as she recalls rolling down the hill, bodies bumping. Then the hugs, feeling him so vulnerable, so alone. She does not understand what is happening to her, what is she feeling? But she likes it. She hurries along home, a strange little smile on her lips.

CHAPTER 48 A Time to Rest

Abby and I walk to the altar set for the consecration of the land. New plantings have been added throughout. It is pretty. Friends have donated much of the new landscape with flowers and bulbs as is the custom.

I have searched for something of Eve's to bury in lieu of her physical body. I chose the small stuffed bear I had given her to celebrate our wedding anniversary. She had to leave so many of her favorite stuffed bears and animals back on Earth, I had a local seamstress sew one.

Abby chose Alex's necklace. She had created it for his birthday from local stone and beads. The catch had stuck and she was repairing it for him. And for baby, that same small brush Eve was using that last, fateful day.

The stone mason and I etched the names on a plaque to honor all.

Merlyn and Dagwood are pleased.

Vanessa would officiate the rites to consecrate the lands and many friends will attend.

We gather at the appointed hour and take our places. First the altar and the items upon it are consecrated.

As the ceremony continues, Vanessa steps to the altar, arms wide and announces, "All are welcome of good heart and spirit. Please join me!"

A gentle breeze whispers the trees.

Twas a good omen!

"Sir Frank, please begin?"

I raise a small container of dirt towards the north. Fitting, since I so enjoy working the soil.

"Guardians of the North I call upon you to mark as sacred this Circle we call 'Eden'. We designate this consecrated garden as a physical and spiritual resting place for our loved ones as we fulfill our duties and return their remains to Our Mother."

"Let the energies of Camelot keep the circle safe and secure. Let this be the home of Love and remembrances, sanctity and happiness. A place where we honor the gods of our traditions. Guardian of the North, element of Camelot, we honor you as well and keep you in our hearts." I reach into the urn, take a handful of soil and sprinkle the ground as representative of blessing the entire gardens.

Vanessa nods to Jackie. He pledges the same prayer but to the Guardian of the East holding a feather representative of the element of air. As he finishes his prayer, he flies the perimeter of the gardens landing nicely back upon the altar.

Abby turns to pray to the Guardian of the South and the element of Fire. So proper since she has become the light of my life, our Manor's life and no fierier personality I have ever met! Her pure white candle sputters in the breeze. As she finishes, she tips it, spilling molten wax to further consecrate the gardens.

Then Kaye turns to the Guardian of the West, the element of water. She prays for the blessing and safety upon the lands. She does beseech the plants thrive and our Mother accept the offerings as we use these gardens to return Her servants back to Her land. She dips her fingers into the cup and sprinkles water.

Vanessa then bids us to return our offerings to the altar.

All in attendance join hands.

Kaye begins. “Guardians of the Elements, Gods of our ancestors, we congregate to ask Thy blessings and protections upon this garden. Watch over those resting here, guide their spirits. Teach us all the true understanding of thy one true tenet, ‘Do No Harm!”

“We thank you for this day and for all those you may grant us. Thank You Mother, for all the help and blessings.”

Something startles a flock of birds and hundreds rise up as one overflying the altar.

Abby thanks all for attending and directs them to join us at the small rock display to bid a final goodbye to our spouses.

Many know something of the accident, where a magickal backlash had taken our loved ones but not all was told. Some things need to remain unsaid.

Abby is as nervous as I. We lovingly place Alec's necklace around the bear’s neck and Baby's brush onto its chest. We place all into the small wooden pine box I have built, cover it with the lid and Abby places it reverently into the opening. I cover it with soil.

I think we did an adequate job. It is difficult to see through the tears. She reaches across and grasps my hand.

Jackie, setting upon Kaye’s shoulder speaks. “Eve, Alex and Baby – May you all rest most peacefully in this lovely garden. May your spirits know peace and joy and until we met in the unfolding may all sing your praises!”

“So Mote It Be!” Kaye exclaims.

Helped by our friends we plant bushes, flowers, bulbs and even catnip to decorate the landscape.

We include several of Eve's special roses. The reds for the love we shared with our spouses. White for the purity and sanctity of their spirits and the yellow roses we plant for the gladness of them being in a better place and at peace.

At the end, we meet in our main hall where refreshments await to feed the body; and friends await to soothe our souls. We shed many a tear that day, some even in laughter at remembrances.

CHAPTER 49 Puzzlement

"I still cannot understand, Judith. Someone must be doing chores for us. Eggs are gathered, leathers are mended, rows are hoed; could there be such things as fairies?" he half-jokes.

"I am sure there is a logical explanation to all this. Fairies do not appear. Mayhap, if we take a look around the farm, we will find some clues." She shakes her head at her lover. Soon they will be hand-fasted and she will not feel as if they are doing something against the Mother. People living together should be hand-fasted. But with their circumstances being what they are, there is little opportunity. And Sir Frank and Miss Abby have no qualms about them living and working together.

With a sly smile on her face, "But not today. Now we go see Rebekah and Jonathon. I think they have news for us. I believe that she is with child!" A big grin comes to her face. She is happy for her dear friends and also a bit sad that it is not her expecting a little one. But soon enough.

Alistair knows what is expected. He gives his girl a huge hug, tells her he loves her and goes to hitch the wagon to the horse.

CHAPTER 50 The Choice

Deborah decides to help. She has an old dress she can rip and re-sow. She places it into her pack; swings it over her shoulder and heads for the castle. She is due at the library today.

She enjoys the work and the perks of borrowing books. Mayhap she can pick up extra treats from the main room. Some meats and fresh bread will be welcome additions she thinks.

Robert, the page is in the front gardens. He is always on the lookout for her, wanting to be near, to talk. He seems nice enough and all. Tall and she guesses, handsome. His Da is over-seer here. Though Robert is older, Peter seems mature.

Why is she even comparing the two she wonders? She does not want to talk to him today. She is afraid she may say something to make him suspicious of what she is doing. Though she is not doing anything wrong.

No one owns that shack. And Peter did rebuild it to make it usable. He takes care of his little sister. He is not stealing, actually. Just helping someone who needs help and cannot pay money for it. All these thoughts run through her mind as she walks past Robert.

"Hello Deborah," he smiles shyly. "You are here to clean in the library?"

He knows it is the reason but he is hoping she has come to see him, also. He has a crush on her and tries to find any reason to be near her.

"Yes Robert! Miss Abby is expecting me. Then I need to hurry home to do chores. So, I shall not be here long."

"May I walk with you for a bit?" he asks, almost afraid of a rejection.

"I do not want you getting into trouble with Sir Frank, should he be needing you to run errands."

"I would like to escort you to the library in the event you need an errand run!"

"I will be fine and there will be others to help clean today," she explains, trying to get him to stop following without hurting his feelings. "Mayhap I will see you in the main hall later?"

With a smile, he takes the hint, leaving her to her thoughts.

Why does she feel guilty talking to him? Peter has no hold on her, so why does it feel as if she betrayed him?

She spends the next hours enjoying her work. Dusting, cleaning and generally putting the books in some order is rewarding. And after several hours of toiling, it also makes her hungry. She gathers her pack and wanders down to the main hall to eat.

She avoids Roger, enjoys a quick meal and conversations with other young girls who work the manor. She fills a pack with meats and fruits, enough for several meals for Peter and Willow, too. She spies sweet rolls by the door and several go into the pack.

Janet, a kitchen worker stops to say hello. She carries old rags and odd dresses.

"What are you doing with them?" she asks Janet.

"They are headed for the rag bin, why?" Janet asks.

"Can I have those?" she wonder.

"Sure, anything for a friend, Debbie."

"Thank you," she smiles back, looking them over. Sizing the remnants to Willow's size, she makes her selections and then leaves.

With what she already has; these will add color with enough left to sew an apron. Funny, how quickly she took the young girl under her wing; and Peter suddenly settles in the upper most part of her mind.

It is a new feeling for her.

Over the next days of visits, bringing foods and the dresses, she brings a book to read to them. It is becoming obvious which boy she prefers. Robert is a nice boy, but Peter is a fine young man. Not to take anything away from Robert, he works hard at what he does but if he can not work, he and his family will still eat.

With Peter, if he does not work, Willow will starve and be in danger if he is not around to protect her. Peter seems to grow into the job. He is also trusting her more.

She will try convince him to ask Miss Abby for help.

With Debbie's continuing visits, Willow begins to express herself better, much to Peter's delight.

Two days later Miss Abby questions her about the extra foods she is taking.

"I have a shy friend." She tells the woman.

Miss Abby reminds her if she needs to talk or needs help to come to her or Sir Frank. "But until then I will trust your judgment, Debbie!"

She is overjoyed at that pronouncement and can hardly wait to tell Peter.

Her parents are also questioning where she is going. She told a partial truth of helping to care for the little girl, Willow. She feels bad not telling the entire story but it is not up to her; she has promised to keep the secret. So, to help her ease her conscience she stays home to do extra chores until she feels drawn to see Willow, and Peter of course.

She has another dress for the little girl; not the prettiest of dresses as she is still learning her stitch work but it is serviceable and the colors are vibrant. The yellows with a touch of pink will make Willow smile, she is sure.

Peter is nearly at a mindset to ask for help. Debbie reminds him that it will get colder and the shack will not be warm. She is worried that in a large snowfall he and Willow can be trapped and freeze without firewood. And if he cannot get out to check the traps, may starve.

It seems the grown-up thing to do. But that is for later, until then, he has the garden to hoe and weed.

It is still warm so he takes off his shirt. The sun bounces off his newly bulging muscles. It does not surprise him to see Debbie coming along the trail. She is far enough away, leaving time to hoe another row. Debbie is only a girl after all, but she has that pretty smile and he enjoys her visits more than he thought he would.

She peers towards the cabin and spies Peter, outside working shirtless. The sheen of his sweat glistens in the sun causing her to hesitate in her tracks.

He glances up, pauses to smile and wave.

She waves back with another quick step. A sound, a rattling; then excruciating pain shoots up her calf. She screams, falls, trying to roll out away from the next attack of the deadly rattle snake. She lay in pain, staring into the fangs of that killer.

Peter hears the scream, sees Debbie fall. His heart stops as he lights out running; reaching her in moments, moments that seem to take forever.

The snake hisses, coiling, ready to strike again. Blood oozes from Debbie's leg.

Willow, hearing the shriek runs to catch up to Peter.

"Rattler!" He cautions, tossing his shirt at his sister. With a stick and the shirt, she contains the snake.

Peter bends to examine the bite marks, thinking what to do. Her chance of survival without a healer are nil. The closest help is Sir Alistair. He will carry her. He sweeps her into his arms as if she weighs nothing, and runs. Sir Alistair will have to help them.

He cradles her tightly, "It will be all right, Debbie, I promise. It will be all right!" He cries in one breath.

And in the next breath, *"HELP! HELP!"*

How could he have been so stupid to live out here all alone? No one nearby to help, no close neighbors.

Debbie lay in his arms wincing at every step, tears stream down her face in blinding pain.

Two stray cats he has been feeding run up. "Not now!" He cries. "I need help. She is *dying*!"

They meow.

A mysterious woman miraculously materializes in front of him. He stops dead in his tracks, petrified, afraid to move. He gawks, nearly dropping Debbie.

The Lady takes one look, the wound on the young girls' leg catching her attention. She snatches Debbie from his arms and is gone in an eye blink.

He stands there; eyes wide with terror, panicking. He has lost Debbie and knows not what to do.

Willow comes up behind him; her mouth open in disbelief at what she witnesses. The dead snake is wrapped in his shirt. She had trapped it with a stick while kneeling on its tail as her Grand Da had taught. Cutting off the head of the foul beast, she pushed the tail into its open mouth. Even in death, it automatically bites down. Her Grand Da taught her that trick, also. He said that was the safest way to handle the deadly vipers. If it was not needed, she would skin it later for dinner.

But now, they stand looking at each other. "What happened to Debbie?" she cries.

Peter shrugs.

An old man with a large walking stick poofs in.

"Are you Peter?" he asks.

The lad could only stand and nod. Suddenly, after a dizzying moment they find themselves magically transported to a large room. People bustle, platters clang sliding onto tables, conversations echo around. The two children cower, frightened, not used to this much noise or this many people.

CHAPTER 51 Back to Me

I take them aside. "Miss Abby is working on healing Debbie." The snake hangs from the rag that was once a shirt. "Is that what bit her?"

The little girl with big eyes nods.

I reach for it carefully and beckon for a page to remove it.

Two cats see the snake then scamper into the other room.

"Good! That saves me from running to tell her what type of snake."

Willow is not happy losing supper and vocally lets me know.

"If you want to eat that snake, I will have them bring it back to give it to Ana to prepare. But the rest of us will be eating venison, pork or lamb. With potatoes and carrots, string beans and a sweet roll. But you can have that snake if you really want it."

Her jaw drops at the mention of those foods.

"John, take Peter to wash up and get him some clean clothes, please. And send Ana to me?"

John points to the short woman with a broad smile entering the room. "Here she is, Frank," as he herds Peter from the room. "Ana, this is... What do they call you?" Looking down at the scared, young girl.

"My name is Willow, Sir." She realizes this man is someone important and she should show manners and respect.

"Ana, this young lady is Willow. Would you see that she gets a bath and some nice clothes, please? Maybe get someone to clean her knife. She used that to catch and kill a rattle snake. I have someone skinning it for her. I am sure she wants the skin and rattle as a keepsake," I tease.

She gapes up at me surprised I figured that out.

"Go with Ana. Once you and your brother are presentable, we can eat and talk."

She stands a moment longer taking it all in. "Am I going to be working here?" she asks.

"Why would you be working here, do you not have family?" This is unreal.

"No!" She answers with a head shake. "Just Peter and me."

"Well, we will talk about it later after we have eaten. Take her and get someone to look after her?"

Ana walks the girl towards the baths. She knows enough women to get the girl nice clothes.

Abby returns looking pale and drained with a tired little smile on her face.

"Debbie will be fine. I managed to get the poison out before it did much damage. She will take several days to heal," she explains.

"Good!" I exclaim. "Now, tell me what the hell happened?"

Merlyn meows up at me.

"That's it," she agrees, looking down at the feline.

"What?" I ask again.

"Somehow that boy Peter blasted out a mental SOS as you once did. I homed in on it, poofing to the exact spot to find them."

"That was how I was able to send you right back to get the other two youngsters," she explains piling food onto her plate. "Healing takes much out of me." She smiles as she eats.

I sit patiently awaiting the rest of the story.

"She told me some of it. Peter and Willow are orphans. Their family was killed in a mining accident some months back. They traveled a ten day to get here after their cabin burned."

She has that sorry look on her face, as if falling for stray kittens again. I feel Merlyn as she says, "*What!*" and hear the verbal meow.

"I am kidding Merlyn."

I get an odd look from Abby.

"So why didn't they come to us for help?" I wonder.

"Peter is convinced they would be split up and sent to work houses for the rest of their lives," she explains.

"That explains why the little girl asked if she was going to be working here." I search around for Robert and find him nearby trying to overhear our conversation. I remember Abby mentioned that he seems to have feelings for the girl.

"Debbie will be fine. Miss Abby helped heal her. Find young Wizard Matthew and ask him to attend, please?" Robert smiles, relieved and takes off running.

"What are you planning to do," she asks.

"Hopefully we can find where this mine is and see what happened. Maybe there are relatives to take care of them," I mention.

"Well, from what Deborah said he was expecting to hide them until his fourteenth year and then go back to work the mine on his own," she explains.

"Seems no one told him you needed to be sixteen to own property here," I laugh.

"She also said he was the one who was helping Alistair. He would go at night do chores and bring back leathers to rework." She looks down to pick at something on her plate. "I already sent for them."

Young Matthew appears. He is an apprentice wizard and reminds me of one of my own grandsons.

"Can we get Merlyn to see if the cats can find out where the mine is?" I ask Abby. "It may save some aggravation."

She shrugs and communes with Merlyn.

"Matthew, I need you to take a stone with you. Travel a ten day walk west, look for the remnants of a burned-out cabin and a mine entrance near it." He peers at me for an explanation. "We have two small children who are orphaned. Their family was killed in a mining accident. I want to find the place, check it out and if we can give their family a proper burial."

He glances askance at me.

"I feel bad for the kids. Maybe we can find a way to give them some hope. When we get the report from the cats, we can give you an exact location."

"I will report in as soon as we find something, Sir Frank." With a small bow towards Abby he poofs out. "I wish he would use the door like everyone else," I chuckle.

I make sure Abby eats enough to replenish her energies. Magicks and healing extract a price and we always pay it.

Willow returns with a broad smile, nice clothes and a dolly held tightly in her arms. Beverly, the cook's assistant has taken the girl under her personal supervision. She saw that she had a bath, her hair fixed and explained how things run. She also supplied the clothes for the girl.

I said I will repay for whatever Willow has gotten. Beverly smiles, says it is her pleasure. The clothes were her daughters who has outgrown them. Willow is welcome to them.

Peter has cleaned up and sits with Debbie.

We had Tom and Sarah Jane poofed in to be with their daughter. Their two other children, John and Souzie come running over to Abby. She has become their surrogate Grammie and Souzie is climbing onto Abby's lap. Plates are being filled and little mouths are being fed.

Tom has gone to talk with the lad.

Sarah Jane thanks Abby for healing her daughter. "I am concerned, realizing those two were unchaperoned," Sarah Jane mentions trying to pick Souzie from Abby's lap.

"*No!* Stay with Grammie Abby," the toddler declares. Which got a huge hug and another cookie from 'Grammie'!

One of the young kitchen girls helped Willow decide what to eat.

Judith sits with an apprehensive look, not sure what has happened, why they are summoned to the castle. Still not long from under the Black Dragons' rule she worries. Alistair is escorted out of the hall right after arriving and she has not been told where he has gone.

He was taken to Debbie and introduced to Peter. Finding that the lad is the 'elf', he asks why Peter had not come forth to ask for help. They had a lengthy conversation.

Back in the hall the noise level rises as people enter for their meals.

"Merlyn informs me through Abby they have found the mine along with a burned-out cabin."

A quick look at Willow, "Your cabin burned the same day of the mine collapse?" Abby asks.

The child looks up shyly and nods.

"Can we get an expert out there to check to see if we can work that mine?" I ask quietly, not wanting Willow to hear we are removing her family's bodies. The less she knows for now, the better.

"The apprentice, Wizard Harry has family who are miners. We will send him there," John suggests.

"Good idea," I admit.

John waves a page over and gives instructions. The young boy takes off running.

Several minutes later, Sir Harry strides into the hall.

"How can I be of assistance?" He neatly bows. Being a handsome young man with manners, he will be a fine catch for any woman.

Abby beckons telling him what we need and to return when he has made arrangements. He poofs out only to poof back immediately.

"All is in ready, Miss Abby."

"I will send you to the spot you need to be, then you can bring your experts in to evaluate the mine and take care of the other thing," she advises.

With a slight nod he is ready and she sends him away.

I see Willow nodding off in her plate and motion to Abby who smiles at the girl. One of the local women helps her up to a room and to bed.

Peter enters, sees his sister as she passes and smiles at the pretty clothes. He seems subdued and contrite. I imagine someone told him 'I told you so,' a time or two.

Alistair has returned and is having a quiet conversation with a very relieved Judith.

Peter still doesn't look convinced that we aren't sending him to a work camp, somewhere.

There are long pauses and strained moments as we ask him what has happened.

Between bites of food and sips of juice we get the details.

Matthew and Harry poof back in to report on the mine.

"We were able to extract the bodies carefully from the mine," Harry reports. "They did not seem to suffer." He finishes before I could caution him on what to say.

Peter jumps up, "You got my folks from the mine?" He glares around, bewildered, "But why, how?" And then he breaks down in tears.

Harry apologizes for not seeing the boy.

Tom reaches over and places an arm around the young man.

"The cave in was not terribly large," Matthew continues when I prod for answers. "Most timbers held. But where the men were digging, well, they had not thought to add extra support." He stops to shake his head at losing fellow miners.

Then he continues, "And several feet into the mine timbers were rotten. Those collapsed killing his Ma."

"Tell them what else we found," Harry pushes.

"The lode of ore they were starting to dig seems to be high grade and a large vein." He explains that whoever owns the mine will amass a tidy sum of coin. Plus, the other minerals they found will add to the overall value.

"But can that mine be made safe," Abby queries. "It does no good to put people there to work if they are going to be in danger."

Harry agrees and confesses, "There is always risk in mining, but we can increase the size of the timbers to help support the loads during the earth quakes to be fairly certain of the safety factor."

Matthew jumps in that no one is holding that piece of property. At least no one has filed any claims.

I mention to them. "Find John and file a claim on that property."

Abby's eyebrow goes up questioningly and I nod towards Peter.

He still has not looked up so only hears the words. "*That was my Da' claim!*" jumping from his chair staring straight at me. If looks could kill. "Why are you stealing it?" he demands

"We are not stealing it, son. It cannot belong to your Da. First, he is gone and secondly, no one ever made a claim for the property. Anyone that wants it can claim it." I try to explain. "If you went out there to work the mine any local Holder could kill you, take the mine and send your sister off. You are not of age to hold property so you cannot claim it." I finish

"So, you are stealing it," he screams, demanding his property. He takes several threatening steps towards me. "So, you are using me to get this property, stealing it?" Another two steps closer, blood in his eye. Two of my guards draw their swords and move to intercept him. I wave them away.

"Sit down, Peter?" I ask him. He gives me a defiant look.

"Sit!" I point to the bench.

He sits, still with a killer look at me.

"Understand something. First, I have no need for your property."

"But you are claiming it…" he protests again.

I put my hand up to forestall the arguments, nodding towards Matthew. "The land there is good for farming?" I inquire.

He concedes it is, "But we need to divert the flow of water."

I nod at him to continue.

"At one time it cascaded down the front of the mountain, running near where the cabin stood. Now, with the earthquake, it pours down into the caves and comes out the side. We can divert it to be out of our way and have it fill a small hollow forming small pools or ponds. It would be good for swimming and fishing along with irrigation if things get very dry." Matthew completes his explanation.

I look to Harry, "What can you tell me of the mine? Can we move miners in and get enough yield to make a good profit?"

"More than enough," he confirms, "and with the farm running enough food to cut the costs on supplies."

By now Peter is livid. One guard has gone to physically restrain the lad.

I stare him down. "What did you expect me to do? Let you go back there and get killed in the next cave-in, leaving your sister all alone?"

"It would be better than watching you steal it from my Da." He screams. "I should have known better. My Grand Da warned me about land owners, not to trust them. Where do you send me? A workhouse until I am old and gray?" He is losing steam. It has been a long, emotional day.

"If you will sit and be quiet you will learn what will happen to you and your sister." I point to the bench he nearly knocked over trying to reach me. I nod to Judith and Alistair.

"If you would like, you and Willow can live and work with us until you are old enough to hold the property?" Judith offers. Peter sits with his mouth open. "We are a small farm but you and Willow would have your own rooms." Alistair continues. "I saw the work you did for us and I think you will make a great farmer, someday. And then you can go out on your own," he finishes with a hopeful note in his voice.

"And how do I get enough coin to buy property and get out on my own?" he throws back vehemently. "We have nothing!"

Alistair peers down at the boy and shakes his head, "You still do not get it boy, do you?"

"What do you mean?" still upset and muddleheaded.

"Sir Frank is claiming that property for you and Willow; holding it until you are old enough. Did you not realize?" Alistair stands up and points. "Do you not see all the happy people here? If Sir Frank was cruel and mean would they all be smiling?" He glances back down at the lad and lets it sink in. "We all want to help."

The lad gapes round, taking it all in. Then peers up at me as if he was sucker-punched. "But we were told land holders around here were out for more and cared nothing for the people. Just use them and spit them out."

"Well, Peter, we are not from around here," I admit. "But this is how it will work. My people will take over the mine and give you the farm. In the next day or so we will travel there so you can pay your respects to your family. My men will build a pretty garden to lay them to rest in." I let that sink in. With misty eyes, he slowly nods.

"Then we can decide where the new cabin can go, along with the other out buildings. Some land needs to be set aside for the miners, also." He nods at that.

"It will be several years before you can work the land, mayhap we get another family out there to work part of it. Then with the mines we will split the profits after deducting for the claims against the land," I finish.

Peter looks up with eyes blazing again. "There are no claims against the land."

"Ah, but there will be. Timbers are needed to shore up the mines. Lumber and furniture for the cabins and out buildings. Then, horses and livestock, seed, plows and other incidentals." I tick off the items on my fingers. "Then when that is done and paid for, you will split my half with the miners and all I want is a small portion of the profits for special projects. The rest is for you and Willow."

Abby peers over at me, "What special projects?"

"We will discuss it all later. I will need your input," I explain.

Peter calms down and smiles. He is a handsome young boy. He and Debbie will have a long and happy marriage.

"So, do we have a deal?"

He seems contrite, nods to Judith and Alistair, and then as if someone has whispered to him, "Thank you, all."

But still being the young lad he is, he helps himself to a handful of cookies.

Judith leans over to hug him. The look on his face says, okay, enough. I am thirteen and want to leave.

We all laugh. Well the adults do, anyway.

He gets up and Sarah Jane asks, "Where are you going?"

"To visit a sick friend."

She gives Tom a quick, worried look.

"Oh, let them be Sarah. I am sure that at this point they can be trusted."

We sit and enjoy the food, the company and the entertainment. All in all, a normal night here at the castle.

CHAPTER 52 A Healing

Many are called.

It is nothing aloud; nothing verbal or untoward. Just a mere whisper on the breeze, an urge to go.

And we assemble.

I don't know how many are summoned. But we come; singly, in pairs or several together. No one knows why. We gather in the field; we hunt up deadwood, pile it and then stand in a semi-circle in front the Old Willow. Several wizards and spouses materialize. Kaye arrives, Jackie perching upon her shoulder fidgeting from claw to claw. A quick question into my mind as to why.

I think I know.

Dean and Beth arrive with his parents.

Thankfully the moon is full, casting beams upon the meadow. Enough light to perceive shapes and recognize friends. Rebekah and Jonathon find Kaye, a question upon their lips, as on all lips, "what is happening?"

It is confusion but not noisy. Quiet conversations as wizards materialize. Clouds would dot the moon and then scud away, bringing back the light. Abby stands by me, my hand in hers.

Then there is quiet. A quick buzz in my head and a soft touch of a whisper in my brain.

Abby walks out in front of the assemblage.

"WELCOME TO ALL GOOD AND GENTLE SPIRITS! COME, JOIN US AT THE FIRE."

And the deadwood we have piled in a depression that seems made for it bursts into flame, almost as if on its own volition.

I think Abby will officiate this rite but Kaye takes the lead and she seems as confused as the rest of us.

But something drives her.

She looks around the gather, raises her hands and in a melodic voice heard by all,

"GODESS OF THE MOON,
OF NIGHT SKY YOU ARE QUEEN.
KEEPER OF UNIVERSAL
MYSTERIES AND ALL THAT HAS BEEN,
MISTRESS OF THE TIDES,
EVERCHANGING, EBB, AND NEAP.
FILL US WITH YOUR POWER
AND KNOWLEDGE DEEP.
I BEG OF THEE TO SHIELD AND
HEAL US WITH YOUR CHARMS
AND HOLD OUR WORLD,
IN YOUR HEALING ARMS
PLEASE, BESEECH THE SPIRITS
FROM HEAVENS AROUND
TO HELP MAKE OUR WORLD,
OUR HOME, HEALTHY AND SOUND.
BRING THE HEALING STRENGTHS
TO OUR LITTLE PLOT,
HELP US SAVE THIS WORLD
WE LOVE NAMED CAMELOT!"

She faces the fire, the Willow in her sight and she prays,

"We call upon the tides to shift and bring forth all that poisons.

We ask the stalks that carry leaf
to make well all horizons

To the roots we also plead draw up those feckless parts.
Expose them to the healing moon, cleansing soil and our hearts.
Camelot's Soul she gives us, though selfish we be named
Make calm our troubled spirits, turmoil and illness be tamed."

Her spine stiffens and she convulses as if taken by the shivers. Her arms, rigid; palms rising.

Something draws my attention, our attention, skyward. A small light pulses as if a flickering star but much brighter, stronger. A beam of purplish hue bathes Kaye's head.

Abby gasps, "A healing light?"

It moves down Kaye's body, girdling her then spreading out along her arms, circles back to her head continuing to infuse her with a soothing luminescence.

Her Robe falls away, her body rises to hover above us. Uncovered, her soul exposed to all, the light radiates into the soil. The beams from her hands search, picking others who wear stones of healing.

Abby first, then Beth and Madeline. Cook follows her sister, Ana and then several others. Thirteen in all bathe in purplish hue, levitating.

Bodies revealed, souls bared to heal our World, Camelot. The gentle rays emanating from woman to woman then outward to bathe all the congregation.

As I am touched, it soothes, easing my soul; elation fills my being.

I watch as my fellow practitioners glow, their stresses dropping away.

The Willow changes. The color transforms from the sickly browns and grays. Beginning from the bottom. Purples, then greens tinge the stem. The bark appears healthier, the branches strengthen.

Something pervades my consciousness; a sound knocks on the door of my mind. A *purr*? First Merlyn, then Dagwood and then more of the local cats sing to the willow.

Now the tree radiates a darker purple, the bark and branches brighten, the leaves sparkle; new growth bursts forth. The soil flames, the purple light discharges outward, spreading healing energies throughout the world. Moving as a ripple when a pebble is dropped onto a quiet pond.

The purring ceases, the light fades and the healers drift to the soil collapsing in heaps, drained and satisfied.

That was the word which came to my mind; '*Satisfied!*'

I wrap Abby in her robe, help her up to protect her from the chilly air.

She smiles with great satisfaction. "Now I know some of what you felt during your Reiki session."

The women are exhausted. Something strange and unknown seems to have happened in those minutes or hours during the ceremony. There was much said. Many signs and signals from Kaye and Abby to the rest of the healers. It was nearly as a ballet with the music only heard in their heads. A choreographed ceremony of healing is the impression I get.

Wizards helped transport many of the congregation to our manor. Pages and sculleries on alert, the food and drinks served and consumed fast and furious. I had to forcibly hold Ana down as she tries to get to the kitchen. It is good she is so weak or I could never have kept her at the table.

All the healers are depleted, run down, flat out tired. This session is the most exhausting in history.

After Diana analyses the samples, we should find the infected areas healing and well. From what I feel they healed the entire planet.

The cats visited, rubbing against people, sharing comfort as they wander the hall. Abby explains, through bites of cheese and sips of juice, “the cats were called to lend their psi talents to facilitate the healing.”

But from whom did the orders come? Who could alert the cats to join the rite? The *Guardian*? Maybe?

Several friends find their energy to stop by our table to talk, asking questions we have no answers for or to thank us for the hospitality.

Kaye is off in a corner resting on a bench with a scullery offering food and drink. Jackie hops from table to table checking on everyone while keeping a close eye on her.

As nourishment is taken and people rest, some wander off home. Some need to stay, feelings not clarified and the want and need of being close to the center of the healing, to the center of the planet.

Kaye manages to hobble over. She and Abby still have little idea of what has happened.

“We were used,” Kaye gasps still trying to hold her emotions in check.

I guess when taken that way, channeling that much energy, that much power; it must take a toll on the body and mind.

Abby agrees with a shudder, “It seems to be an immense amount of healing power from some entity in the universe?" she whispers, not having enough strength left to even lift her head.

Merlyn sits next to her leaning against her one hip. Dagwood sits between her and me leaning against her other hip.

Jackie hops to the table. "It seems the consensus of all the participants that you were used. None seem the worse for wear, none act like they were abused, but you women were all used."

Kaye peers over at him and beams, "We hope that the entire episode is worth it!"

"We will need a report from Diana after she runs an analysis on the stability of the planet," he states. "By the way, has anyone seen her?"

Almost on cue, she bursts into the hall, "Please, help, it's Allain," she cries.

"What's wrong?" I query.

"I'm not sure. A scullery knocked on his door, and when no one answered, she entered. He screamed, *'Leave me alone!'* Rose to slam the door, then collapsed."

All this as we rush up the stairs. Jackie has arrived first, having poofed up. I will have to remember that.

Several burly men deposit the poor lad upon his bed.

He appears wretched; unshaven, ill-kept and unwashed, not the 'Allain the Bard' we know.

"Allain," Abby whispers, a perplexed expression upon her face. "Where did all this come from?" she asks.

"Where did all what come from," he wonders, perplexed at seeing all the people crowd around.

She points to the writings and drawings on the table.

He shrugs. "The last few days have been a blank, Miss Abby. I remember sitting here for what seemed like hours looking at a blank sheet then I would imagine something in my mind; harmonious healing light would fill my head." He glances up at her as he holds his wrist.

The serving girls arrive to share their stories, and how they tried bringing food. He would rant and rave about the interruption throwing them from the room.

"What's wrong with your hand," she inquires. "Are you hurt?"

"I have very little feeling in it and the pain shoots up my wrist and arm," he explains.

Abby reaches down, taking hold. I see his pain fall away and his complexion brighten. Even in her weakened state she has helped.

"Thank you, Dear Lady for that. Please tell the young ladies how sorry I am for their mistreatment. I would never throw a pretty girl from my room; especially when they bring food." He apologizes sheepishly, "I do not know what overcame me."

I read the papers. Words, music, hand motions are all on the sheets. I am amazed at the complexity of it all.

Abby also thumbs copies. "Did you make this all up, read of it somewhere?" she continues her line of questioning.

Jackie, reading over my shoulder, well, technically from my shoulder now hops to the table itself as I show him the pages.

After a moment of inspection, The Crow asks, "Do you know any healing?"

"The usual things, pressure on wounds, keep cuts clean and what herbs to use for different ailments, what to use for headaches and hangovers," he admits.

"But no healing spells?" the crow questions.

"*No*! I can do no magicks," is the reply

"These gestures here and here," Jackie points to several drawings with his wingtip, "are healing spells. I can read them though they are ancient."

"So where did they come from," I ask. Jackie and I stand looking to Allain for an answer.

He merely shrugs!

"I wanted to create a new song so I sat with clean pages and fresh inks." He looks up at us from whence he sits. "I am told that was several days ago and I do not recall much of anything else."

Abby peers over my shoulder and then grabs the sheet from my hand. Showing it to Kaye, "does this sound familiar?"

She gasps, stutters, "These are the words I used tonight for the healing. I have never before heard those prayers and have no notion of where they come from."

We all stare at the poor man, lying sickly upon his bed.

All he could do is shrug.

CHAPTER 53 A Visitor

It is a wonderful spring day, but it is always spring here.

I lie in my hammock, LH at my side. Abby sits on a stool in our garden picking leaves for teas.

I sip coffee, she sips a 'dew'. Merlyn and Dagwood nearly doze on the hand-made picnic table, enjoying the dappled sunshine. They keep an eye on two chipmunks who busily gather nuts. They might have chased them but both felines are of an intelligence there is no need to do that.

Merlyn looks up at me with a quizzical look. Well, I guess unless they want to. It is an almost nod she gives me and goes back to her watching.

There are trees in varied states of maturity in the forest, so nuts and fruits will be mature throughout the year.

Allain is on his way to his travels moments ago so the cats need something else to occupy their days. He will return soon and Diana will be waiting.

She traveled home to tie up loose ends. Abby tuned a summoning stone so Diana could call us when she is ready to come back to await Allains' return. She will live in to Abby's manor and help keep various endeavors running properly and in good health.

It is a typical, beautiful morning; the ones' we enjoy here in Camelot. The birds sing, frogs from the nearby pond croak their sonnets along with the chirps of crickets, a quiet that most modern people will never experience.

Here, there are no extraneous noises of cars, trains or busses. The ringing of a phone is unheard of. Turbine engines running power plants do not exist. It is a quiet that lulls and super-sensitizes your hearing. It brings a peace; making you uniquely aware of sounds out of place.

The cat's ears go up. I hear nothing along my link with Jackie, so it isn't him. He will announce himself first. But a slight noise in the front of my head; a buzz, officious in nature it seems. Abby also seems affected.

'Hail the Manor!' comes softly to us all. *'Am I welcome?'*

Abby's smile goes ear to ear. My thought is she invited him in since we watch as the stranger approaches from the lane.

Both felines rise to their paws, respectfully it seems. And we are soon face to face with 'The Guardian'.

He is tall, thin with slightly graying hair, clad in a tan robe and sandals. He enfolds Abby in his arms as a brother would after a long journey. He reaches out and shakes my hand. If his ears have been pointed, I would have thought 'Sarek'[9] from Star Trek.

"I have come to bid thee fare-well," he announces, leaning to scratch both cats. "It is time for me to continue on my way."

9Sarek, Commander Spocks' Father, portrayed by Mark Lenard (1924-1996) first in the original Star Trek series, 'Journey to Babel', 1967, then later in several of the motion pictures.

"But we thought you trapped, your consciousness intertwined amongst the rock and the planet," Abby reminds. "And your body destroyed."

"When the healing energies surged through Camelot, I was one of the things cleansed. The power removed each bit of consciousness from each bit of rock. I was able to direct it all back into a cohesive energy. Little by little it grew until I had all of me reassembled. It was then I realized my body lie in a temporal zone hidden by my powers to survive. I still have not imagined all the parameters of it."

We stare at each other, stunned by the news of his leaving.

"I came to thank you all for your kindness and help. All that time alone, I had forgotten the niceties of companionship. Now I leave to be among my own kind and to my work in other existences."

A wide smile lights up his face. "If you are ever in need of aid you can search me out amongst the alternatives!"

He turns and walks away. One hand rises in a parting gesture and with each step he slowly fades.

But one quick, final thought, *"Beware, the Crow has learned of the stone!"*

I gulp!

Abby smile wryly, "The birds are gone, again!"

And the quiet that envelopes us was nothing like we have ever felt before.

***That Crow is coming*.**

He is enraged.

He is incensed.

He is infuriated; flying hard and fast.

He lands at high speed, barely back-winging; I grab him before he slides off the table and hurts himself. I don't think there is enough coffee or meat to soothe *his* savage breast!

"***DO YOU KNOW WHAT THAT STONE IS****?* He yells at me as he stomps up and back on the table. "**DO *YOU*?"**

"Jackie, calm down. You will burst your feathers."

"***THAT THING WAS WATCHING ME IN MY OWN WORKSHOP!"*** Now he stands, hopping from claw to claw. ***"MY OWN WORKSHOP!"*** His wings out and flapping in near hysteria.

Abby laughs so hard she upset his coffee cup, which she replaces.

I try to sit but I was laughing so hard I fell off my hammock, on to my backside.

The Crow continues his rant for another moment until he reads the humor in my brain. And with permission granted from Merlyn he reads her mind as she lay along the table, tail twitching showing the most emotion I have ever seen from her in a long time.

After taking a sip of coffee, he confesses, "I guess the last laugh is on me. All these years that stone has been sitting there watching. From my Great- Great something or other relative down to me. We watched while it watched back"

We eventually calm enough to enjoy a small snack and some light conversation.

CHAPTER 54 It Makes Cents

Later, as we get comfortable in bed, "What special projects do you have in mind?" Abby queries.

"You saw what happened to Peter and Willow. It almost happened to Deborah and her family." I take a breath to get my thoughts in order.

"I want to set up a fund to draw from to help others in an emergency. I don't want families to worry where or how they will live. We might not be able to bring loved ones back but families can stay together or get new properties. Maybe money to live on while getting an education. Or capital to start a business."

"Maybe it isn't needed since we can do magicks but it is just something I think we should do. We can do it with many of our enterprises. A bit of the profits put to the side. Maybe we will mint coins with my countenance engraved. We need to have good looking coins," I joke.

She playfully slaps my arm.

"You can be on a coin, too," I offer. "But I am serious. What would have happened if you had not heard Peter's call for help? Debbie may have died and we wouldn't have known."

"Those two children may have starved or been attacked by wolves or bears. They may have died from exposure. All from fearing being sent to a work house," I conclude. "And who threatens their kin with work houses? We don't have them in this world."

Abby sits up, looking towards Merlyn. "What?" she asks of the feline.

"What?" I echo wonderingly.

"Merlyn says two of Dagwood's watchers were sleeping under the cabin. Peter had been sharing food with them."

"Why didn't they alert us sooner concerning the children?" I ask.

"Oh, right!" Abby relays. "Nothing needed to be reported up until that point. Dagwood knew Debbie had been bitten as soon as it happened. Merlyn was alerting me when she heard the boy in my mind."

I sigh, "Well thank you all for keeping everything under control and the populace safe. I am going to sleep since everything is taken care of," I joke. "Wake me if you need me for something important." And I roll over pulling the covers along with me.

I feel and almost immediate tap on my shoulder.

"What? I'm sleeping!"

"I need you for something," she reports.

"Ask the cats," I smile.

"They can't hug me like you can."

I give a quick wink to the felines as I move to en-wrap her in my arms.

"Some things are just best left to us humans. No offense, Dagwood!" I whisper.

THE END

Still to come.
BOOK THREE in

TAILS OF THE CROW
"THERE IS AN ALTERNATIVE."

Just a few random thoughts

Sometimes, late at night, I sneak into a corner of my brain, travel to that small hidey spot where I keep my most private thoughts behind lock and key. I unleash scenarios where the improbable are mundane, the impossible are everyday and the slightest wish might send others screaming into the night.

Maybe somewhen I'll be caught on the other side as that door creaks slowly closed, the lock clicks shut and I am forever trapped within, 'ENDLESS POSSIBILITIES'!

Looking to go home again,
but I missed the exit ramp.
Yearning to return at last,
But the map is torn and
damp.

I am lost amidst the roads of life
And the way is blurred with tears,
Trying to find my way back to you,
But I am gone too many years!

We can't change the love we once
had
Or re-capture the days of yore
The streets of time are all one
way and
You can't enter the exit door.

But the sun will shine once again,
The birds will warble their song;
Trees will leaf and flowers bloom.
Then our love won't seem so wrong.

Frank J. Sconzo, Sr

~~~~~~~~~~~~~~~~~~~~~~~~~~
~~~~~~~~~~~~~~~~~~~~~~~~~~

WE HAVE FOUGHT MANY BATTLES
THROUGHOUT ALL OUR LONG YEARS
SOME HAVE RESULTED IN VICTORY
WHILE MOST LEFT SCARS AND TEARS

BUT EACH TIME WE'D RISE AGAIN;
BRUSH OFF THE DUST AND GOOK.
TAKE A STEP TOWARDS A BRIGHTER TOMORROW
WITH NARY A BACKWARD LOOK.

WE'LL SMILE AT OUR DETRACTORS AS WE
TELL THEM WHAT WE HAVE PLANNED.
THEY WILL LAUGH, CALL IT ABSURDITY
BUT WE'LL MAKE ANOTHER STAND.

WE'LL TAKE ANOTHER RUN AT HAPPINESS;
ENJOY LIFE FOR ANOTHER DAY.
PUT OUT HELPING HANDS TO EACH OTHER –
BECAUSE FRIENDS ARE FRIENDS,
ALWAYS...

www.ingramcontent.com/pod-product-compliance
Lightning Source LLC
Chambersburg PA
CBHW070654180626
46817CB00006B/2368

* 9 7 8 0 5 7 8 8 8 2 6 8 0 *